Double Toil & Trouble

A Story of Macbeth's Nieces

By Peg Herring

For the reader:

Some years ago, I wrote a book about Tessa macFindlaech, and I've always wanted to continue the story to include her sister Jenna. As I finally did that, Jenna gained a twin, Jessie, and the story became two tales twisted together.
If you have not read *Macbeth's Niece,* or you read it so long ago you need a refresher, I've included a synopsis at the end of this book, along with notes on the real Macbeth, the Shakespeare play, and William and Matilda, Duke and Duchess of Normandy.
None of the information is essential to your enjoyment of this story, but it's there if you're interested.

PH

Chapter One

Jenna

They came at daybreak, stalking silently from the grove of spindly trees in business-like formation, eyes watchful, weapons ready. Before the sleepy-eyed Scots could react, the rough men were upon them, pulling the adults from their beds at sword-point and herding them together like sheep. Squinting into the misty morning, Jenna stood with the others, shivering and fearful in the cold damp. Their men glared at the interlopers, furious with them for the assault and with themselves for being caught unprepared.

There was little to hear as Jenna's life crashed around her. Men grunted as they were kicked or pushed into place, a child cried out and was hushed, face muffled against her mother's chest. Jenna heard the mother whisper fiercely into the girl's stiff, reddish hair, "Whist, nae, d'ye hear?" An older girl sobbed, but there was not much sound to it, as if she realized her fears meant nothing to the hard men who stared impassively at them.

Jenna's gaze swept the tiny circle of her family. Meg, her oldest sister, stood with her husband Donald. Nettie and Ailsa, each with a baby on her hip and a husband at her side, watched fearfully, glancing at Meg for courage. Behind them the family's servants and herdsmen stood, children peering from around their parents' legs. Jenna's heart gave a little jump as she realized her twin was not among them. A second, closer scan gave no reassurance. Jessie was not there. Where was she?

Out staring at the night, Jenna decided. When darkness covered the mountain, Jessie often left the smoky house to breathe fresh air beneath the stars. *Tonight, it's a blessing*, Jenna thought. *Jessie will be spared whatever fate awaits the rest of us.*

When members of the clan-hold were assembled within the ring of the hard-faced, foreign-looking warriors, two men stepped from the tree line and made their way forward. The first, a man with starkly-white hair and dark, brooding eyes, moved with a slow and stately gait, as if heading a procession of worshipers rather than a band of interlopers. Though his frame was well muscled he looked shrunken, as if he'd taken little nourishment of late. His solemn face bore an expression of piety, and his gaze focused somewhere above their heads. His heavy sword rode in a scabbard at his back, and his hands were folded before him as if in prayer. Lesser men had done the dirty work. It seemed he had a different role.

The second man, a half step behind the first, was one such as Jenna had never seen before. Taller even than his tall companions, he seemed too perfect to be real: long, silken hair of reddish gold, a face strong yet beautiful with high cheekbones and a smooth brow, and a body formed for pure strength. While the others wore subdued colors and rough fabrics, this man's deeply-dyed garments trumpeted personal pride. His bright blue eyes missed nothing as they swept the scene. When they lingered on Jenna, she shivered but would not look away. After a moment his gaze went on.

The silent warriors who'd torn Jenna's people

from their beds parted to admit the two men into the circle of captor and captured. The dark-eyed one examined the men among them, focusing on each face in turn, his expression almost, but not quite, benign.

When he spoke, his voice was higher than she'd expected. "I seek the men of Macbeth's clan." The words, though spoken in her tongue, sounded strange, the inflections slightly off. Their odd appearance now made sense. The intruders were Vikings.

Long ago, before Jenna's grandfather's father was born, they'd come as invaders. Some had settled along Britain's east coast, carving a place for themselves among the mixed clans and tribes settled there. Along with Saxons, Picts, and Angles, Vikings had intermarried with natives until in some places it was difficult to separate the cultures.

These men, however, were blatantly Norse, with the tall frames and fair hair of the Scandinavians to whom terrible deeds were attributed. Looking at the grim faces before her, Jenna felt her fears deepen. What if the old folks' tales of the Northmen's cruelty were true?

Eyes sweeping the bedraggled group of prisoners, the leader's gaze focused on Donald. "Are you blood kin to the fiend Macbeth?"

Meg's husband was no coward. His rugged face revealed contempt and his voice was firm as he answered, "Our late king was no fiend, though I claim no blood kinship with him."

The stranger smiled thinly. "Macbeth was a murderer and a coward. I am come to avenge his crimes, so my soul and the souls of my family can be at peace."

Donald frowned in confusion. "Macbeth is dead these ten years."

Waving a hand as if the argument had no consequence, the man replied, "I, Leif Arneson, have seen his cruelty. The sight of it would burn the eyes from your head."

The splendid man beside Arneson shifted his feet. Jenna couldn't decide if he was discomfited or impatient. Their eyes met for a second time and his head tilted, like a cat awaking at a sudden noise. She lowered her face, uncomfortable at his interest.

The white-haired man spoke again, raising his voice. "Macbeth ordered the murders of a mother and her sons. The gods have called me to avenge them."

A stir went through the little crowd of listeners. A stranger come at the behest of his gods could not be good for them. "The ageless ones are angry." His voice thrummed with certainty. "The blood feud calls."

There were gasps of dismay. A blood feud!

"Macbeth was killed in battle," Donald said, his voice firm. "There's no call for more blood."

The Viking shook his head. "One death does not suffice. Each squandered life cries for payment."

Jenna shivered. A blood feud was a fearsome

thing. The family of a murder victim was required by honor to exact a life for a life, and the life taken need not be the murderer's. Any family member might suffer in his place, even children. Would they all die today because of events a decade gone? It was unusual but not unheard of, and Arneson's demeanor revealed determination to see it through.

Meg stepped protectively before her husband. "No man of Macbeth's line lives here."

Anger flared in the Viking's eyes. "You lie! Macbeth's brother took his family to the Cairngorms, to this place, when he tired of your nation's constant upheaval."

"My father, long dead, sired only daughters." Meg nodded at her little family. "Nor are there male children in the new generation."

Arneson's posture slackened as if he'd taken a blow to the stomach, but he raised his face piously to the stars. "At least the gods spared us more of his ilk," he murmured.

Meg's chin lifted defiantly. "Our father was as good a man as ever lived." Donald put a hand on her arm, warning her not to tempt a madman. The Viking, ten years late for vengeance, was almost certainly diseased in his mind.

There was a stir outside the circle, and Jenna turned to behold a new, even stranger sight. Four men approached, bearing among them a large shield of beaten metal. On it sat a woman of extraordinary beauty and coloring such as she had never imagined.

Her hair was so pale as to seem translucent, lighting the face it framed. Her eyes were a brilliant blue, and her cheeks showed red against otherwise chalk-white skin.

When the bearers set the shield on the ground, however, Jenna saw that the woman's lower body was deformed, almost barrel-shaped. Probably to disguise this, she sat amid colorful blankets and pillows, only her upper torso visible above the bright fabric, like a vision in a dream.

The newcomer examined the people before her, considering each face. Her gaze stopped on Jenna, perhaps noting that no child clung to her, no man lent his protection with an arm or even a glance. One pale eyebrow lifted before she went on, cataloging each member of the group in a manner known only to herself. "Have you found what you sought, Leif?"

The Viking glanced at her resentfully, but his voice remained neutral. "They say no men are left of his line, Aldis."

"Is this true?" She spoke to Meg, her tone hinting she would know if lies were told.

"My uncle was the last macFindlaech."

Her smile was odd, perhaps haughty, perhaps something else. "Only women speak for the great Macbeth?"

"I cannot speak for him," Meg corrected. "My uncle and I never met."

Arneson stirred impatiently. "No sons to

compensate my loss, Aldis. Who will pay for Macbeth's murder and betrayal?"

"We have heard such stories," Meg said, "but tales may be told of any man once he's dead. The telling does not make it true." Again Donald shifted beside his wife, perhaps wishing she didn't feel the need to defend her kinsman.

Even in their home high in the mountains, they'd heard of it. Folk said the desire for power had led Macbeth and his lady wife to murder and madness. They rejected the whispers, first because it was natural to hope their kinsman had not been a monster, and second because their sister Tessa had known the king in his last year of life. She insisted the stories were lies invented to justify one king's deposition of another.

The Viking's cold gaze seemed to look through Meg, but he responded to her words. "I did not imagine my brothers' cries as Macbeth's men spitted them like hogs at slaughter. I heard them!" He raised his hands dramatically, and spittle flew from his lips as he shouted, "The fiend's line must be stomped out, like the eggs of a serpent!" His eyes searched the crowd as if willing satisfactory victims to appear. The Scots winced at his fury, but no one spoke.

"There are no males of his blood here, Leif." Aldis spoke softly, her hands resting in her lap. Jenna would learn later that she cultivated stillness because movement caused her pain.

The Viking turned on her in anger. "Then you were wrong, and we have wasted weeks."

Though she sat below Leif, Aldis appeared to look down on him. "If a curse were easily broken, it would not be such a dreadful thing."

She turned to Meg again, correctly judging her to be the ranking female. "There was a woman, the stories say, who traveled far to warn the tyrant of his enemies' approach. Macbeth's niece, they say, disappeared during the battle. Is she kin to you?"

"My sister, but we have not seen her for many years." Jenna noted Meg's careful phrasing. Tessa lived in England with her husband, Lord Brixton. She sent letters from time to time, and only the day before a gleeman, a traveling entertainer, had brought one. He must be somewhere in the circle now, though Jenna didn't see him.

Tessa's letters provided a window on the world for Jenna, who had used them to teach herself to read. Knowing little of her younger sisters, Lady Brixton nevertheless wrote each of them a personal note with each missive she sent. Jenna had insisted from the beginning that the reader point out the words to her as he read. She memorized each one in order to puzzle over it later on her own. With letters and the books left behind by her father, she deciphered the connection between sound and form in writing, and from that point was often scolded for neglecting more productive work to "put her nose in a book."

Hearing that Tessa lived, interest lit Leif's eyes. "Does Macbeth's niece have sons?"

Seeing her mistake, Meg hurried to correct it. "When last we saw her, she was a maid."

"And none of these is kin to Macbeth?" Leif gestured at the men in the circle, his gaze determined. Dread gripped Jenna. He might yet order them all killed in order to leave no living drop of Macbeth's blood.

Meg stood firm before his gaze. "These are my husband's kinsmen. You have climbed the mountain for nothing, Northman, for you will not find what you seek here."

Her defiant tone brought a frown to Arneson's face, but his reply was interrupted as another man entered the circle. Broad-shouldered and solid, he moved silently into place beside the blond giant. His plain clothing was outshone by his companion's polished brass brooch-pin and carved sword-case, but he seemed to Jenna more human, perhaps because his brown hair and square build were more like the men she knew. She felt a strange sensation when his gaze lifted and met hers. His eyes widened momentarily, as if he felt it as well. She looked away. He was a Viking, and therefore an enemy.

"Did you find others?" Arneson asked, and the quiet man shook his head. Good for you, Jessie. These Vikings might look like perfect warriors, but one slight girl had eluded them. She looked toward the spot where she guessed Jessie was hiding, but stopped herself, fearing she'd betray her sister's presence.

When her glance returned to the circle, the newcomer was still looking directly at her. She lowered her face, fearing he'd read what she was thinking.

The blond giant also noticed the look she tried to hide. "There is someone else here."

Arneson turned to the dark-haired man. "Lukas, look again."

Without comment, the man turned and left the circle. His direction was wrong for where Jenna guessed her sister was hiding, and she smiled to herself. The Vikings were not as wise as they thought themselves to be.

Arneson turned to the cripple, apparently his seer. "Might one of these women yet bear a son?"

Fear sharpened her sisters' faces. Nettie clutched her oldest daughter to her side, glancing fearfully at her husband. Ailsa clung to Robert, who put a protective arm around her and their baby daughter. Even the servants hunched lower.

The seer took a long time to answer. "A woman will do only if there is no other. You must first make certain the missing sister has no sons."

"How are we to find a woman ten years gone?"

"They know where she is." The giant spoke for the first time. His voice was low but carried easily, and he said it casually, as if to let the prisoners know how pitiful resistance would be. He unsheathed his sword, and a shiver of dread passed through the prisoners.

"Tell me, then." Arneson focused on Meg.

Her expression was stony. "I have said it. We

have not seen our sister for many years."

"Not seeing is not the same as not knowing." Surveying the circle of Scots, the big man stepped toward Ian, a servant almost blinded by cataracts. With a swift thrust, he spitted the old man with his sword. Ian was dead before he could cry out, but Meg's anguished scream filled the air. Others moaned audibly as he fell.

"No!" Meg bent to touch the old man's face, and Jenna put a hand on her sister's shoulder.

"A useless life. We have done you a service." Righteousness vibrated in Arneson's voice. "Now repay the kindness. Where does Macbeth's seed grow?"

Meg looked to Donald, whose face was grim. Everyone understood the message: reveal Tessa's location or see their people butchered one by one. What kind of choice was that?

As the decision hung over them, a man stepped out from the circle. Slight of build and no taller than Jenna, he carried himself with a confidence that demanded attention. It was the gleeman who had brought Tessa's letter. "I can tell you where the woman lives if you make it worth my while," he told the Vikings. "I saw her less than a month ago."

A collective sound circled the little group, part dismay, part relief. Though this man might save them further tragedy, his intervention meant trouble for Tessa.

For her part, Jenna felt only anger. How dare this fellow offer to sell the lives of her aunt's children to these monsters? "If you make it worth my while" indeed! Everyone here knew Tessa had twin boys eight years old as well as two younger daughters. Now the twins might be killed because of this man's cowardice.

"You've seen the woman?" Arneson asked. "Where?"

"I can draw you a map." Jenna searched her mind for the gleeman's name but could not recall it. Whoever he was, he had no right to make decisions for her clan.

The third man returned to the group, shaking his head to indicate he'd found no one. "What's this?" he said when he saw Ian lying dead.

"A necessary sacrifice," the Viking replied in a tone that revealed how little Ian's death mattered to him. "We have learned what we need to know."

The man seemed to object, but in the end he pressed his lips together and said nothing. Angry he missed the sport of murdering an old man, she thought.

Wiping his sword on Ian's tunic, the tall Viking put it away. "We've journeyed all this way and climbed this infernal mountain only to learn we must go somewhere else?"

"The forces of nature lead where they will, Bjorn" Aldis said. "All things have purpose."

Leif seemed not to have heard their exchange. "We will find her, but what of these liars, Aldis? Is it good sense to leave them alive?"

"Bad luck to kill mothers with children," she replied flatly, as if they discussed vegetables. "Put them in their cattle byre and block the doors. By the time they escape we will be too far away for them to stop us."

"Such as these would prove no stop to us, but we will make double sure." Leif Arneson looked around the circle as he spoke. "Swiftly, then. I want this curse lifted before the king's matters move forward."

"You will be ready when he comes." Aldis' somewhat protuberant eyes went wide as if visualizing some future event.

"See it done." Leif's men began herding their prisoners into the cave where cattle were kept in bad weather.

"Wait," the giant ordered, and Jenna's heart stopped as she found his gaze on her. "This one is no mother of children. We should take her with us."

Fear tensed her throat, and although she intended to say, "Don't touch me," only a strangled growl emerged. Meg put an arm around her, a protective gesture and a warning.

"Why, Bjorn?" Leif was focused elsewhere.

Bjorn came close, looking Jenna over as if she were a hunting hound he might purchase. He pulled her chin up with his hand then released it, brushing her chest lightly in an ominous gesture. "A wild flower from high in the mountains," he murmured. She smelled mint. Did he chew it to sweeten his breath, or did he suffer from headaches? Judging from his fine clothing, she guessed the former. Jenna met the Viking's gaze defiantly and opened her mouth to speak, but Meg gripped her shoulder in warning.

Meeting her gaze with a smile, the tall man said, "A hostage will protect our retreat."

Leif shrugged without interest. "As you wish."

Bjorn turned his gaze on Donald. "Do not follow, Scotsman, for her life is in your hands."

After a moment Leif said, "If the sister has no sons, females must serve to pay the price." His voice turned anguished. "I am determined to end this curse."

Donald made his move then, leaping at the Viking in a desperate attempt to protect Jenna. He reached for Leif's throat, but one Viking reached out and slung the flat of his axe against the side of his head in an almost casual gesture.

Seizing her chance, Jenna dived past the Northmen, bare feet churning, and ran for the trees. As the intruders gaped in surprise, she gained the edge of the grove, disappeared into the foliage, and slipped behind a knoll she knew well, having hidden there more than once in the course of childish games.

Peering through the green-tipped branches, she watched the aftermath of her flight. Leif gave a curt order and gestured impatiently. Most of his men continued toward the byre, and Jenna's heart sank as she saw two men pick up Donald's still form and carry him along. Two others, the man called Bjorn and the one with green eyes, followed her into the wood. Bjorn headed down the path with sure intent. The other stopped, looking toward the spot where she lay. From his shrewd conclusion she'd choose cover over flight, Jenna guessed he was a skilled tracker with instincts honed for locating and capturing his quarry. Surprisingly, after a moment's hesitation he moved away, following his companion.

Jenna lay flat, hardly daring to breathe, but she knew she couldn't remain there for long. Dawn was breaking, and the night-robe she wore showed starkly white against the dark ground. With a bit of luck, however, she'd reach a place where the two men would never find her.

The path the Vikings had taken led to a pool that provided the clan's water. The hiding place Jenna sought was there, but she had to approach it from a different direction. With agonizing slowness she moved away from the path, gliding silently through the trees to the far end of the cold, clear pool. A small waterfall fed it, and every child of the clan knew that behind the cascade lay a cave just large enough for one slight female to hide in until her pursuers gave up looking.

Creeping down the steep slope, she reached the water's edge. The bank was soft here, and the pool lay under an overhanging ledge of scrub brush. Jenna ducked under the overhang and crouched beneath it, staying out of the water until she could be sure the Vikings were gone.

That was her mistake. As she waited, listening, a hand reached down from above and caught hold of her night-robe. One of them had guessed her intent, and now he had her. Or did he?

There was but a moment to decide what to do, and no real choice. Twisting her body Jenna slipped out of the loose shift, leaving it in her pursuer's hand. She dived into the pool, hardly aware of the cold as fear drove her onward. Pushing herself deep into the water, she let experience guide her. Her lungs strained as she crossed without surfacing, pushing through the water with powerful kicks. Just as she feared her chest might burst, she felt the pound of water on her shoulders and made a final lunge. Soon she was behind the waterfall, safe from her enemy's eyes and naked as the day of her birth.

Chapter Two

Jessie

The night her world changed, Jessie was watching the moon make its way through forests of clouds in the night sky. So intent was she on the shapes and variations above her that she saw nothing until the Vikings were upon the clan-hold, pushing her family from their homes and their beds with rough words and heavy hands. From a place in her favorite tree she saw it all, though she couldn't hear what was said. She sat frozen, unable to think of anything she could do to help.

At least a dozen large men, mostly fair-haired, forced her family and their small group of servants into the center of the open space, menacing them with heavy swords. Instinctively, Jessie's eyes sought her twin in the group. Jenna was there, her expression fearful but also angry. Meg and Donald stood stiffly together, hiding the dread they must feel.

When everyone was assembled, a man stepped from the trees, an odd combination of youth and old age. He walked as if in a trance, but he questioned Donald and Meg intently. What did he want with them? There was little the world considered wealth here in the Cairngorms, nothing that made climbing the steep mountainside worthwhile. It was why her father had chosen this spot, far from their royal peers.

Meg answered the Viking, her words unintelligible but her manner scornful. Jessie shivered, for she sensed these men would not take defiance kindly.

Though she feared for them all, Jessie's greatest concern was for Jenna, her other half. They shared the same light brown hair, greenish eyes, oval face, and clear skin, and they believed they shared one heart, for they heard each other's thoughts and finished each other's sentences. On the outside they were so much alike that only close family could tell them apart. Donald often said teasingly if they sat still and remained quiet, no one could. "Of course," he always added, "Jenna is seldom still or silent."

Though alike on the outside, their personalities were different. Jenna was the strong one, active, inquisitive, and sure of herself. Jessie was meek and unsure, in large part because of her crippled leg. Flawed herself, she easily forgave the wrongs of others. Jenna abided no insult and found forgiveness almost impossible.

Though Jessie admired her sister's confidence, Meg sometimes did not. "You must not anger so easily," she often advised. "Keep your words to yourself until you've considered them a while."

"I try," Jenna replied each time. "But my chest gets tight and my face gets hot—"

"—And you say what you should not."

It was true, and the worst of her anger was directed at anyone who slighted her twin sister. Jessie had been born with a dislocated left hip, a problem no one noticed until it was too late to correct it. Though the leg could hold her weight, she had a severe limp and had to wear a special boot in order to walk normally. Convinced she needed protection because of her disability, Jenna provided it with a vigor that was often overzealous and even embarrassing. No one was allowed to mention Jessie's malformed leg, and heaven help anyone who called her a cripple. Jenna had even declared herself unwilling to marry, due, Jessie feared, to the belief Jessie was unlikely to wed. Life was hard in the Highlands, and a cripple who was the sixth of six daughters was not a highly-sought prize, however comely she might be.

A few days earlier, Donald had taken up the matter of marriage privately with Jessie. Dougal, a kind but dull youth from a nearby clan-hold, had asked for Jessie's hand. Even Donald had seemed doubtful of Dougal's suitability as a husband, but the unspoken question was who else would have her. "Think on it," he'd told Jessie. "If you agree, we'll tell your sister together."

Jenna would be angry, would insist the niece of Scotland's former king deserved better, but Jessie had asked herself, which should she choose: a spiritless marriage or no marriage at all?

The Viking leader's raised voice brought Jessie's attention back to the scene before her. Jenna's tendency to speak her mind would be dangerous in the present situation, and she said a prayer that her sister would for once remain quiet. She did, but for no apparent reason the beautiful Viking stabbed Blind Ian, who fell to the ground and lay very still. Jessie sobbed aloud, clamping a hand over her mouth. She could do her family no good if she were discovered.

What could she do in any case? Jessie touched her leg resentfully. Since she hadn't put on her boots when she came outside, she was helpless to stop or even delay whatever was going to happen.

As her family stood frozen in horror at the murder of a helpless old man, the leader of the Vikings asked again whatever it was he wanted them to tell. No one moved for a few moments, but then a man stepped forward. It was a gleeman named Alfred who had arrived the day before with a letter from their sister Tessa. What he said pleased the Viking, for his demeanor became more relaxed. He gave further orders, but something caused Donald to react. He sprang at the leader, only to be clubbed unconscious by one of the other men. Meg knelt beside him, but Jenna broke away and ran for the trees. Aware of Jessie's probable location, Jenna angled away to protect her. Once in the woods, Jenna disappeared almost immediately. The leader pointed after her and gave a sharp command, and two men separated from the group and followed.

Jessie watched in fear as they approached the trees. The leaves hid her from a distance, but her linen night-shift glowed ghostly white in the dim morning light. If one of the men looked up as he passed, he would easily see her.

Intent on catching Jenna, the men didn't look up. Instead they followed the trail to the pool, turned to opposite sides in order to catch a glimpse of Jenna. Jessie sent up a second prayer that her sister might elude them and reach a safe hiding place.

The trail dropped near the water, and she watched the two Vikings disappear. Only when they were gone did she realize that on their way back along the trail, their eyes would naturally rise with the ground, and she'd be visible, like a white bird perched in the old tree.

What should she do? She was no match for them in speed. With few choices, Jessie decided to climb down and hide somewhere in the undergrowth until they passed by a second time. As quietly as possible, she left her place on the branch and let herself down to the ground.

Chapter Three

Jenna

Jenna huddled in the tiny cleft behind the waterfall, shivering with cold and fear. Nothing was clear, but her would-be captor's movement separated him from the dim forest. He stalked to the rim of the pool, glaring into its depths, and she saw the creamy fabric of her night-robe float downward as he tossed it into the water in disgust. Not a man used to defeat, she guessed, but he couldn't see where she'd gone.

He was patient. He didn't pace or curse, but waited beside the pool much longer than she could have held her breath under the icy water. A tracker, she thought once more, with a hunter's experience and the will to subdue his anger and wait out his quarry. She smiled to herself. Safe in her noisy nook, she could wait longer than he could.

The man's head turned, and he stepped back from the pool's edge. A moment later a second form emerged from the trees, and she made out the gold-red mane of the Viking Bjorn. He carried something wrapped in white, something that moved. Not something. Jessie!

Her terrified twin flailed blindly, but her weight was nothing to Bjorn. He held her to his side, gesturing with his opposite hand as he spoke to the Tracker. The nameless one pointed at the water, but Bjorn shook his head dismissively. He turned away, and Jenna watched in horror as her twin disappeared up the path, still kicking at her enemy. With a last long look at the pool, the tracker turned and followed.

Jenna let out a strangled sob. She had no hope of catching the men before they reached their companions, and what would she do anyway? For a few minutes she wept bitter tears for the escape that had come at her sister's expense. When she raised her face, her sodden night-shift floated before her, drawn by the inward pull of the waterfall. It lay just outside her reach, offering modesty if not warmth when she recovered her composure enough to take it.

It was some time before Jenna reentered the water, retrieved her garment, and exited the pool. Chilled and miserable, she returned to the clan-hold, stopping frequently to listen for the presence of the interlopers. All was silent. Old Ian's body lay as it had fallen, his sightless eyes truly empty now. His corpse and their tracks in the soft earth were all the Vikings had left behind. They had what they'd come for, Tessa's location and a hostage to protect their retreat. She must hurry, or they'd escape before her kinsmen could catch up and kill every single one of them.

She moved to the byre, calling, "Meg, are you in there? Are you all right?"

"Jenna? Is it you?"

Two heavy timbers wedged the doors shut, and it took longer than she'd hoped to move them. Lacking the physical strength to lift them, she dug a trench, scraping the sod away with a spade. At her command, the prisoners inside pushed together, pushing the timbers along the ground. The boards cracked as the stony ground resisted, but finally one man then another squeezed out the opening. Putting their backs to it, they soon tossed the timbers aside, and everyone poured out of the barn except the two Jenna was most anxious to see, Meg and Donald.

Inside the byre Meg knelt beside her wounded husband, who lay unconscious and bleeding from his ears. Her face was grave. "He breathes, but he hasn't moved."

"Oh, God!" Jenna searched the face of the man who served as her surrogate father. She could picture Donald teasing or working or even snoring, but never had she seen him so still, so pale.

Gentle hands lifted their leader, took him to the house, and laid him on his bed. Meg wouldn't leave his side but gave orders as to what must be done, and Ailsa and Nettie obeyed quickly and quietly. Ailsa stirred the fire to life and added fuel to warm the patient. The acrid smell of vinegar reached Jenna's nose as Nettie brought a bowl covered with a soft cloth. With a healer's touch, Meg bathed the wound, judging its depth. "The hurt is grievous," she said, confirming what everyone had already guessed.

Jenna stood beside her sister, heart aching. Her twin was a captive, her brother-in-law hurt, and her sister close to collapsing with grief. Without Donald's leadership, there was no one to mount a rescue. "I hate the Vikings," she muttered to no one in particular. "I'll kill them all if anything happens to Donald or Jessie."

Meg looked up in surprise. "Jessie? What of her?"

"They took her." It almost choked Jenna to say it aloud, but instead of tears this time, anger rose as she told the tale. "The one they called Bjorn came upon her as he sought me."

Meg's face registered new pain. "They took her."

Jenna pressed her lips together to hold her composure. "I should have stopped them."

"You couldn't. Donald tried, and this is the result." Meg caressed her husband's still face. "We must hope Jessie can escape somehow."

"How? Without her boot she can hardly walk."

"And if we go after them, they'll kill her. They said as much."

"But she will be—" Speaking her sister's probable fate was too painful. If stories told of Vikings were any indication, she'd be raped for sport and killed when they finished with her.

Meg rubbed the line between her brows, unable to accept all she faced. "When night falls, she might crawl into the woods and hide until they leave."

"How will she escape a dozen men?"

"If she can get away, she will," Meg repeated. "There's nothing we can do."

Jenna stared into the fire. "It's my fault she was captured."

Meg looked up, her face drawn with tragedy. "It's not your fault there's evil in the world. How would they know they had a different girl, and would it matter if they did?" She turned back to her husband, unable to dwell further on the question of Jessie's capture, but her words made an impression on Jenna.

"And they'd never know if I took Jessie's place now," she whispered to herself.

Chapter Four

Jessie

Though she did her best to keep up, Jessie could not. Finally one of the Vikings stated the obvious. "There's something wrong with her."

The leader glanced back disinterestedly. "You brought her, Bjorn. See to it." His tone held as much concern for her as for an unwanted kitten.

"I'll rejoin you later." The man named Bjorn took her arm, allowing the rest to move on. His expression sent a chill down Jessie's spine. She wouldn't live much longer, and she'd wish for death long before it came.

The blond woman spoke from her perch on the shield, her tone flat. "Is it sport now to kill girls, Bjorn?"

He answered in a low tone, his voice hard. "Mind your own affairs, Aldis. I won't let Leif forget it was you who brought us all this way on a useless chase."

The woman glanced at the leader, who'd gone on, uninterested in their exchange. Doubt clouded her eyes, and she gave Jessie a pitying glance before ordering her bearers forward.

As the other Vikings passed, one called in a teasing tone, "Be sure of your kill this time, Handsome One. Don't let this one escape as you did the beast yesterday."

Bjorn glared as others chuckled at the jibe. "The animal did not live out the night, I'll wager." He pulled Jessie off the path with a rough jerk. She made no sound, since there was no point in it, but she resisted, clawing at him as she stumbled along. A second jerk brought her tumbling into his arms, and he enclosed her in a strong embrace, his face next to hers.

Jessie heard her growl of objection as she tried to free her arms from the man's grasp. The Viking only laughed low in his throat. Then a firm voice behind them stopped him cold. "I'll take the girl."

Jessie looked up to see the man who'd helped in the search for Jenna. He stood behind them, feet slightly apart, his expression neither friendly nor threatening. The others had gone on; no one heard the exchange but the three of them.

"She's lame. Leif doesn't want her slowing us down."

"My pack pony can handle her weight."

Bjorn frowned in confusion. "What do you care what happens to her, Outsider?"

"There is a code in these matters," the man replied. "Hostages must be treated well and returned to their families once the need for them is over."

"In your world, Norman, but not in mine. I took her, and I'll do as I like with her."

The other seemed unfazed by the implied threat. "I'll see she doesn't hinder us."

The big man took a step forward. "You should not try to stop me, Lukas."

The other didn't even blink. "There is no trying here. If I must stop you, I will do it."

Bjorn's glance flickered in the direction of the retreating band. The sounds of their passage were dim now. Jessie heard only muted footsteps and the beating of her own heart. Rage glittered in Bjorn's eyes, and his jaw tightened. "She is nothing to you," he said, but the objection sounded more petulant than threatening.

"And even less to you, it seems."

For a time Bjorn measured the man he'd called Lukas. Then he turned abruptly and stalked after the others, leaving Jessie partly relieved. Had Lukas spoken the truth, or did he want her for himself? She chose to behave as if he'd acted out of goodness. "Thank you."

"We are not monsters." That was all he had to say on the subject. He led her to the path, where he took some of his pony's load onto his own back, providing a place for her to sit. "How did you hurt your leg?"

Jessie hesitated. If she admitted she was permanently lame, he might conclude she was indeed an impediment. "I twisted it when he captured me."

Accepting that, Lukas set her on the animal's broad back. "Hold on, for the way is steep."

That was the end of conversation for the day's journey. They made their way downhill, rejoining the others. Bjorn gave them a baleful glare, but no one commented on the turn of events. Jessie had to concentrate on keeping her seat as the pony navigated the steep slope. When shadows fell, they found a fairly flat spot and made camp for the night.

Lukas helped Jessie dismount, which was a good thing, since her aching muscles refused to hold her upright at first. As Lukas secured the pony for the night in a copse of trees, a dour servant who'd walked beside the woman on the shield all day approached and said curtly, "My lady will speak with you."

Jessie turned to see the odd woman regarding her. She sat on a bearskin, surrounded again by her colorful pillows. An equally colorful tent was being set up nearby. Curious but a little fearful, Jessie followed the servant to where the odd woman sat. "I am Aldis," she said when Jessie reached her.

"Sit here." She pointed to a place near the fire that had begun to warm the evening chill. Meekly Jessie obeyed, thinking Jenna would have refused. But then, Jenna's leg would not be aching from unaccustomed exertion.

She had trouble understanding Aldis' speech at first due to her heavy accent and a slight slur, as if her jaw didn't always obey her intentions. "You are kin to Macbeth?"

Jessie tilted her head in confusion at the question but saw no reason to lie. "He was my uncle."

"Did you know him well?"

"Not at all."

"I see." Aldis sat very still, an exotic goddess rising from colorful smoke. "I hoped you could tell me why he ordered the deaths of a helpless woman and her children."

At home they had spoken of this. "One shouldn't believe stories when those telling them have reason to blacken the king's name."

"But there is a witness to this one." Aldis glanced at the Viking leader, who'd set up a small altar and now knelt before it. "Leif was there when your uncle's men murdered his mother and her children. It is why he has sworn a blood oath on the males of Macbeth's line."

Jessie moved a little to the side to avoid the smoke from the campfire, which made her cough and obscured her view of Aldis' face. "Why would the Scottish king murder a Norwegian family?"

Aldis frowned delicately. "Leif is a Scot who came to Norway as a boy."

"And how does he know my uncle was responsible for this deed?"

"The nurse who saved him, distant kin to my uncle, often told the story of the day when the king sent men to kill everyone in the castle, even the servants. She said Macbeth's line should be ended in revenge for the deed."

Jessie's mind raced, interpreting what she'd seen but not heard at the clan-hold. They'd found no men of Macbeth's line, so where were these men heading now with such purpose? If Leif knew their sister Tessa had twin boys, he would go to Brixton. "This Leif would kill children?"

Aldis' face remained blank. "His brothers were children, and it did not save them. If his nurse had not hidden him in the root cellar, he too would have died." She seemed eager to explain Leif's behavior, perhaps to excuse it. "In recent days Leif has had great misfortune. He has concluded there is a curse on him."

"He asked you to find the cause of it." Jessie guessed Aldis' physical limitations were balanced by heightened powers in the magical arts.

Aldis closed her eyes briefly, as if tired. "It is my duty to help others if I can. Searching the bones, I saw signs that Leif had neglected loved ones." A flicker of emotion crossed her face. "Believing the omens point to those long-ago deaths, he's come to avenge his family."

A watcher of people, Jessie guessed Aldis disagreed in some measure with Leif's decision. She'd read the omens but hadn't expected the results she was now experiencing.

And why had they come to Scotland? "Surely he knows Macbeth is dead."

"That should have ended the call for blood." Aldis' tone hinted that was her wish, but she went on, "Last winter Leif's pregnant wife and two sons died in a fire. He believes it was a punishment from the gods, because he did not act to end

Macbeth's line."

"I don't understand."

Aldis gazed into the fire, apparently seeing a picture within it. "Leif's father was a Scottish lord, what you call a thane. Leif was second oldest of four brothers. One day when he was almost ten, their father came home to say he was no longer safe in Scotland. Leif recalls that his mother cried, asking if Scotland was safe for her and her children. Leif's father said she'd be well if she simply denied knowing his whereabouts.

"Several days later, as Leif and his nurse Sigrid were storing vegetables in the root cellar, they heard screams from the house. Leif wanted to help, but Sigrid held him back. He struggled against her, but she was strong, and soon all went quiet in the house."

Jessie shivered, imagining the chaotic sounds, the boy's panic, the servant's determination.

"In time someone came to the cellar. Sigrid pulled Leif into a dark corner, behind some bags of turnips, and they huddled there, terrified. Leif said it seemed like hours before the man turned to go. He peeped out once and saw a sword stained with blood in the man's hand.

"It was a long time before Sigrid tiptoed to the door, listened, and determined it was safe to leave their hiding place. Stepping into the castle yard, they saw the first of the bodies. There were more inside the house: Leif's mother, his brothers, and the servants. One was Sigrid's own son, run through with a sword. She said the killers must have thought he was Leif."

"How terrible!"

"Sigrid and Leif walked all the way to Angle-land, where her sister lived. There they learned the murders had been ordered by the Scottish king, Macbeth. Anglish troops were gathering to kill the monster and restore the true heir, Malcolm, to the throne. Sigrid wanted no more of Scotland, though. She believed the only way to keep Leif safe was to return to her childhood home in Norway. There Leif became Svenn Arneson's foster son and, eventually, heir to his lands.

Jessie was silent, considering the tragic tale Aldis had related. Had her uncle really been responsible for the deaths of the thane's wife and children? She knew little of her father, but by all accounts he'd been a good man. Could his brother have indeed been such a monster?

Aldis abruptly changed the subject. "You are shivering." Shadows had deepened, and a chill descended on the camp the fire couldn't adequately combat. Jessie shivered in her thin night-robe. "Hnossa," Aldis said without turning. "Give this girl clothing. Shoes, too. Your second pair."

The woman's bottom lip pushed toward her nose as if to keep herself from objecting. Stepping into the tent, she took up a cloth bag, removed what was probably her only spare outfit, and tossed the clothes and a pair of felt slippers into Jessie's lap.

"Thank you," Jessie said, grateful despite the woman's ungracious manner. To Aldis she said, "You're very kind."

"A small good deed may balance somewhat an error in judgment," she said obliquely. "Go into the tent and put them on."

Jessie obeyed, glad for the privacy. The tent smelled of herbs and flowers. There was a small chest at one side, a soft sleeping pallet nearby, and a blanket that probably served as Hnossa's bed.

When she emerged, dressed in a linen skirt and over-blouse only a little too big for her, Aldis nodded with satisfaction. "Now you must return to Lukas. I will not invite you to dine with me, since you wouldn't enjoy the fare I require."

Jessie turned to see Lukas waiting a short way off. He nodded gravely to Aldis, whose stoic face melted into a smile. Repeating her thanks to both women, Jessie returned to her captor.

Leading the way to a grassy spot, Lukas opened the bag he'd carried on his back so she could ride. He removed several food items and laid them out on a kerchief. "Eat." A man of few words.

"What does Aldis eat?" she asked.

"She drinks a concoction of cowbane, juniper, and lemon balm during the day and mandrake with poppy-seed and vinegar before bed." Lukas almost smiled, and Jessie thought his face benefited from it. "You'll do better to dine with me."

Jessie took a withered but edible apple and a piece of white, hard cheese with a strong smell and a sharp tang. "Thank you." She ate hungrily, having had nothing since supper the night before. As Lukas took cheese and a handful of nuts for himself she asked, "Why do you care what happens to me?"

"It wasn't necessary to take a hostage." He glanced at the knot of Vikings engaged in eating their own evening meal. "I'll do what I can to convince Leif to set you free when we reach Glamis. Until then, stay close to me, and you'll be safe. Do you understand?"

"Yes."

"Good. Now I must bind your hands, or someone else will do it." She submitted meekly as he tied her hands before her then secured the rope's other end to a high tree branch. Unable to reach the spot from the ground and unable to climb up to it with her hands tied, Jessie had reasonable range of movement but no way to escape. It was cleverly done, not that she appreciated his talent.

Seated on the ground, she regarded Lukas with curiosity, wondering what made him different from the others. Bjorn had called him Outsider and Norman, which meant he wasn't a member of their band. He'd promised to secure her freedom if he could, yet he tied her so she couldn't escape. What sort of man was he?

Though she didn't know why, Jessie felt safe with the taciturn Lukas. He seemed uninterested in rape, which was more than any woman taken prisoner by Viking marauders could hope for. What *was* he interested in? Seeking the most comfortable spot she could find on the hard ground, Jessie resolved to stop thinking on it and rest. No telling what tomorrow would bring.

Chapter Five

Jenna

It took Jenna only a few hours to catch up to the Vikings. She followed the familiar path as the sun came to full strength, turning the chill and dew of the morning into memories. Once she heard them ahead, she slowed her pace, aware she could do nothing until nightfall. They made no attempt at stealth, shouting back and forth as if on a pleasure outing. *For them it is*, she said to herself. *A Viking's only happy when he's just murdered someone.* The image of Blind Ian's lifeless body returned, and the desire to avenge the harmless old man's death burned inside her.

She had to rescue her sister first. True revenge would be for Donald to pursue. Once he was well again, he would assemble the Scots and hunt down the Viking murderers. If they let her come, Jenna would herself kill the one who'd come so near to catching her, the one with the tracker's eye and heart. Recalling that first glance, when he'd seemed to read her thoughts, she shivered. Evil lurked behind that intriguing face.

She vowed to remember Donald, still and pale, and Ian, even more so. Vikings were born to violence and raised with no respect for human life. She'd heard fireside tales of their raids, of Christian priests gutted, of nuns and other innocent women ravaged. They were old stories, but the Scots had long memories. Vikings were different from normal folk: blood-thirsty with strange gods and disgusting customs. Barbarians.

When the group ahead of her stopped, Jenna climbed a tree to watch their preparations for night. A serving woman led Jessie to a tent set up for Aldis. As Jessie and the seer talked, the servant gave Jessie some clothing, though not willingly. When Jessie had changed, the tracker led her to a spot where he'd spread two blankets on the ground, a few feet apart. Gradually, the camp went quiet as one by one the Vikings made beds for themselves under the stars. The leader, Leif, sat before a second tent, speaking seldom, apparently existing in a world of his own making. Aldis and her serving woman disappeared into their tent, and shortly afterward Jenna heard singing. She couldn't tell if Aldis sang or was soothed by her maid's soft crooning.

The tracker and Jessie sat together, away from the others. He laid food out between them, and Jessie, always too trusting, ate it. Sharing his meal brought the man no credit with Jenna. He was only keeping his captive strong enough to survive another day. Still, as he spoke to her, Jessie's fearful expression relaxed a little. Something he'd said had relieved her mind.

After they'd eaten, the tracker tied Jessie to a tree then stretched out on the ground some distance away from her, closing his eyes. Soon after, the man called Bjorn approached Jessie and pulled the knots that held her hands tighter, so that she grimaced in pain. He grasped her chin, holding her so she stared into his eyes. Jenna's heart froze. Something he said made Jessie lower her eyes.

The tracker shifted slightly, calling attention to his presence, and Bjorn moved off, satisfied to have taken away any peace of mind their prisoner had gained from the other man's reassurances.

A watch was posted, a young man whose interest in the captive was obvious. Ignoring him as if used to the leering gazes of strange men, Jessie made herself as comfortable as she could and slept—or pretended to. As the night grew darker, the sentry moved close to the fire, poking its depths with a stick from time to time and idly regarding the forest around him. Sounds faded as birds went to their rest and movement within the camp slowed. After an hour, the sentry's boredom was obvious. Jenna guessed they were lucky the tracker hadn't taken first watch.

After what seemed like a long time, the sentry's head began to droop. Bringing his knees close to his chest, he folded his arms and dropped his head onto them. Another ten minutes and he was, if not asleep, at least so drowsy Jenna felt safe approaching the camp as long as she remained outside the fire's glow.

When Jenna touched her sister's shoulder, she stirred immediately, as if her unconscious had remained on guard amongst her enemies. When Jenna bent close so Jessie could see her face, she smiled and put her hands out so Jenna could untie the cords that held her. The rope was rough, and as Jenna worked it grated softly against itself. They both stopped, breathless, as the tracker roused, grunting softly. Jenna stepped back into the shadows and Jessie relaxed her body as if asleep. Raising his head enough to see she was still there, her captor found a more comfortable way to lie and settled back to sleep.

Once his breathing slowed again, Jenna returned and finished freeing Jessie's hands. There was a second near-disaster as the sentry roused, stood, and began a circuit of the camp, peering into the darkness. Jessie feigned sleep while Jenna retreated into the trees, glad she'd changed to dark clothing and a deep hood she could draw over her face. When he'd satisfied himself that all was well, the young man added wood to the fire and settled again, staring into the flames until his chin once again drooped and he slept.

With painful slowness, Jessie rose to her feet and moved toward Jenna, who stood at the edge of the firelight. The girls tensed with every noise and movement, but the Vikings slept on. Clasping hands, they retreated farther into the trees, where Jenna had left Jessie's boots. She sighed in relief at the feel of them. The special boot their old servant

Banaugh had designed had a built-up sole that compensated for her damaged right hip and allowed her to walk almost normally. A barefoot escape would have been almost impossible. Now they had a chance.

When it was safe to whisper Jessie asked, "Donald, is he alive?"

"When I left, yes, but gravely hurt."

"What if the Vikings return?"

"They won't find us asleep a second time."

Jessie nodded, hastening her steps. "We must give as much warning as we can."

"One of us must reach home." Jenna had promised herself her sister would not be a prisoner again.

Sooner than they'd hoped, a noise made them go still. On the trail only twenty feet to their right, moonlight revealed the face of the man Jenna thought of as the Tracker. Behind him was a second man, his face hidden by shadows. They moved almost silently, and without a moment of brightness in the cloudy sky, the girls wouldn't have known they were there.

The men stopped, listening, and the twins held their breath, fearing their probing eyes could see through the darkness to their hiding place. They couldn't, of course, and they moved onward, the Tracker leading in his deliberate, watchful way. The odor of mint wafted toward them: Bjorn.

When they were out of sight Jenna whispered, "Exchange clothes with me."

"Why?"

"Do it!" Used to following Jenna's lead, Jessie obeyed. Soon Jenna wore the clothes that had once belonged to

Aldis' maid. "Now stay here, out of sight, no matter what happens. If I can, I will follow you home, but you must continue alone once they are gone."

"No!"

"The clan must be alerted," Jenna insisted. "And tell Meg to send someone to warn Tessa, someone who can travel faster than the Vikings." Jessie opened her mouth to ask how Tessa was involved, but there wasn't time. "It must be this way," she told Jessie. "I can run farther and faster than you can."

Jessie grasped Jenna's arm fiercely. "Don't try to outrun them. Once they begin chasing you, hide until they give up looking."

"I will." Recalling the tracker's determined expression, Jenna doubted he'd give up, ever.

It was a bitter parting, with no time to speak their grief. "I love you, Jenna."

"And I love you. Don't start for home until you're sure they've gone." With a last squeeze of Jessie's hand, Jenna hurried away, heading toward the path and the men who hunted them.

Chapter Six

Jessie

Jessie listened intently, interpreting events she could hear but not see. There was a shout as one of them spotted Jenna scrambling through the woods. Twigs cracked, leaves swished, birds called out in confusion. Jessie tensed with each new sound, and her stomach ached with the urge to spur Jenna on with her own spirit. After a while the sounds faded, and she was alone.

For the first time in her life, Jessie was afraid of the dark. Until now, darkness had been her friend. Often she stole outside alone after the others were asleep to listen to conversations among the trees, the stars, and the air. Alone in the night, she was free of eyes that noted her ungainly walk. The black night hid her deformity.

Now, far from home, fearful, and exhausted, night seemed threatening. There might be a Viking behind any tree or rock. She might have lost her beloved sister in the darkness. She might lose the pathway home and fail in the task Jenna had set for her.

A night bird called and she jumped, staring into the trees. *Courage,* she told herself sternly. *Jenna said what you must do.* But Jenna wasn't here. She could no longer borrow courage from her. She must reach home and warn Meg, who'd send Tessa a warning. But a part of her mind whispered, *You can't. You're a crippled, timid mouse who needs Jenna to lean on.*

Jessie had always been the fearful one. Ornery cattle, serpents, even spiders, made her shrink away. Jenna had always stepped in, slapping the cow on the nose, shooing away the snake, and gently moving the spider to another location. How many slimy, scary things were between Jessie and home at this moment?

Fiercely she pushed her misgivings aside. Jenna had led the pursuers in another direction. Jenna was enterprising and quick, so she would escape capture. Home was uphill; all she had to do was let her feet feel the incline. Setting her lips, Jessie rose from her place of hiding and moved toward the trail. She heard only the usual night sounds now, the swish of breeze in the new leaves. Whatever else was happening was far away. The trail was clear in the moonlight, a silver band shining up from the darker green of the forest. With a last look back at the spot where it disappeared around a curve, Jessie started for home.

Chapter Seven

Jenna

The Vikings moved up the trail, the one she thought of as the Tracker stopping every few seconds to listen and scan the trees. Jenna hesitated, doubting her chances for success. She'd chosen her course, however, and it was too late to change her mind.

Picking up a twig from the ground, she snapped it in two, making a sharp sound. The giant turned, gaze sweeping the mountainside. The moon showed for the briefest moment, lighting three shapes, two tall men, one slight girl. Bjorn stiffened like a dog on the hunt when he caught sight of Jenna. Then he was running. The moon disappeared, but she imagined the second man joining the chase, moving effortlessly toward her on strong legs. Plunging into the depths of a large stand of pines, Jenna ducked under low branches that scraped her back and arms. Her hope was that the taller, wider Vikings would find it impassible.

The drawbacks of her plan soon became painfully obvious. The pursuers' longer legs carried them closer with every step. Quiet was all but impossible, so while she fought her way to an unknown destination, they simply followed the sounds of her passage. And the shoes she'd taken from Jessie were useless. Within seconds she'd lost one. The other followed soon after.

It was a pitiful effort, and when a hand gripped her shoulder, almost pulling her off her feet, Jenna was as angry at herself as at the Viking. What had made her think she could elude these hateful men? She comforted herself with the thought Jessie was safe to continue homeward, where their people would protect her.

Twisting her arm painfully, Bjorn said, "I thought I tied you well." She said nothing. Let him believe he made a mistake. Let him think on his failings.

Taking a coil of rope from his knapsack he grasped her hands, pulling them behind her. "That isn't needed," the other said. "Look." He pointed at her right foot, where blood showed black against her white skin. She hadn't even known she was hurt, but once she was aware of it, the cut throbbed painfully.

"She can hardly walk, much less run," the Tracker said.

Bjorn sniffed. "It appeared she couldn't walk earlier today, yet she moved well enough just now." He couldn't deny her injury. Would they carry her back to their camp or simply kill her and leave her body for the wolves? She didn't think the cut was crippling, but if they thought it was, she might get a chance to escape.

Bjorn's next comment sounded odd, as if his voice had undergone a change. "The others will wonder what has happened. Return and tell them we've recaptured her. I'll bring her when I've bandaged the foot."

There was a pause, and in those few seconds, Jenna imagined her future. Bjorn wanted his companion out of the way. Her skin crawled as if his hands were already upon her, and she bit her lip with dread.

"You go back and tell them." She'd heard little of the Tracker's voice, but she sensed a challenge in the words. He didn't like Bjorn.

Fair hair moved in the moonlight, a gesture of irritation, perhaps anger. "Why?"

"I trust myself with a helpless female. I have no such knowledge of you."

There was another pause, and Jenna sensed Bjorn trying to decide whether his response would be confrontation, wheedling, or reluctant assent. In the end, he managed a laugh of derision. "All right, if you would play priest and physician to a worthless Scotti girl, I won't fight you over it." His voice turned hard. "There'll be another time." He stepped closer, using his height in an attempt at intimidation, but the Tracker didn't move. "If she escapes again, I'll see that her family up the mountain dies, to the last babe. Their blood will be on your head."

They looked at each other a moment longer—Bjorn angry, Lukas calm—then Bjorn moved off. In moments the sounds of his departure faded. The two were alone.

The Northman stirred, letting out a deep breath as if starting over. "Sit," he ordered. Jenna sat, her back against a tree, while he knelt, took a bag from his shoulder, and began making a fire, using flint from the bag and twigs from the ground around them. Once a tiny blaze lit the night, he fed it bigger bits until it burned cheerily in the darkness. Taking a cloth from the bag, he wet it with water from a small skin.

"Have you a feather bed and a magic hen in that bag as well?" she asked sarcastically.

"I don't like to be without resources," he answered.

When he moved toward her Jenna shrank back, but the Tracker took her foot and began cleaning the blood away with a gentle touch. The cut wasn't deep, but it went all the way across her instep, and she felt it pulse with each beat of her heart. Frowning, the Viking went once more to his pack and returned with a foul-smelling paste that he smeared on the cut. Wrapping the cloth around her foot, he held it tightly for several minutes. Once the bleeding stopped, he tied it in place.

Standing, he looked around, and Jenna followed his

gaze. The forest floor was a burnt-orange hue, thick with old pine needles. The trees screened the wind, closing them in so it felt as if they were far from everywhere.

"Pine makes soft bedding," the Tracker said. Jenna glared at him. A Viking speaking of bedding was ominous. If he intended rape, he wouldn't win easily.

Instead of approaching, however, he sat down near the fire, back against a tree, and regarded her with curiosity. "Did you not believe what I said before?"

She didn't know what he'd said, but it didn't matter. "Nothing you could say would make me think well of you, Viking."

Noting her defensive posture, he answered an unspoken question. "I don't take unwilling women. Enough come to me of their own choice to satisfy me." Reaching for his pouch, he rummaged through it for a piece of bread and tossed it to her. "Eat this."

The bread was hard, but Jenna ate it all. She needed strength, for she planned to escape as soon as possible. He seemed to read her thoughts but said nothing, merely handing her the skin of water so she could wash down the dry morsel. As he did, he noticed fresh blood on the bandage on her foot. Deftly he untied the knots and redid his wrapping, tightening it until she winced.

Reaching into the pouch again, the Tracker pulled out a leather jerkin. With his knife he cut two rough circles from the back of the vest. Using laces from the front of the garment, he tied the circles around Jenna's feet, making primitive boots that would protect her from the worst of the terrain. Finished, he surveyed his work critically. "They're better than nothing." His eyes glinted with humor in the firelight. "I hope you appreciate the sacrifice of my best vest for your comfort."

Jenna was at a loss. Despite earlier discussion among the Vikings of killing her, this one seemed concerned for her comfort. "I'm grateful, um..." She didn't know his name, and "Viking" or "Northman" didn't seem appropriate at the moment.

He shrugged as if to say it was not worth consideration. Rising, he put out a hand to help her stand and test the injured foot. Without thinking Jenna accepted the tacit offer, and a jolt struck her as if lightning traveled up her arm and into her body. When his eyes met hers, she realized the Tracker felt it too. They hesitated, neither aware of anything but each other as it seemed the world slowed around them. His free hand rose and came toward her face, but he didn't touch it. The hand hung in the air, apparently pushed in one direction by some emotion and pulled in the other by something else.

"I am Lukas." His voice was softer, hesitant and almost choked. Jenna opened her mouth to say her name, but nothing came out. For once anger failed to protect her, and she vibrated with the rhythm of his pulse. What was happening to her?

Taking a deep breath, she forced herself to remember where she was and with whom. The frightened faces of her family rose in her mind. This was her enemy. She took a step back, releasing her hand from his. With the spell broken, anger poured in to replace what she'd felt a moment before. "I'll be less trouble to you now, Viking."

Lukas read the message in her tone. "Rest," he said evenly. "When the bleeding stops, we'll go on." He sat down at the opposite side of the fire. "What's your name?"

"My name doesn't matter."

He raised his eyebrows in a patient gesture. "Nevertheless, I would like to know it."

"I am Jenna." She wondered if Jessie had told him her name, but it seemed she had not.

"Jenna. I haven't heard this name before."

She didn't explain that her mother, Kenna, had refused to name her last two children, so distressed was she at the prospect of more daughters. Jenna had heard from the servants how her father Kenneth took over their care, naming Jessie after his wife's mother and Jenna with a similar name to his wife's. As far as anyone could tell, she had not been impressed.

Jenna recalled no hint of affection from her mother: no caress, no soft words, no notice most days. When their father died, it seemed as if they'd been orphaned. Kenna had lived a few years more, wrapped in self-pity, but the love the twins got came from others, not from her. Jenna's most vivid memory of her mother was being told, so young she was barely able to understand, that she'd caused her sister's infirmity. "Two babies in my womb was too much," Kenna told her healthy daughter. "The larger one broke the smaller one's bones."

Though Jessie never blamed Jenna for her lameness, Jenna blamed herself. She did everything in her power to protect and provide for her twin. Perhaps because of Kenna's harshness, others in the clan coddled Kenneth's last two children: their old servant Banaugh, her brother-in-law Donald—

That reminded Jenna of Blind Ian, murdered by these men. She steeled herself to forget the past and concentrate on her hatred of Vikings. And on escape.

They were silent for some time, staring into the flames. "He was my hearth-brother." It took a moment for Jenna to realize he meant Leif. "He seeks to regain his battle-luck, for a leader is no good without it."

"Battle-luck?"

"When Viking warriors fight, they follow leaders they choose. A man who is cursed will have no men to follow him, and thus will gain no glory."

"What battle?" Jenna sensed he referred not to some nebulous future fight, but one coming soon.

Lukas didn't answer her question. "Leif does what he feels he must."

Viking battles were none of Jenna's affair, but Lukas' desire to talk signaled a relaxed mood. Time to seize her chance. "I must go into the trees."

He understood her meaning but hesitated. "You'll run again."

"How can I, with my foot sliced like an onion?"

He chuckled bitterly. "Do you take me for a fool?" Rising to a crouch, he fed a twig onto the fire. "I'll make you this bargain. You may go—not far, and you must sing all the while. Do you sing?"

She sniffed in disdain. "Not at such times."

His laugh was genuine this time. "That's the bargain. Sing, so I know where you are. If you stop singing, I'll come after you." His expression sobered. "Think of your family. Bjorn doesn't make idle threats."

Jenna didn't bother to say what she thought of Bjorn's vow. Exaggerating her limp she went into the trees, searching her mind for a song that conveyed her disgust for Vikings. She settled on one she'd heard Donald and his cousins sing when they were deep into drink. It concerned a Viking named Ivar the Boneless, making sport of his nickname and a possible sexual explanation for it.

When she'd gone as far as she dared Jenna stopped, still singing as she measured the opportunities her surroundings offered. The moon was out for the moment, but looking up, she saw it would soon be hidden by clouds. If she chose the right direction, one he didn't expect her to take, she might find a place to hide where he couldn't find her.

Downward, then, because he'd expect her to head uphill, toward home. Off to the right, a steep outcrop of rock jutted. If she could swing herself under the ledge, she might hide in its shadow until he gave up looking for her. Falling silent, Jenna moved quickly toward her goal. At that moment the moon went dark, and the night covered her.

The drop was steeper than she thought, and it was impossible to tell what lay beneath the outcrop. She had no time to wonder. Sliding down the face of the rock, she gripped the edge with both hands and swung herself under the ledge. Pain shot through her foot at the effort, but she ignored it. Better pain than capture.

Sounds of Lukas' pursuit soon came. He walked back and forth above her, no doubt straining to see movement that would betray her path. There was a soft grunt as he knelt on the outcrop to look down. To her great relief, the underside of the ledge was deep enough to put her out of sight to all but direct inspection.

She almost smiled, imagining the Viking's frustration at losing her a second, actually a third time. He'd thought kind treatment would induce her to accept captivity, but he was wrong. A Scot would die rather than live under the control of others, and when the others were Vikings, it was that much worse.

Jenna huddled on the jagged hillside, her wounded foot throbbing. The Tracker's boots scraped on the rock above her. He'd picked up a stick from the fire to use as a torch, and the light it cast moved back and forth as he tried to discover where she'd gone. Soon he moved away, pushing branches aside as he scoured the area for signs of her passing. Hope he'd give up faded. This Viking was not one to do that.

A long, low growl from above made Jenna cringe even farther into her shelter. There was no mistaking the sound of a wolf. She almost cried out a warning but forced herself to remain silent. The growl came again, lower and more ferocious. Did Lukas have the sword he'd laid aside while he tended her wound? How would he face a wolf bare-handed?

The growl rose to a snarl, and the animal's claws scrabbled on the ledge as it charged. A terrible scuffle followed, and it was impossible to separate the sounds of feet scraping on the rocks, snapping teeth, and involuntary grunts of released breath. Growls mixed with cries of pain, both human and animal. Jenna clenched her teeth, unsure what to hope for. Finally she heard a high-pitched yelp, followed by silence. The struggle was over.

When the quiet continued longer than she could abide, Jenna emerged from her hiding place and peered over the ledge. Nothing moved. Using both hands and feet, she crawled up the steep slope until she reached firm ground. The moon had emerged from the clouds, revealing a dead wolf with a knife protruding from its chest. Beside it Lukas the Viking lay, inert and pale, a dark stain spreading from a deep wound in his side.

It took Jenna the better part of the night to get Lukas back to their rough camp. She couldn't carry him, and in the dark it was impossible to tell how badly he was injured. First she returned to the fire, adding fuel to keep other beasts away. Then she found a blanket in his pack and took it to where he lay unconscious. With great difficulty she rolled him onto the woolen square then dragged it to the camp. It was a struggle, for he was half again her weight and longer than the fabric by at least a foot. Once back at the fire, she set to work saving her enemy's life.

The wolf's teeth had caught him at the soft flesh of his side, just above the hip. Although the bite was deep, no great gush of blood signaled rupture of an artery. Examining him by the firelight, she found scratches on his thigh where claws had ripped the skin. Those would be painful but not life-threatening. A bump on the back of his head led her to guess he'd been knocked unconscious as he fell backward under the beast's attack. She thought she could stop the bleeding from the bite. Unless he'd cracked his skull when the beast landed on him, he might live. Though she told herself she didn't care, Jenna couldn't leave him to die.

Without letting herself consider the consequences, she removed Lukas' trousers. Fabric left in a wound made it likely to fester. She cleaned the gash, using the last of the water to rinse out dirt and bits of cloth. Locating the smelly salve he'd used on her foot, she applied it to the wound then bandaged it with strips torn from the bottom of his shirt. Following the sound of dripping water, she located a tiny waterfall and refilled the skin. Returning, she dipped another strip of cloth in the cold water and placed it around his head. She didn't know if that would help but doubted it could hurt. Having exhausted her small store of medical knowledge, Jenna sat down near the fire and watched for signs of recovery.

After what seemed like a long time, Lukas' eyes opened. At first he tensed, ready to fight his attacker. "It's all right," she said soothingly. "The wolf is dead."

His eyes met hers blearily, and he mumbled, "Prettr." She didn't know what that meant, but he added groggily, "You sing well, too." His face slackened and he drifted off into a sleep she sensed was restful, not dangerous. Adding more fuel to the fire, she settled down beside him, figuring she too should rest.

She woke to find herself surrounded by Northmen. Leif stood over her, his face pinched with curiosity. "What happened here?"

At the sound of voices, Lukas' eyes opened. "I was attacked by a wolf, probably the one Bjorn wounded," he said. "The girl took care of me."

As his hands moved beneath the blanket, Lukas' eyes widened. Looking beyond Jenna, he saw his clothes lying where she'd tossed them as she tended his wounds. She suppressed a tiny smile of revenge. You saw me naked, Viking, but you no longer have an advantage in the matter.

There was much ado among Lukas' companions. Following Jenna's directions, two of them retrieved the pelt so Lukas would have both a memento and a warm cape. Others cut saplings and made a conveyance that allowed their wounded comrade to lie almost prone while two men pulled him, using leather straps tied around their chests. Soon they were on their way down the mountain again, and by noon they'd rejoined the main group.

Aldis listened closely as the story of the wolf's attack was told. "What made you stray from the fire in the dark of night?" she asked. Lukas pretended not to hear the question, but his cheeks reddened as if he'd told a lie, which in a way he had.

Chapter Eight

Jessie

As the sun reached its zenith Jessie stumbled into the familiar clearing, exhausted and anxious. People moved about, following their daily routines, but they were subdued. No one sang or called out a greeting or a teasing comment. A shout went up when someone sighted Jessie, and soon she was inundated with questions. Would the Vikings return? Had they harmed her? And worst of all, where was Jenna?

Promising to tell her story later, Jessie went to the main house to find Meg. Her sister dozed in a chair beside the bed where Donald lay, and Jessie went to her on tiptoe. Donald's hand was warm when she touched it, but he was pale and still. The herbs used on his wound gave off a sweet, pungent smell.

Sensing her presence, Meg opened her eyes. "Jessie? Jenna brought you home?"

Jessie shook her head. "She helped me escape, but I think the Vikings caught her. She said I must tell you she will try—" The terrors of the last twenty-four hours caught up with her, and she began to cry. She flung herself at Meg, who wept with her as they held each other. When they parted, each wiping her eyes, Jessie asked, "Has he awakened?"

Meg looked at her husband's still form. "No, but perhaps it's best that way. His body must repair the hurt, so perhaps he should not know enough to think and worry." She smoothed the blanket that covered Donald. "I fed him soup a while ago, and he swallowed it like a dreaming child."

"Then his body indeed knows what's best." Jessie repeated Jenna's message. "We must prepare to defend ourselves in case the Vikings return, and we must send word to Tessa that she's in danger."

"I should have thought of that." Meg explained the peril Tessa's boys faced from the Vikings, her dull tone revealing that she was still overwhelmed with shock and sadness. "We must tell her they're coming, but how can it be accomplished?"

Jessie had thought about that as she walked home. "Is the singer still here?"

"I suppose so."

"He could go to Glamis and send a message. Tessa will recognize his name and trust that his words are true." Jessie glanced again at her unconscious brother-in-law. "I'll find him and ask."

Meg's expression showed surprise at Jessie's initiative, though if it had been Jenna, she wouldn't even have noticed. Too exhausted to question it, she nodded agreement.

Jessie began her search with a servant named Anne who was feeding Ailsa's two-year-old. "Where is the gleeman who brought Tessa's letter?"

Anna's face took on an odd expression. "I couldn't say."

"When did you see him last?"

Her lips thinned in disapproval. "After those men left, we all saw him." She turned back to the child, and Jessie moved on, confused. When two further requests for the gleeman's whereabouts brought similar responses, she became suspicious. Finally she went to find Rob, a dour, crab-like herdsman who lacked the ability to lie or dissemble. He was tending a cut on the hind leg of a ram, as gentle with the animal as he was ungentle with his fellow humans. "Rob, where is the gleeman?"

His face went still. "Gone."

Her eyebrows rose. "Gone? I didn't pass him on the

53

path."

Rob's eyelids drooped. "That one wouldna want t' meet wi' one o' us."

Picking up the threat in his tone, she asked, "What did you do?"

"We dinna hurt him." It was said too quickly, and she knew it for a lie. "It were no' his place t' speak out. He needed a lesson t' teach him t' keep his mouth shut."

"You beat him."

Rob looked away from her. "We let him ken no' t' stick his nose in again."

"What did he do that was so terrible?"

Shaking a finger at her, Rob said, "Th' lad told them murderers where Tessa lives." Rob released the bleating animal. "Now they'll gae an' harm her babes."

Jessie recalled the scene she'd witnessed from the trees. Leif had been demanding, Donald hesitant. Then the big Viking—Bjorn—had murdered Ian. The gleeman had saved their lives by telling where Tessa's boys could be found.

Her people had taken their grief and anger out on the gleeman, sending him on his way with blows and curses. She must have passed him on the path, but he'd no doubt hidden when he heard her coming, unwilling to face either Scot or Viking.

Leaving Rob to his work, Jessie started back to the house. She'd hoped to convince the young man to go to England and warn Tessa. Alone, he'd move faster than the Viking band. He knew the way, while Leif and his band would have to find someone to guide them. He could have given Tessa and Jeffrey time to ensure their children's safety. But he was gone, and he'd be unwilling to help them now.

They'd exchanged a few words the night before the attack, when all was well in the clan-hold. She'd liked his smile, ready laugh, and melodious voice. Alfred—his name came to her—had been kind, ignoring her limp and complimenting her hair. She hoped her overzealous clansmen hadn't hurt him badly.

Unsure of what to do next, Jessie surveyed the area. Though momentous events had occurred, the clearing appeared unchanged. Ringed by pines that scented the air and blocked the worst of the wind, the clan-hold was familiar and reassuring. Her family's house, a little larger than the others, sat against the mountain. People moved in and out of the dwellings and outbuildings with silent efficiency, carrying tools that signaled what chore they'd take on next. Closer observation revealed a difference, however. The men who possessed weapons wore them today, strapped to their backs or hanging from their waists. Everyone was watchful, eyes sweeping the area every few seconds, ears tuned to each unfamiliar sound. A new grave served as a reminder of their reason to be on guard.

With Jenna gone, Donald hurt, and Meg focused on tending him, the rest of her people would have to take on more tasks. Sheep didn't care if a person got sick. Crops didn't wait for a good time to ripen. No worker could be spared at this time, for the whole year's harvest depended on a few short months of summer work. And not one of them knew the way to Brixton. England was far away and alien, a place conjured in Tessa's letters but not real to them, as Scotland was.

Who could warn Tessa of the danger? Who was determined enough to find the way but able to be spared from the work here? The answer came with a deep sigh.

There was only her.

Arguments arose in Jessie's mind. She'd spent her life in the Cairngorms, had little sense of the world outside. *But there is no one else.* She was lame, unable to outrace a dozen Vikings. *But there is no one else.* She had only a name, Brixton Manor, and a vague location, somewhere near York. *But there is no one else.*

Donald had given her a pony, a shaggy little beast that could walk all day, though it refused to run. She called him Foot, for he gave Jessie freedom her own feet did not. "A one-woman beast," her brother-in-law pronounced him, since Foot was likely to kick anyone else who approached him. Even Jenna, usually able to charm man and beast, had never won Foot's favor. More than once she'd suffered double bruises when the pony's hind hooves caught her on the thigh as she tried to sneak up behind him with a halter.

Jessie readied herself, telling no one what she was up to, and waited until it was dark and the household was asleep. Tethering Foot to a tree, she returned to the house a last time. Meg slept in a chair beside Donald's bed in case he should wake. Ailsa sat by the fire, ready if she were needed. Jessie touched her arm, signaling quiet. "I'm going to Glamis." Her sister opened her mouth to protest, but she said, "No one else can be spared. I will send a message to Tessa and return."

Ailsa was shocked, used to Jessie tending babies and knitting stockings. No one expected her to take decisive action in a crisis.

But she had to now. "Tell Meg in the morning. And tell her—" She stopped to steady her voice. "I'll seek Jenna in Glamis. If the Vikings are there, I'll go to the castle for help." The thane would force the Northmen to release their prisoner. At least she hoped he would.

Leaving Ailsa with mouth agape, Jessie took up the bag she'd prepared earlier and added food from the larder. On a hook she found a canteen Donald had fashioned for himself and filled it with water from a bucket. With a brief hug for her sister she went out into the night.

Foot snuffed in curiosity at her approach, as if to ask if she were sure of this night-time adventure. There was a guard at the trail-head now, a precaution in case the Vikings returned. Leading the pony to the starting point, she explained that Meg had sent her to find a special herb for Donald. "It must be picked at midnight to be fully potent."

The guard nodded understanding. "'Tis often so, I've heard."

That lie told, she thanked him, feeling tears in her eyes at this last contact with someone she knew.

As he helped her onto the pony, Jessie took a last look around the clan-hold, so much the same yet so changed. Two of their number were gone, one dead, one a prisoner. Their leader was gravely hurt, his wife paralyzed with grief. Although home looked the same, it would never again be so for Jessie. Without Jenna, it seemed almost an alien place.

Urging the pony on with a soft click of her tongue, Jessie admitted to herself that her trek down the mountain was as much in hopes of saving the sister closest to her as it was to warn the one she hardly knew.

Chapter Nine

Jenna

When the sun rose pale over the hills, the Viking party prepared to continue down the mountainside. Leif gave orders in his own tongue, and while the words and the cadence were unfamiliar, Jenna understood the gestures. She figured out that she, Lukas, and Aldis, along with her new guard Rothgar, Hnossa the maidservant, Aldis' four bearers, and two men ordered to pull Lukas' "land-boat," would continue down the main path, a slope less taxing than the meandering, skinny trails that turned off from it. The rest went off along those trails, probably hunting meat for the evening meal.

At midmorning it began to rain, not a gentle mist but a downpour that made the pathway treacherous and the travelers miserable. Jenna trudged stoically along beside Rothgar, a taciturn, lumpy-faced man who said little other than, "Move!" or "Faster!" He'd tied her hands behind her, making walking even more difficult. The cut on the ball of her foot throbbed with every step, but no one offered sympathy. Poor payment for saving the life of one of their own, she thought. Lukas was behind her, so she couldn't tell how he was faring. She guessed the jolting was agony for him.

They didn't stop at midday, though Jenna's legs were wooden with fatigue and her stomach growled with hunger. She caught a scent and saw Rothgar take a chunk of dried fish from his pouch and chew it as he walked. The others were apparently content with nothing. No one considered Jenna's needs, and the bread Lukas had given her the night before was a distant memory now.

As they trudged along, she considered how she might escape. The woods were thick in places, and they would hide her if she had enough time to get out of sight. Two things argued against that: her tied hands and Rothgar's vigilance. If she veered to one side, he swatted the back of her head to remind her only forward movement was allowed.

By the time they stopped at nightfall, Jenna had no thought except putting one foot in front of the other. Her face was covered with scratches, since she couldn't push brambles out of her way. Her feet were bruised, the right one bloody, for her makeshift shoes couldn't protect her from jagged rocks. Her muscles ached, arms from immobility, legs from the long trek, and back from constantly adjusting her balance to keep from falling on the steep terrain.

When they stopped, Rothgar pointed at the ground, indicating she should sit. The rain had ceased for the most part, but the ground was damp and uncomfortable. After helping to make camp, he brought Jenna a piece of dried fish and a chunk of bread almost too hard to bite. Sitting down beside her, he ate his own portion, apparently used to the meager fare.

As she gnawed at the bread, the last supper she'd had at home came to Jenna's mind. Meg had made mutton stew with still-warm, crusty oat bread to dip into it, and she recalled the heat and the tenderness of it on her tongue. If only she could return to the past! At home she was a macFindlaech, kin to the former king of Scotland and daughter of a family respected for honesty and leadership. Tears rose but she blinked them away, encouraging instead hatred for those who'd separated her from home. She'd never forgive these men, ever.

The Viking nudged her, indicating she could share his drink. She would have liked to refuse, but the food was so dry she needed something to wash it down. She tasted the liquid carefully, frowning at its bitterness. He laughed, saying something she didn't understand. As she handed back the skin, he put one hand in her hair and pulled her toward him.

"Prettr," Rothgar said, mouthing the words with exaggeration as if that would make her understand. When she didn't react, he rolled his eyes in concentration until he found the word he wanted. "Bonny." Pleased with himself, he repeated it. "Aye, bonny." She recoiled, but his grip was firm. He leaned toward her, his leering grin revealing what was on his mind.

A terse command ended the encounter, and Jenna turned to see Aldis frowning across the space between them. She said something more in a commanding voice, and Rothgar rose, his resentful glance revealing a measure of fear as well.

"Come!" Jenna followed him to where the woman sat. With a resentful nod of obeisance, Rothgar returned to his former place.

Aldis' luxurious fur was spread atop an oiled skin to protect it from the damp ground. Once again her legs were invisible under her pillows. She wore a simple woolen dress covered by a woolen cape against the evening chill. It was fastened at her shoulder with a brooch from which hung a cluster of metal objects that served as both decoration and tool-kit. On short chains hung scissors, sewing implements, and other items a woman might want close at hand. When she moved, they jingled against each other, making soft music.

Untie her hands," Aldis ordered, and her maid obeyed without once looking at Jenna's face. As she rubbed her chafed wrists Aldis said, "I told Rothgar you're cursed, being part of Leif's blood feud. If he touches you in lust, he will share whatever fate awaits you." Jenna didn't know how to respond to that. Did Aldis believe her own words, or had she made up a convenient lie to frighten the guard into leaving his prisoner alone? "You lost the slippers I gave you."

Jenna managed a wry grin. "They weren't well suited for

running."

Glancing at her foot Aldis said, "It's bleeding. Does it hurt?"

"A little." She'd walked on her toes all day, trying to keep her weight off the cut.

"Hnossa, tear some bandage strips and get water and salve." With a glare of resentment, the woman went to obey. She returned, dropped the items abruptly, and stalked away. Ignoring her, Jenna went to work. The cut was clean; Lukas had done a good job. She hoped for a moment she'd done as well for him, but then she recalled he was her enemy. She wouldn't let herself care.

When Jenna finished, Aldis leaned in and examined the bandage. "Tomorrow we will do that again to assure it does not fester."

Jenna searched Aldis' face, trying to guess whether the woman was friend or foe. "Why do you care what happens to me?"

"We spoke of this already; have you forgotten?" Jenna guessed it was Jessie who'd heard the explanation, so she didn't press. Aldis breathed a sigh. "I tire of Hnossa's gossip and long to hear a new voice. What do you Scots do in these hills when winter comes?"

All evening Jenna sat at Aldis' fire while Hnossa fussed like a determined bee. Aldis ignored demands that she cover her head, eat a few more bites, and chew carefully lest she choke. The servant, whom Aldis called her thrall, made no secret of her dislike for Jenna, giving her baleful glances and stepping on her fingers once as she moved around the fire.

"Hnossa's clothes fit you well," Aldis remarked. That explained the woman's animosity. "You shouldn't have tried to escape. Bjorn vowed to hunt you down and kill you, but

Lukas said a hostage can't be slain without cause. Bjorn didn't like it, but he won't cross Lukas."

The Tracker had saved her life. It didn't make her hate him any less, but Jenna wondered why he cared if she lived or died.

The men sat at their own fire, speaking in muted voices. Every now and then a laugh rose above the hum of conversation. Ignoring them, Aldis questioned Jenna about the Scots' ways. She answered reluctantly, unable to forget these were her enemies.

Noting her terse replies, Aldis said, "You hate us."

Jenna would not lie. "Yes."

"It is a hard thing, I know, but Leif must do something to change his fate."

"By killing children?" Jenna sneered. "You're his seer. Tell him this is madness."

"I do not control the destinies of men." She looked down as if ashamed. "We are called *vitki* among the Norse, and we simply report what we see."

Had Aldis' gods failed her, or had Leif put an interpretation on the message she hadn't expected?

"You made no call for a blood feud."

Her eyes turned toward the fire. "It's true. I saw nothing of Alba or Macbeth in the runes."

The camp had begun to settle in to sleep, and Hnossa stomped to a spot between Aldis and Jenna and stood glaring at them. Rolling her eyes in exasperation at the silent nagging, Aldis dismissed Jenna. As she returned to her guard, Jenna glanced back and for the first time saw Aldis' legs. Thin and misshapen, it was clear they couldn't hold her. She needed the maid's support to walk into the tent. Jenna turned away, unwilling to let the vitki see the pity in her eyes.

Rothgar tied her hands, linking the rope to his own girdle so that if she moved in the night, he'd feel the tug and awaken. Jenna was less fearful now, believing Aldis' hint of a curse would protect her from rape though not from rough treatment. Settling herself as comfortably as she could, she soon fell asleep, the drone of voices and the hard surface beneath her unnoticed in her exhaustion.

Two days of slow travel followed. When possible Aldis rode on her shield, borne by what she called her Fire Horses. Horses were important symbols to the Northmen, she explained to Jenna, and fire referred to gold, a prized metal. The vitki's four serving-men were indeed gold, both in the color of their hair and the service they provided, making mobility possible.

When the path slanted too steeply or became too narrow, one man carried Aldis in a soft leather chair that strapped to his back. Another dragged the oversized shield while the remaining two rested, relieving their companions at intervals. The process involved much stopping and arranging, but Jenna didn't mind, since her own legs often shook with fatigue. Each day brought a little rain, so her clothes were damp most of the time.

No one spoke to her during the day, but neither did anyone trouble her. She remained alone with her thoughts, which always strayed to home. What would Meg do about her abduction? Had they sent someone to warn Tessa that her sons were the focus of a Viking blood feud? Leif was apparently rich and powerful. Men served him, mad or not.

One night as they sat by the fire she asked Aldis, "If Leif's luck is gone, why do these men follow him? Why would they kill for him?"

"Leif is strong," Aldis replied, "and our people admire strength above all else." Her expression turned rueful, perhaps because she lacked that quality. "These are men of the old ways, men who seek battle rather than hearth and home, vengeance rather than love or even lust. Leif promises great rewards in the days to come, either here or in Valhalla."

"Valhalla?"

"The life after this one, where warriors rise each day and go into battle. They die in glory, are reborn the next day to again go into battle. They return to the drinking hall each night." She paused before going on. "A Viking who dies in his bed goes to Hel, a cold, dreary place. No one wants that, certainly not Leif."

It sounded strange to Jenna. "They are not Christian, then?"

"Some of my people have converted to your faith, but the old ways die hard. Your Christ's message of peace is a hard lesson for a soldier."

"And you?"

Aldis took a sip of the foul-smelling concoction she drank for sustenance. "My gods are many, some good, some evil. They explain how I have such afflictions along with my gifts."

Jenna knew better than to argue religion with a relative stranger. "Leif seeks to restore his battle-luck so he can die gloriously, as the old religion requires."

"Yes. A battle is coming soon that will bring glory to many. A curse must not interfere with our success, so the blood feud must be resolved."

Scots understood the blood feud, family being both a person's greatest support and most sacred responsibility.

"Still," Jenna said, "taking vengeance on innocent children is wrong."

Aldis set her lips. "He believes it is necessary. I would not destroy his hopes, even if I could."

You're in love with him. Jenna almost said it aloud but for once caught herself in time. Aldis had no hope of a normal life. She'd never truly be a wife or a mother. Her only chance in life was to become important to someone and receive, if not love in return, at least gratitude. She would encourage Leif's dream of redemption as long as she could be part of it. Where, then, would the killing end?

With the death of Tessa's twins, if Leif found them. Jenna wanted to prevent that, but her power at this point was limited. Presently, with her hands tied, she couldn't even scratch the spot on her shoulder blade where an insect bite seemed likely to drive her as mad as a Viking.

Chapter Ten

Jessie

The trip down the mountain was moonlit and quiet, but Jessie had to force herself to continue onward. Though the trail was easy to follow, she imagined she'd lost her way a hundred times. Other fears rose, too: sword-wielding Vikings who leapt from the trees to spit her as they'd done to Ian. Wild animals stalking her and her beloved Foot. A fall on the steep slope that might lame the pony and end her journey.

Despite that she traveled on, straining to see between the dark branches that lined the way. She listened, too, focusing on sounds other than those Foot made as he plodded steadily on. The pony trusted she knew what she was doing, which meant she'd be responsible if anything happened to him.

A noise to the right caught her attention, and Jessie pulled on the rope halter. Something moved in the trees, low to the ground but larger than a rabbit or squirrel. A deer? A beast more threatening? What should she do? Hurry on? Remain still and hope whatever it was didn't see them?

The noise grew fainter. Whatever it was moved away. When she heard it no more, Jessie resumed her trek.

When clouds gathered over the moon, she and Foot rested for a few hours. Morning, when it came, was rainy, but Jessie munched on nuts as her sure-footed conveyance plodded on. Highland ponies were not noted for speed, but endurance was another matter. Foot ignored the rain completely and was content with a ten-minute respite every few hours, where he grazed contentedly on what plants were nearby and drank daintily from any available stream.

Near noon on the second day, Jessie heard singing in the distance. She stopped Foot, turning her head as she tried to locate the source. There! It was off to her right. Reluctant to leave the pathway, she listened to the rain dripping onto her shawl, unsure what to do. Singing had never signaled danger before, but the world was a different place of late. As she listened, she recognized the tune and then the singer. Leaving Foot to graze, she crept into the trees.

The gleeman sat strumming his lute and singing, but he looked much worse than when she'd seen him last. His tunic was torn, his right eye ringed by an ominous rainbow of black, blue, purple, and yellow. Still he sang as well as he had at her fireside a few nights ago.

"Alfred?" She stepped out from her hiding place.

He jumped to his feet, but when he saw her, he relaxed. "Jessie? Is it you?"

Most couldn't tell her from Jenna, and many avoided saying their names as a result. Alfred had discerned their differences right away and made it a point to say her name the few times they'd spoken together. She found she liked that very much.

Jessie thought Alfred very talented, though she hadn't heard many gleemen. Their mountain home was too out of the way for most to bother visiting. Music spoke to Jessie in a way that few other things did, and she recognized that Alfred's voice was better than most. The first time she heard him it seemed he sang to her alone, but of course that was due to craft. Gleemen made each female in the audience feel special, every man contented. It was how they made a living.

She stopped a few feet away from him. "I heard what happened, Alfred. I'm sorry they beat you. It would never have happened if Donald were himself."

Alfred touched his bruised and swollen eye regretfully. "They were angry, and I was in the way of their anger. They didn't listen when I tried to tell them I lied."

"You lied?"

He nodded. "I would never betray your family, Jessie. I told the Vikings that Tessa lives in Norwich."

"That was cleverly done. They'll find nothing."

"Unless they're wise enough to check my story in Glamis," he said, and her smile dimmed.

"That's true. They could easily learn the truth." She put a hand on his arm. "But you tried to help, Alfred, and my kinsmen punished you for it."

He shrugged. "I'll be myself again in a few days."

"It's good of you to forgive them."

He tried for a smile then grimaced when a cut on his lip made it painful. "Forgiveness might come later. For now I only try to understand." He stood, brushing leaves from his clothing. "I saw the Northmen take you. How did you escape?"

She told him of Jenna's rescue. "I hope to save her in return," she finished. "But I'm not sure how."

Alfred was silent, and she guessed he was trying to decide how to dissuade her from her mission. He undoubtedly believed a naïve, crippled girl had no chance of success. Still, who else would do it?

In the end he said, "I can accompany you to Glamis and help you send a message to Lady Brixton from there. The fishing trade is lively between here and York, so there's sure to be a boat leaving soon." He frowned. "As for your twin, the Vikings must pass through Glamis. We'll ask the thane to make them give her up."

His use of the word *we* made Jessie feel better. Determined as she was to accomplish the tasks she'd set for herself, it was heartening to hear someone say he would help. "Let us be on our way, then. My sister Meg will see you are rewarded."

Alfred grinned again, winced, and put a hand to his split lip. "Your company is all the reward a man could ask for." Jessie lowered her gaze in response, and he led the way to the trail. *A gleeman's gallantry is always at the fore,* she told herself. *The words mean nothing: a showman's rehearsed response.*

Chapter Eleven

Jenna

When the Viking party stopped for the night the second day, Lukas fell into an exhausted sleep. The jolting of his crude sleigh probably sent waves of pain through his body at each step, but he made no sound of complaint.

Aldis invited Jenna to sit with her as Hnossa wove her mistress' pale hair into complicated knots. Aldis peered into a polished brass square to see the result and when she noticed Jenna's interest, she offered it. For the first time in her life, Jenna saw her reflection in something other than water. She was fascinated, turning her head to watch the image do the same.

"Bonny," Aldis said. "Was that not Rothgar's comment?" Jenna made a negative sound, handing the mirror back to Hnossa. Her hair was wild and matted, her face scratched and dirty. "You need some care," Aldis said archly, "but he is right. You are quite lovely."

Eyeing Aldis darkly, Jenna remained silent.

"Why did I save you from their pawing?" Aldis' piercing eyes read her thoughts. "First, it costs me nothing, and I enjoy putting fear into their superstitious hearts. Even Bjorn is afraid of my magic, though he pretends not to be." Her expression was hard to read, but Jenna thought the vitki was a little afraid of Bjorn too. She went on, "Second, you are able to help with Lukas, and I would see him restored to health. And last, I enjoy talking with you."

Jenna reminded herself Aldis was partly responsible for Leif's vow to end Macbeth's line. If he didn't find Tessa's sons, she would no doubt serve as substitute. In that event, Aldis would no doubt frown disapprovingly but do nothing.

Almost as if she'd heard the thought, Aldis said, "I will help you if I am able. I wish no harm to innocents."

"He's mad, and you smile at him and ignore it."

Her face became a cold mask. "The victim of a curse sees the source of evil better than others. I must trust Leif's instincts."

In her mind, Jenna counted the men who traveled with Leif. Though strong, Aldis' bearers were servants, not fighting men. That left ten Viking warriors. She'd assumed that was all he needed to subdue a small clan-hold, but perhaps ten were all he could command. How long would even these ten warriors follow a cursed chief? She saw why Leif was desperate to change his luck, but how could he believe his misfortune stemmed from a man dead ten years?

"You're blind to his evil because you love him." Jenna was hardly aware she'd spoken aloud.

Aldis' lips puckered. "I will rest now." Hnossa helped her rise, and the two women went into the tent without further word.

The next day Aldis' mood was forgiving. "Let the Scotti girl walk beside me," she ordered, "and untie her hands. She's far enough from home that she may have some comfort." The smile she gave Jenna hinted she found pleasure in ordering large men about.

Travel was more bearable without arms that ached, and Aldis' chatter helped pass the time. At the vitki's bidding, Jenna tended Lukas' injury as best she could when they stopped to rest, changing the bandages and insisting he drink plenty of water. She used the same salve on him he'd used for her foot, curling her nose at the smell.

When he thanked her, she dismissed him curtly. "I would do the same for a sick hound, Viking."

His jaw tightened. "And even a dog would be grateful."

That evening as they sat around the fire, they heard heavy footsteps approaching. Rothgar seemed unconcerned, and in a moment Jenna understood why, for the other Vikings joined them, loud with good humor. Slung on a pole was a freshly-killed deer, and though she wasn't glad to see the Northmen, fresh venison was welcome after days of dried food. While the meal was prepared, someone unearthed a skin of strong drink, and by the time it was ready, the men were generous. Jenna's share was as large as anyone's.

Lukas was gaining strength, and Aldis ordered him brought to her side, where she fed him choice bits of meat. Her eyes lingered on Lukas' face, and he talked with her as with an old friend, relaxed and smiling. Had she misread signs that Aldis was in love with Leif? She seemed very fond of Lukas, as well. Did she love both men? It seemed to Jenna Viking women were not as true-hearted as Scotswomen.

The next day, at Leif's behest, the group separated again. "Stay with Aldis," he told Lukas, who was still unable to walk unassisted. "We will go ahead and prepare for our journey."

Lukas made no objection, but his eyes flickered to Jenna. "And the girl?"

Leif peered at Jenna as if he'd forgotten about her. "Aldis craves her company."

Bjorn said in a languid tone, "I, too, crave her company. You'd hardly know she is with us."

"No," Aldis said firmly. "Lukas needs gentler hands than Rothgar's." Lukas' gaze had turned on Bjorn, hard as granite. Bjorn pretended not to notice, but he didn't argue. Instead he made a mocking bow, hinting there'd be other times, other chances.

Jenna was relieved she'd soon be free of Bjorn, whose constant gaze made her uneasy. She was also glad to be done with Leif, as dangerous as Bjorn but in a different way. She'd have a better chance of escape with only a cripple, a few servants (Aldis called them *carls*), the Fire Horses, and a wounded Viking for company. Catching Lukas' gaze on her again, she looked away. Whenever she met those sea-green eyes, it seemed he read Jenna's thoughts as if she'd said them aloud.

Leif and the others packed their belongings and left, some still bleary-eyed from drink the night before. Stoically hefting their burdens, they took their places in a line that disappeared briskly down the mountain path.

Aldis' party moved at a more leisurely pace. First she asked Jenna to assure that Lukas was as comfortable as possible on the sled-boat. He insisted he felt no pain, disgusted with his own weakness. Indeed, Jenna thought, it would have been rude to complain when Aldis spent her life being carried from one place to another. Meeting Jenna's gaze, Lukas made a shrug of acceptance, which she ignored. She also ignored the warm feeling that rose in her chest at the thought he'd sought her attention.

Lukas was like all the others, she reminded herself: crude, unfeeling, and primitive. He was handsome in a stern way, and she noticed he was more fastidious than the others in his habits, chewing with his mouth closed and carrying a small scrap of cloth in his belt for wiping his hands or his nose when necessary. Nevertheless, he'd ruined her life as effectively as if he'd run her through with a sword.

Who knew what fate awaited her? Aldis' protection had kept her from rough treatment so far, but she was a prisoner, at the mercy of savages, and it was as much Lukas' fault as anyone's. She wasn't sure why she'd saved his life that night, why she hadn't run for home as his blood flowed into the earth. That was what a Viking deserved. Still, the fact she nursed him created a bond between them, and she admired his strength. She quashed that feeling, for she'd be gone when an opportunity arose.

Despite his improving condition, the journey down the mountainside was still hard for Lukas. His jaw often tensed with unspoken pain as he tried to find a position that didn't jar nerves exposed by the wolf's claws. Turning her eyes to the hills, Jenna resolutely forced her mind off Lukas' discomfort.

About mid-morning, Aldis asked, "Tell me about this Tessa, the woman Leif seeks?"

Jenna answered, careful not to give details. "Tessa is my second oldest sister. At sixteen she was sent to live with our uncle, the thane Macbeth, in order that she might be wed."

"Of course," Aldis murmured. It was common practice to send extra females to distant relatives' homes, where they might find husbands and end their burden on their family.

"Long ago she was kidnapped by a spy. Our uncle believed her dead, but she and the spy fell in love."

"A romantic story." Aldis impatiently pushed away the blanket Hnossa tried to drape around her shoulders. "It's too heavy. Take it away."

Jenna grimaced. "Their path to happiness was not smooth at first."

"Is he important, this spy?"

Maybe the Vikings would give up if they heard Tessa was married to a powerful man. "Jeffrey's a laird. A lord, as the English say it."

Aldis' perfect brow furrowed. "Your sister lives in

England? We were misinformed."

Jenna paused in shock. The gleeman had lied to the Vikings. That meant she still had a chance to reach Tessa first. Let it be so, she prayed. Leif would soon learn the truth, since Tessa's story was well known in Glamis, but if Jenna could escape tonight, she'd have a head start. Aldis estimated they'd reach Glamis tomorrow. Tonight is the time to steal away.

The little party stopped for night in the foothills. The spot Rothgar chose was almost level, and a soft carpet of grass made it comfortable, which Jenna hoped meant her captors would sleep soundly. Somehow she'd have to get her hands free, for she was still tied at night.

The mood in the camp was relaxed, the strain of the steep descent behind them. Their last day's travel would be over flatter, softer ground, and Aldis expressed pleasure at being once more able to ride her "ship" as she called the shield. "It's more dignified than hanging on a man's back. I don't often feel in control of my life, but at least up there I can see where I'm going."

"Do you mind telling—" Jenna broke off, unsure if Aldis was willing to discuss her disability.

"I suppose everyone new to me wonders about it."

Jenna blushed. "I have a—" she stopped herself in time and said, "—a relative with a crooked hip. She is a twin, and there was not room for both of them in the womb."

"I've heard of such things."

"My friend learned to walk with a special boot, but the hip cannot tolerate running."

Aldis looked down at her spindly legs. The difference between her perfect face and pitiful body was hard to fathom. "Mine is a condition of birth called 'glass bones.' No one knows why it happens, and often those afflicted have short lives."

"How terrible!"

"The bones harden somewhat at puberty, but it's too late for them to be of use. We have limited movement and constant pain."

"I'm sorry." Jenna indeed felt sorry, for Aldis faced life bravely despite her condition.

The vitki gracefully accepted her sympathy. "Some with the condition have fared well. Ivar, a warrior called the Boneless One, captured the English town of York, which we call Jorvik."

Recalling Donald's ribald song, Jenna suppressed a smile. The true explanation had nothing to do with the man's sexual prowess. "He was a chieftain despite soft bones?"

"Ivar was an excellent bowman. His practice of being carried around on a shield gave me the idea and some measure of freedom." She chuckled dryly. "It came at a cost, for Leif decided that on my shield, I could accompany him on this enterprise."

"I see pain on your face sometimes."

"You see more than most, for I learned early to hide what I feel." Aldis looked at the hills behind them, lost in the past. "My father would have drowned me at birth, but my mother would not hear of it." Her tone indicated doubt at the wisdom of her mother's choice. "Oddly enough, it was my father who died that year, not I. After a difficult childhood, my condition stabilized somewhat. There's no longer danger I'll break a bone simply by picking up a hairbrush, but rough treatment or a bad fall could bring about my death."

"I'm sorry."

Aldis smiled thinly. "Perhaps as compensation, I was blessed with the Sight. Leif is convinced I can turn his luck." The whites of her eyes were a bluish gray, probably a sign of her disease. "If I'd known the result, I might have hidden what I saw. Now it is too late."

There was something in Aldis' voice. Was she afraid of Leif and his madness? Whatever her feelings, she couldn't change things now. What choice did a cripple have except to make herself useful to someone with the power to support her?

"You said that first day you are promised to a boy," Aldis said. "What will he do now that you're gone?"

Jenna pulled some burrs from the hem of her skirt in order to give herself time to think. Why had her sister shared information with this woman that she hadn't shared with her? Jenna had to answer as Jessie would.

"He'll find someone," she replied. If Jessie had done as ordered, she was back by now with whichever young man had spoken for her. Meg would have sent someone to warn Tessa, and, if Fate was kind, Donald was recovering from the wicked blow he'd received at the hands of these men. If things had gone well, only her own life was changed beyond recognition.

"I'll try to convince Leif to release you before we leave Glamis."

Jenna tried to appear grateful, but what would she return to? No special young man waited for her at home. Would anyone want her after she'd spent several days with a band of Vikings? No doubt Meg grieved for her, but she had responsibilities and heartaches enough. Jessie would be most affected. They'd never been apart, but she'd get over the loss. She'd have to.

Seeing Aldis looking over her shoulder, Jenna turned. Lukas was trying to stand, his lips tight with pain.

"See to him," Aldis ordered. "He will fall and open his wound again."

Jenna rose obediently. Some part of her objected to approaching the Viking, but unwillingness to see him suffer overcame it. *He is your enemy,* logic whispered, but she could not stand to see him in pain.

Lukas was standing when she reached him, but he swayed drunkenly and she stepped under his arm to support him. The same rush of feeling came each time they touched, but she'd learned to ignore it through force of will. "Sit. You're weak as a newborn lamb."

"I must—" He grinned weakly. "I must go into the trees and sing."

"Oh." Jenna looked around. "Wait here." Assuring herself he was balanced on one foot, she went to a tree, chose a forked branch, and broke it off, fashioning a usable crutch. Handing it to Lukas she ordered, "Use this."

Lukas blushed. "I thank you." He stumped slowly into the woods. While he was gone, Jenna borrowed some pillows from Aldis' supply to make his resting place more comfortable. When he returned, she helped him sit and covered him with a blanket.

"Can you eat something? Meat or bread?"

He nodded. "I've begun to regain my appetite, which is good, for I must rejoin the others."

Her warming feeling toward him evaporated. *He's eager to get on with what Vikings do best, killing old men and innocent children.*

She brought him food, though there wasn't much left. Aldis' carls were as greedy as they were crude, and no one went out of his way for their injured companion except Jenna and Aldis. Lukas ate a handful of dried cherries and a pear, tossing away only the stem and the seeds.

"I should look at your wounds," she said when he'd finished, but he shook his head.

"I can tend them myself." A flush betrayed embarrassment at her earlier care.

She sniffed. "I've seen naked men before you, Viking." It was almost true. She'd seen her kinsmen bathing, so she knew how a man's body differed from a woman's. It gave her a small jolt of pleasure to speak of it casually and see his flush deepen.

"I'd have bled to death if not for you."

"As I said before, I'd have done it for anyone." Was that the truth? It was hard to say. Was the reason she'd stayed there Lukas himself or her inability to let any man bleed to death alone in the forest? It had to be the latter, though she thought she might have been able to leave if it had been Bjorn who was dying.

She rose to go, but he asked, "Where is this woman Leif seeks?"

Jenna's voice turned cold. "I don't know."

"She is your sister. You know where she lives."

"My home is all I know of the world."

His look revealed irritation. "I have told you I can help."

Help with what, Viking? Killing two nephews I've never seen? Killing Tessa as well, for she will die before she lets your lawless band murder her sons.

Reading her thought, he looked away. "You have no reason to trust me."

Once again she turned to go, but he touched her arm. The now-familiar surge of heat went through her as he said, "I mean your people no harm, please believe that. If I'd known—" His words echoed Aldis'. Leif was beyond understanding, they implied. "To find the one who killed a kinsman is a man's duty and honor. But I swear to you I didn't know Macbeth is dead all these years." His eyes met Jenna's again. "And it's a great wrong to kill a child."

She fought against accepting his words. How could she believe a man meant no harm who'd seen an old man murdered, helped to take her prisoner, and torn her from her home?

"You're right. I don't trust you." With that she left. Lukas looked after her helplessly, but she did not see. Nor did she notice Aldis watching, her graceful brows arched.

Heavy clouds had gathered, which suited Jenna well since the night was dark as pitch. She lay awake, waiting for the camp to settle in to rest and working to free her hands, stretching the leather strips Rothgar had used to tie her. It wasn't going well.

Movement made her stop and pretend to be asleep. The next thing she knew, someone tugged at her sleeve.

It had to be Lukas. Maybe what he'd said earlier about not wanting to see her harmed had been a veiled promise to set her free tonight. She felt a rush of warmth toward him. He'd had to wait until he was stronger, but now he'd come to release her in return for saving his life.

Another tug indicated she should rise. Next he'd free her hands. She'd steal away in silence, get a head start, and reach Glamis before dawn.

In an instant, her hopes were dashed. Her visitor jerked hard on the rope, turning her roughly. A hand covered her mouth, and a muscular arm wrapped like a fibrous vine around her waist. Pulled off her feet, she felt hot, foul breath on her cheek and recognized Rothgar's stench. This was no friend come to her rescue.

Barely able to breathe, Jenna could make no sound. She clawed at her attacker clumsily, but her bound hands made poor tools for self-defense. Once he found his balance, Rothgar headed into the trees with her draped over his shoulder.

Her panicked brain didn't understand for a moment what happened next. Letting out a yowl of pain, Jenna's captor dropped her. She fell to the ground, and her face hit the earth only slightly after her shoulder.

"Run!" a voice whispered as she rolled over, shaking her head in confusion. "Run!" it repeated. This time the urgency came through, and in no time she was up and off, her feet flying over the grass-covered earth. She looked for shelter in the woods, knowing her best chance was cover, not distance. Behind her the camp awakened. "She's getting away!" "Go after her!"

For days Jenna had thought about what she'd do if a chance to escape arose, and her plan was better this time. With the few precious seconds of confusion as the Vikings figured out what had happened, she made the dark her friend. Once in the trees she slowed her pace, looking upward. Her plan this time wasn't headlong flight through the woods.

Nerve-wracking sounds behind her revealed the camp's confusion. Jenna worked at freeing her hands, using her teeth. When the knots loosened and her hands slid free, she rubbed her wrists to restart blood flow. Once she thought her fingers would obey her commands, she examined the tree closest to her. No low branches. She moved on to the next with the same result, but the third tree had a sturdy limb within reach. Pulling herself onto it, she climbed quickly, feeling her way along and bumping her head a few times. Within seconds she was as high as she judged the tree could take her. Straddling two branches, she clung to the trunk, her face pressed against its rough bark as she quieted her gasping breath.

The Vikings had begun to organize, making torches out of firewood and dividing the area into quadrants. They moved around below her for what seemed like forever, stopping often to listen for betraying noises. Jenna clung to the tree and made none. Then she heard Aldis' voice, as clear as if she sat beside her. "Come back. You'll never find her now." They trudged back resentfully. Aldis wasn't the one who'd suffer when Leif learned of the night's events.

The vitki spoke again, her voice different now. "What made you strike out with your crutch like that? You nearly lamed poor Rothgar."

Lukas' voice rang with innocence. "I thought we were being attacked."

"She was escaping. I tried to stop her." Rothgar's voice revealed both anger and pain.

Recalling the whispered command to run, Jenna knew Lukas had seen Rothgar take her, discerned his intent, and acted to save her. In doing so he'd also given her freedom. She wished she could thank him, but that was silly. It was his fault she was there to begin with. Best if she never saw another Viking again, even one who'd saved her life.

Chapter Twelve

Jessie

Jessie and Alfred traveled down the mountain, alert for sounds ahead of them lest they blunder into Leif's band of cutthroats. Alfred made her stop to rest from time to time, though she insisted they had to hurry. When he heard the babble of a brook or saw a bush laden with edible berries, he'd stop. "It won't benefit your sister if you injure yourself and are unable to continue," he argued. "You've never made such a long trip, and your leg may suffer from too many hours on horseback."

Most people called it "Jessie's problem," which always made her feel as if it was a shameful thing. Alfred approached her disability as a matter to be dealt with but not pitied, and she found that made it easier to admit, like disliking peas or being left-handed.

She fared well with Foot's steady pace and the singer's assistance in getting on and off the pony's back. They talked as they traveled, and Jessie began to feel a little jealous. Alfred had been everywhere, all over Britain, and she was at that moment as far away from home as she'd ever been. Time passed quickly with Alfred's tales of humorous characters, near catastrophes, and impressive castles he'd visited. Having the gift of apery, he could make his voice sound like anything from an old woman to a lisping child. His puckish face lit when he told his stories, and she listened, rapt. What a life he'd had, and not much older than Jessie herself.

"I started traveling with my father after my mother died," he reported. "I was six, and my aunts were horrified, but Father said I was old enough to go. He taught me the songs, the stories, and the route, so by twelve I was a practiced gleeman." He gave her a sideways smile. "He even taught me to read."

Jessie knew few people with that skill. "You read whole books?"

His ready laugh sounded, but he wasn't laughing at her. "Father owned a book, and he used it to teach me." His voice turned regretful. "It was ruined last spring when I crossed a river." Chuckling, he added, "Well, I almost crossed it. I was swept downstream and lost some of my things. If there hadn't been a fallen tree, I might have lost everything."

"Our rivers are dangerous in spring," she acknowledged.

"There's a bright side to it," Alfred said. "I came out determined to learn how to swim. What good is such an experience if we don't learn from it?" He walked on a few steps. "If I had a book, I could teach you to read."

"Could you?" Jessie rode along in silence. The idea was inviting but also frightening. What if he found her too dull to learn the letters? "Jenna taught herself to read."

"Really."

"She's very clever."

"As are you."

"Jenna's the one who figures things out. I am—" She stopped.

Alfred pulled Foot up sharply. "What are you?" he demanded.

It seemed important to be honest with him. "First, I'm a cripple. I can't do what others do, so I make myself useful minding the little ones and stirring the stewpot. Second, I'm shy. I haven't got Jenna's spirit or courage." She smiled lest he think she felt sorry for herself. "A person should accept herself as she is."

"I'd agree," Alfred replied, "if that person knew her worth." Seeing a grassy spot ahead, he stopped the pony and helped Jessie dismount. When they were seated and Foot grazed contentedly beside them, he took up the topic again. "Jessie, you have as much spirit as your twin, though it's a quieter kind. You're wise; that shows each time you speak. And courage? You left home alone on a quest to save your sisters. That's a momentous thing for anyone, and even more so for a girl who's lame."

It always came back to that. She was a cripple, and no matter what she accomplished, people—even this kind young man—would speak of her in light of her disability. How she wished to be known for something else, something admirable that was truly her own.

Alfred's next comment surprised her. "You have a great talent that Jenna does not."

She smiled, disbelieving. "What might that be?"

Plucking a stalk of grass, Alfred chewed on it, falling into his story-telling style. "After your kinfolk, um, encouraged me to leave, I was unable to walk very fast. Once I was away, I rested for a while and repaired the damages as best I could. As I lay there, thinking it might be best if I died and went to heaven, I heard an angel singing."

"An angel? Wonderful!" Jessie had begun to see the joke, and her eyes lit with humor.

"I peeped out from the leaves and saw the angel, riding by on a pony. I had never seen a sight any lovelier, nor heard such a voice."

"It was you!" she said, laughing. "I heard noise in the woods and feared it was a Viking."

"Only a poor, wandering poet and singer of songs." Alfred paused, but he had more to say, and the words came out in a rush. "You sing beautifully. And I say you're prettier than Jenna, for I like women who are…I mean, that's what I think."

Jessie blushed. "You're very kind, Alfred." She could think of no more to add, and apparently he couldn't either. They rose to start down the path again. As she rode, Jessie's face felt warm for some time, as if a small fire burned in each cheek. No man had said such things to her before, and despite knowing gleemen were practiced in gallantry, Alfred's words rested comfortably in her heart.

Chapter Thirteen

Jenna

Jenna stumbled along, so exhausted she hardly cared if the Vikings caught up with her. At first she'd tried to run, but after crashing into stumps and branches a few times, she'd slowed her pace and tried to avoid obstacles in her way.

So tired that her head drooped, she almost missed the flash of firelight ahead of her. She was close when she finally saw it and stopped. Fear shot through her, but there were no Vikings around the small campfire. It was three women who stared intently into a cauldron they'd placed on the fire.

Moving closer, Jenna saw that they were an odd threesome. Their clothes were tattered, their hair matted and filthy, and their slitted eyes seemed to see everything and nothing at once. As she pondered whether to skirt the clearing and avoid the women or pass by where they sat, one of them spoke, startling her.

"Come closer, Pretty."

Her first reaction was to do the opposite, but a second woman spoke. "Safe, you are."

The third smiled without looking at her. "Safe."

Timidly Jenna stepped from the trees and came to where the women ringed the fire. "I'm on my way to Glamis—"

"France," the tallest woman corrected, and the other two repeated it.

"France."

"France."

"You have great things to do," the first woman said, and again the others repeated.

"Great things"

"Great things."

Jenna grew impatient with the women's ridiculous statements. "I am in some hurry, so I will be on my way. I won't keep you from your, um, work."

"Go," the woman who seemed to be the leader said, "but know this: Contentment will come only when you find the two missing pieces of your heart."

The village of Glamis appeared across the river as if rising from the morning mist: a rooftop, then a large cross in the square, then a shepherd who drove a few sheep before him onto the hillside. The castle that had once been Macbeth's appeared last, blending in with the mountain's gloomy aspect until she was quite near.

The mists were a boon, since Jenna meant to slip into the town without passing the guards at the gate. She'd been to Glamis once with Donald, and she recalled staring at the gray castle and the fierce-looking men who guarded it. She remembered as well that there were several lesser gates, which Donald said were unguarded except in times of trouble. The outer wall and gates were only preliminary defenses, meant to slow an enemy's advance while the people hurried inside the castle's thick walls to safety.

The hardest part would be crossing the bridge between her mountain and the town, but the mist was thickest over the water, obscuring her approach. She crept quietly across and turned sharply right, tracing the riverbank. There were huts scattered along the way, but no one saw her except an old man who was relieving himself into the river. He waved his free hand, and Jenna nodded, amused.

Finding an unguarded gate on the southwest side of town, she slipped inside and sat down to wait until daylight, when people began to stir. Though it was hard to do nothing, Jenna wasn't sure what she should do. She'd considered going to the castle and asking the current thane for help, but he'd received Glamis from King Malcolm as a reward for his assistance in defeating Macbeth. The thane would not be eager to help Macbeth's remaining family.

Jenna had to go to England and warn Tessa. She was days ahead of anyone Meg might send, so she could outrace their enemies. Still, she had no money, no friends in the village, and no idea where York was.

The sun appeared, the mists cleared slightly, and folk began to stir. As Jenna walked the high street looking for inspiration, curious glances followed. Strangers were rare enough, and a lone woman dressed in foreign-looking clothes was even more noticeable.

"Good morrow, lass," said a voice behind her, and she turned to see a man so round it seemed if a strong wind came upon him he might roll into the river. A brown robe, worn and grease-stained, revealed his priestly profession.

"Good morrow to you, Father," she answered politely.

Tilting his head to one side he said, "I think you're a stranger here."

"I am."

"And you are unsure of your direction. I could perhaps help you." When Jenna didn't answer, he took her silence for mistrust and smiled reassuringly. "Christ requires kindness to strangers, for we never know when we might entertain angels. Are you mayhap an angel?"

She smiled in return. "Merely an earthly soul on my way south."

He regarded her for a few seconds. "Forgive my blunt speech, but you are tired and perhaps hungry too. I was this very moment thinking of breakfast, which I'd be pleased to share with you." He patted his ample belly. "I have plenty, for I never refuse the bounty of God's earth."

Ten minutes later Jenna sat at a slab table while the priest bustled around his kitchen, ladling porridge into two bowls and sliding one toward her. Setting a pitcher of milk between them, he pulled a pan of sausages from the warming shelf of the fire, using a fold of his robe as a hot-pad. "Sausages on Saturnsday," he said, regarding the circular morsels with satisfaction. "God provides animals to sustain us, and we must not refuse what He offers." With some difficulty because of his protruding stomach, he stepped over the bench and sat opposite her.

"Here." He handed Jenna a wooden spoon for her porridge. "After we thank God for his providence, you must tell me your name and why you've come to Glamis."

She waited while he said grace, joining him in "Amen." Taking a spoonful of the warm stuff into her mouth, she swallowed and said, "My name is Jenna."

"A lovely name," the priest said, "and one I have not heard before."

"My mother was Kenna, and Father liked the similar sound."

"Your father was a poet, then."

"I cannot say. He died when I was young."

Bowing his head in prayer, the priest said, "The Lord knows what's best, but it's sad when a child loses a parent."

"Thank you."

"And would I have known your father?"

Jenna avoided his eyes. "I think not. We're a mountain clan."

"Ah. I thought when I saw you on the street you had not been among so many folk before. You looked a bit lost. And hungry," he added with a smile.

Taking his words as an invitation, Jenna spooned more porridge into her mouth. "Good," she mumbled.

The priest tasted his own bowlful and nodded. "I am Dominic, shepherd to the folk here for a dozen years. I know most people within thirty miles of Glamis. Before that, I was a novice at Scone. If your father died so long ago, I never met him."

"You were here, then, when the old king reigned?"

"Macbeth?" The priest's face took on an interested expression. "Yes, I knew him."

"What was he like?"

Dominic regarded Jenna closely. "He was once well-regarded by the folk hereabout. It's not my place to judge, but if he'd asked, I'd have counseled patience. Things went wrong because he could not wait for events to play out."

She nodded, not really understanding. Right now she needed to prevent a lunatic from spilling his anger onto innocent children.

"I must get to England."

"England?" He pushed the sausages toward her, and Jenna took one with a nod of thanks.

"I must travel quickly." She ate the sausage, wiping the grease on the hem of her skirt.

"A ship would be fastest, I suppose. Have you money for

passage?"

Jenna's face fell. "No."

"That is a difficulty then."

She returned to her porridge. "It means life or death."

Regarding her across the table, Dominic asked, "Does this have to do with a group of Vikings who passed through here some days ago?"

She turned in surprise. "You saw them?"

"A hard lot to ignore." Spooning the last of his meal from the bowl, he set it aside. "I believe they are up to no good, but they're generous with the shopkeepers and charming to the castle's chatelaine." Smoothing his beard, he added, "They asked about Macbeth."

"Yes." Jenna's voice was almost a whisper.

Dominic folded his hands and leaned his ample chin on the resulting brace. "Why don't you tell me the whole story?"

Though she had no reason to trust him, Jenna did. It was good to have someone to talk to, and she sensed he would help if he could. The story of who she was and what had happened over the last few days came tumbling out, and the priest listened with no comment.

"You don't know Donald's condition?" he asked when she finished.

"He was alive when I left."

"I've met him a few times, and he seems a good sort. If he'd had an inkling of danger, those men would not have taken your people by surprise."

"I suppose the watcher fell asleep," Jenna said. "With peaceful times, we became careless."

"I hope Donald did not pay for it with his life."

She closed her eyes briefly. "Amen to that."

Dominic's manner became businesslike. "Are you certain you can take on this task? York is a long way from here, and you're inexperienced in the world."

"There's no one else, and good must win over evil. Vikings are evil, folk say, and now I believe it."

Dominic sat back, arms folded. "Men of all nations are the same. Some are evil, others less so. Some are misguided, set on an evil purpose though they see it as something else."

Jenna didn't argue the point. Vikings were the worst sort of men, but a man of God had to believe no one was beyond saving. Lukas' face appeared in her mind but she forced it back. Lukas had stood by as the harmless old man died. Where was the good in that?

The priest was thinking his own thoughts. "I know of a ship that will leave tomorrow if the wind is favorable. The captain, a friend and a good Christian, might agree to take you along."

"Wonderful!" She leaned toward the priest, tiredness gone. "I'll be days ahead of them."

"But there is a stop to your purpose. Christian my friend may be, but he is a true Scot, as well. He'll expect passage money."

She considered that. "What if I promise to pay when I reach York? My sister's husband is a rich man."

Dominic frowned. "I trust what you've told me is true, but a businessman might not."

Her enthusiasm faded. "Could I work for my passage?

I'm strong, and I learn quickly."

"Sailors would never abide a woman on their crew." Dominic's face grew serious. "If the weather turned, they'd toss you overboard to change their luck."

"They'd have Lord Brixton to deal with if they did away with me."

Dominic slapped the table, making Jenna jump. "Lord Brixton, you say? God is good!" Closing his eyes, he said a brief, silent prayer. Finished, he went on, "We know God is always good, but especially today, His blessings shine on us. The ship I speak of belongs to Lord Brixton, and the captain is Brixton's agent."

There remained the problem of convincing the captain of Jenna's authenticity. She admitted she didn't look much like a lord's sister-in-law with her soiled dress, makeshift shoes, and matted hair. "Make yourself presentable," Dominic ordered. "I'll arrange passage on the *Madeline*." He dragged a large wooden tub from the corner, and Jenna set to work filling it with water.

After she bathed, Jenna washed her hair with the priest's hard soap and rinsed the dullness away with vinegar. She washed her clothing in the tepid water and hung it before the fire to dry. Wrapped in a blanket, she awaited Dominic's return, dozing until he bustled in with good news.

"Captain Neville will take you aboard, he says. I saw hopes of a bonus in his eyes as I described your unfortunate situation." At her questioning look he explained, "You are a nun who plans to visit your sister as you leave one convent and enter another, but you were robbed on the road and lost your belongings." He raised his brows. "Pretty as you are, the disguise of a nun is wise, and it simplifies your need for clothing."

Moving to a tiny closet under the stairs, he rummaged

noisily through the items in a large leather bag, muttering to himself, and pulled out a dark robe. "There are no nuns here at this time, but we have this." Handing Jenna a black robe, he returned to the closet. "I think there are boots as well." In minutes Jenna had a complete costume that was only a little too large for her. "The hem trails the ground," Dominic remarked.

"I can fix that, if you have needle and thread."

"But you should rest before you journey so far."

With the resilience of youth she replied, "I'll sleep on the boat once we're under way."

Chapter Fourteen

Jessie

When Jessie and Alfred entered Glamis together, she waited fearfully for the guards to question their reason for coming. When Alfred said they'd provide musical entertainment at the castle, there were no questions. The guard stared at her, but his manner seemed more appreciative than hostile. She smiled grimly, knowing several days' travel had done little for her looks. A clear pool they'd rested beside had provided a disturbing glimpse of her hair, no longer neatly braided, and her clothes, travel-stained and dusty. Alfred didn't look quite normal yet, though his injuries were healing. They'd made the best repairs they could at the river, washing their exposed skin in the icy water and brushing the dust from each other's clothes. "At least we look less like miscreants," Alfred joked.

Once they were inside the wall, Jessie insisted Alfred take his leave. "You've been kind, but I would not keep you from your work. I'll manage from here."

"But what will you do?" Helping her dismount, he patted the pony's rump, raising a cloud of dust.

"I'll go to the castle and tell them the Vikings are holding a Scotswoman prisoner. They'll be arrested, Jenna will be freed, and Tessa's family will be safe. Then Jenna and I will return home."

"I could go with you to the thane," he suggested, but she shook her head. Alfred had done enough for her, and she didn't want him to feel he had to stay to help the poor cripple.

"Helping me get here was enough."

"It's no trouble—" he began, but she held up a hand.

"Alfred, I might not be able to walk normally, but I can

speak for myself."

He chewed his lip. "All right. Promise to be careful?"

"I will."

"And promise to remember what I said. You are your sister's equal."

Jessie almost laughed. Jenna's equal? No one could claim that. "I'll think on it."

"All right then." He took a step closer, touching a curl that lay on her shoulder. "When I return in a few months, might I climb your mountain to see you?"

Surprised by the question, she answered shyly, "I'd like that."

"Well, then. Until we meet again." Alfred gave her a courtly bow. "I'll pray for your sister's safe return."

As he walked away, Jessie touched the lock of hair he'd caressed. "Good-bye, Alfred," she whispered. She wanted to call him back, to confess she was afraid and needed his support. But her affairs were not his. She must do this alone.

It wasn't as easy as Jessie had made it sound. When she approached the castle, a fierce-looking guard with a mustache the size of a hedgehog stepped in her way. "What do you want, girl?"

"I must speak with the thane."

The man laughed. "Oh, you must, eh? Well, girls don't just ask for the thane and have him come running."

"He'll want to hear what I have to tell," Jessie said.

"If he did, he couldn't," he said. "He's gone to Scone."

"Gone?"

The guard leaned down, putting his nose almost against hers. "Gone. So get yourself away, lass, before you make me angry."

"Could I speak with someone else? The thane's wife, perhaps?"

"Out shopping, I think. She won't want to see you anyhow. She's having a dinner tomorrow and she's all agog with preparations."

Disappointed, Jessie turned away. In her imagination, she'd turned the whole problem over to the thane, who had soldiers and the law on his side. Now it was up to her to rescue Jenna and warn Tessa. Pushing her fears aside once more, she considered the problem. The message to Tessa should come first. Then she'd have to devise a plan for finding Jenna.

Looking around, she sought someone who might give advice to a stranger. A guard stood at the castle gateway, this one younger and more approachable than the other. "I must send a message to England," she said. "Can you tell me how that might be done?"

He grinned at her. "Glad to help a pretty lass."

Jessie blushed, wondering how Jenna would have replied. Thoughts of her sister recalled the urgency of her task. Jenna needed help, if she was still alive.

She explained the message had to go to York, and the guard pondered her request. "There is a boat that will soon sail south. You might ask the captain to take it."

Jessie hadn't considered how the message would be sent. "Do you write, perhaps?"

He laughed. "Me? No, lass, nor anyone I know. But a ship captain will have a man who can write, to do his accounts and such."

Thanking him, Jessie hurried off. Directions were unnecessary, for the river edged the village and she simply walked along its bank until she found the vessel the guard had mentioned. Though it was larger than the local fishing boats, it smelled strongly of the same cargo. Overseeing the loading of several large barrels was a stocky, red-faced man. Evidence of learning rested in his hands, a journal he made notes in as the cargo was loaded.

"Your pardon, sir. May I speak with you?" The man gave her a quick nod and continued his count as she told her tale, speaking loudly to be heard over the rumble of cart wheels and groans of men. When she finished he was silent for a few moments, never taking his eyes off the men who were loading barrels. When the last one was in place, he turned to Jessie.

"This ship is headed to London, not York. However, the captain might stop at Scarborough and send someone inland with your message if you can pay."

Jessie had brought the only thing of value she owned, a ring given to her by her father. It was her dearest treasure, both because it was gold and because it had been his, but she'd guessed it would have to be sacrificed. She handed it to the clerk, who examined it then put it into a bag at his waist. "I'll see it done."

She hesitated, aware she'd put her trust in a stranger. If he kept the ring and tossed the letter into the river, she'd never know. The clerk noticed her uncertainty. "I'll not fail you, lass, and the captain is honest. He'll find a trusty soul to take a missive to your sister. Shall I get you something to write on?"

"Will you write it for me, sir? I don't know the letters."

"Why should you?" he said. "Teaching a female to write is a waste of time and effort."

The clerk gravely took down Jessie's words, looking up with interest at the mention of Vikings. "They threatened your family?"

"Yes."

"Godless savages!" He spit to one side in disgust. "When I saw the knarr in the harbor, I knew it boded evil for someone."

"Knarr?" she repeated.

"A Norse ship that's larger than their long-ship. No doubt they chose it for this voyage because of the crippled woman."

"Is the ship still here?"

He pointed eastward with an ink-stained hand. "She's anchored at the river's mouth."

Jessie's hopes rose. If the Vikings hadn't yet sailed, perhaps she could save Jenna.

"Have you seen them today?"

"It's said they're gone hunting. Their women and the carls wait on the shore near the boat."

Aldis, was here. "Was there a girl with them who looks like me?"

He squeezed the back of his neck to ease a cramp. "I saw only two women, one crippled, one plain."

Thanking the clerk, Jessie hurried to the place where the Viking ship lay. It was easily identified, for it was different from the other boats along the bank: wide bodied, about fifty feet long, and fitted with a single mast to support the large square sail now rolled and tied to the boom. It looked deserted but seemed faintly threatening, bringing to Jessie's mind old stories of Viking raiders who'd pillaged Scotland's shores.

Creeping on hands and knees in the brush along the riverbank, Jessie saw the serving woman, Hnossa, and a single guard talking outside Aldis' brightly colored tent. The maid flirted openly with the man, though he was many years her junior. When Hnossa went into the tent, the man moved off, scanning the shore watchfully before turning his eyes to the sea. How long before the others returned and they set off for York? Would her message reach Tessa before they did?

For some time Jessie watched the tent, wondering if she'd done enough to warn Tessa and if she'd ever see Jenna again. If she'd returned to the village she'd have seen, coming to the wharf, a priest and a familiar figure dressed in nun's robes. The nun embraced the priest before boarding the ship, the deep cowl of her robe hiding a face like Jessie's own.

Chapter Fifteen

Jenna

Shaking off its moorings, the *Madeline* headed to sea, following the coastline southward and stopping at several places before coming to Scarborough. There, "Sister Mary" was told, she'd be able to travel inland on a smaller boat. "Since you're bound for Brixton, you might do me a service," the captain told her. "I was given a letter for the lady of the house."

"Really."

"The clerk in Glamis said it's urgent." He handed Jenna a rolled parchment sealed with red wax. "You might use this to pay for your transport." Digging in his pocket, he produced a ring Jenna knew well.

Jessie had sent a letter of warning to Tessa, which meant she was alive and well. Jenna's shoulders relaxed a little, though she hadn't realized they were tense.

"I'll take the letter, and I'll see Lord Brixton pays you for my passage." Rather nervously she blessed him, as Dominic had advised she must do to maintain her disguise.

By the time the little ship reached Scarborough, Jenna had decided to walk to Brixton. Her nun's robes should keep her safe on the trail, and keeping Jessie's ring was important to her. She was well ahead of the Vikings and used to walking. With the directions the captain provided, she was sure she'd make good time.

Except for her worries, Jenna's trek would have been pleasant. The weather was fine, and she was captivated by the land around her. The flat, green fields were larger than any she'd seen before, the soil so deep and rich that the bare feet of a farmer plowing on her left disappeared in its soft depths. Nothing she'd seen in the mountains prepared her for the soft greens and browns of England along the slow-moving Derwent River.

Mid-afternoon of the second day, she came to Brixton Manor, slightly back from a river bend, its front facing the water. More house than castle, defensible but not warlike, it sat in place as if grown from the sun-warmed ground, comfortable and contented. A garden off to one side contained vegetables, but rows of flowers at one end demonstrated love of beauty as well. Near the riverbank were stables, pens for animals, and outbuildings necessary to the running of a large estate. Her nose caught odors of manure, and she recognized several species, cattle, horses, sheep, and pigs. Farther down were the cottages of those who worked the land for Lord Brixton, and beyond that were small patches of land allotted to each family, marked with posts to identify the owners.

A boy trudging across a field noticed Jenna, and she followed with her eyes as he ran to tell the nearest adult. The man looked where he pointed then spoke to another. The news passed from person to person, so that by the time she reached the edge of the manor proper, a dozen pairs of eyes watched. Though their gazes weren't unfriendly, she guessed they were eager to know who she was and what she'd come for.

The boy had alerted the house, and when she approached the front doors, they opened to reveal a tall, spare woman in a black dress of fine fabric that hung loosely on her bony frame. An apron covering the dress was spattered with flour, revealing that baking had been interrupted. A white cap covered the woman's hair completely, emphasizing the sharpness of her face and the paleness of her complexion. Though she'd never be called attractive, her gray eyes missed little. A frown narrowed her brow, quickly replaced by something else.

"You are kin to the lady of this house."

Relieved to be spared long explanations, Jenna asked, "How did you know?"

"You are the very picture of our Tessa." A smile made her face less homely. "Which one are you?"

"Jenna." Though she remembered to curtsey, she wasn't sure it was well done. Practicing with Jessie hadn't prepared her for the real thing.

Before she knew it, Jenna was engulfed in a hug that was all sticks and white dust. "How wonderful to meet you! I am Madeline Brixton."

Jeffrey's aunt and Tessa's friend, often mentioned in letters as a woman of great age but strong constitution. And strong affection, it seemed, from the embrace Jenna received.

When Jenna was released she asked, "Is my sister here? I have important news."

"Tessa is visiting our cousin Cecilia. She's expected home by nightfall."

"But she is in danger." Suddenly Jenna was so tired she could hardly stand. All that had happened seemed to settle on her shoulders at once, and she sagged with its weight.

The older woman reacted immediately. "Come in, child, and sit down. I'll send for Jeffrey, and together we'll hear your news."

Leading Jenna into the main hall, Madeline led her to a bench near a sunny window fitted with thick, bubbly glass. Calling a servant, Madeline sent him to find Jeffrey, who was out with his reeve choosing trees to cut for timber.

A short time later, Jenna met her brother-in-law for the

first time. Jeffrey Brixton strode into the room, tall and confident, background in soldiering evident in his bearing. He was dressed for work, his dark hair caught in a practical knot at the back of his neck. A stray lock fell over his forehead as he entered, and he brushed it back absently. It stayed only a few seconds before falling over his eyes again. He was attractive, Jenna thought, for an older man.

"You're Jenna? Tessa's sister?"

"Yes."

"Jeffrey Brixton." He bowed briefly but went on, "You say she is in danger?" Family stories of Tessa's adventures flooded her mind. Jeffrey was a man who could defeat Leif's plans.

"And your sons."

"What?"

Jenna told her story, finishing with, "The Vikings can't be far behind me."

Jeffrey had trouble grasping the threat. "But Macbeth is ten years dead."

"Leif's luck failed, and his wise woman claims it is due to unavenged blood."

"Madness! How far behind are they?"

"I think the gleeman sent them in the wrong direction. It was a clever distraction, but it won't delay them for long. Too many people in Glamis know Tessa's story."

Jeffrey looked around the room as if searching for an enemy to fight. "I must find her."

"Go," Madeline urged. "I'll see Jenna is looked-after."

Calling for a servant, Jeffrey ordered a horse saddled.

Opening a chest in a corner, he removed a sword and scabbard. As he slipped the sword-belt over his shoulder, he turned to his guest. "Thank you, Jenna. What you have done required courage, and we are indebted to you."

Feeling a glow of pride, Jenna lowered her head modestly. They weren't out of danger yet. Who knew what evil Vikings would conjure? When she looked up, Jeffrey was gone.

Madeline showed her to a small room and had a maid bring a dress she thought would fit Jenna. "You may rest in this closet until Jeffrey fetches Tessa. Then the two of you shall have a wonderful visit. Now sleep, so you're refreshed when she returns. We will decide together what must be done."

The room was windowless and dark, scented with sweet-smelling herbs. The bed was narrow but comfortable, its mattress stuffed with straw. Once she was alone, Jenna put on the dress she'd been given and laid her nun's robe in a corner. Sure she couldn't sleep, she lay down on the bed and covered herself with a blanket, as the old woman had ordered. It was the last thing she remembered until a hand touched her shoulder.

"Jenna, is it really you?"

She sat up, momentarily disoriented. A candle burned on a small table beside her, and in its light she saw a face familiar yet strange. "Tessa!"

As they embraced, the emotion of the past days overcame her and tears welled in Jenna's eyes. Fighting the sob that rose in her throat she said, "I came to warn that your sons are in danger."

"So Jeffrey told me. I can hardly believe it."

"If you'd seen them, you would. They are horrible

creatures!"

"Oh, my dear, I don't doubt your word. It's hard to imagine, though, that someone could blame my boys for what our uncle is said to have done so long ago." Staring at the wall for a few moments, she shook off whatever memory had stirred. "You must be starved."

Jenna was indeed ravenous. Father Dominic had given her a parcel of food, but not knowing how long it had to last, she'd eaten only small amounts for several days.

Tessa guided her to the hall, where tables had been set up and food was being carried in from the kitchen. Jenna marveled at the food set before them, grand enough for a feast in the Highlands but merely a normal meal at Brixton. There were trays of meat and an array of side dishes whose smells made her mouth water. The room was noisy with conversation and the people of Jeffrey's household took their places. Jeffrey and Tessa sat, heads together, at the main table, their faces serious. Madeline took Jenna's arm and led her to a seat beside Tessa before taking her own place beside Jeffrey. Four laughing children entered, unaware of the adults' somber mood. The two boys were so alike that Jenna gasped at the sight of them: identical twins, like her and Jessie.

Two little girls followed their brothers, one about eight and the other perhaps six. They had their father's dark hair, and Jenna guessed they'd soon tower over their tiny mother. She recalled their names from Tessa's letters. Eleanor was older, Meg the baby.

Jenna's nieces and nephews came shyly to greet her. The boys bowed with youthful dignity, their faces flushed with the effort. "Which of you is Edward and which is Kenneth?"

Jenna saw deviltry in the eyes of the one on the right,

and she thought of times she and Jessie had fibbed about which twin was which. The other, an earnest sort, answered honestly. "I am Kenneth. You can tell us apart by the scar on Edward's forehead. He fell on a pitchfork when we were children."

She nodded, noting a tiny scar near the boy's hairline. Edward looked faintly disgusted at his brother's candor but she said, "I am also a twin, as like my sister as you two are on the outside. But inside, we're quite different." Glancing at each other, the boys grinned, acknowledging her understanding.

Used to the informal ways of her clan, Jenna watched Tessa and, doing as she did, managed not to embarrass herself. Many of the foods offered were new to her, though Tessa said they lived simply at Brixton compared to some English manors. Everything she tried, Jenna found delicious.

After supper Jeffrey excused himself, his wife, his aunt, and Jenna, saying they needed time to catch up. The little girls wanted to stay with "Auntie Jenna," but their father was firm that closer acquaintance must wait until tomorrow. They went off with their nurse without further argument. The boys took advantage of the mild evening to go outside and practice with their cudgels, improving their coordination and strength. Everyone else, relatives, retainers, and servants, settled in to do small chores like harness repair or sewing while they sang, recited poems, and gossiped.

Jeffrey led the three women to his office, which also served as a storeroom, and closed the door to muffle sounds of conversation and laughter. It smelled of bleach, and a stack of white linen fabric revealed why. It was a great deal of work to turn flax into linen and bleach it blinding white, but a household such as Brixton required white table linen for meals and fine shifts and shirts for the family.

Clearing items off several trunks so Tessa and Jenna

could sit, Jeffrey offered the only chair in the room to Auntie Madeline. He stood, pacing the length of the tiny room as they talked.

First he asked Jenna to tell her story again. As she spoke Jenna focused on Tessa, who seemed familiar though they'd been long separated. Tessa looked like a combination of Meg and Jenna herself, although she was by far the tiniest macFindlaech.

When the story was told and their questions answered, Tessa hugged her sister. "You poor thing, facing those terrible people alone! I'm glad you're safe with us now."

"But are you safe?" Jenna asked. "They are many, and trained soldiers as well."

"They won't dare to attack Brixton," Jeffrey said firmly.

"They did not attack the clan-hold. They came like cowards in the dark and took us by surprise."

"And you've spoiled their surprise this time." Tessa smiled to reassure her. "We have the advantage."

Jeffrey looked glum as he picked up a piece of parchment from the table before him. It rattled softly in his hand as he glanced at the writing on it. "It isn't as easy as being prepared," he said. "Today I was called by the king to gather my men and defend the coast."

Tessa's eyes widened. "Why?"

"We'll hear the details when we assemble, but there's rumor of a Viking invasion."

Leif's concern for recovering his luck had been urgent. Aldis had assured him he'd be ready when "they" came. "Leif Arneson will be part of it," she told them, explaining what she'd overheard in the Viking camp.

"The Norwegian king claims right to the throne," Jeffrey said when she finished. "This man is no doubt one of his liegemen."

"Who wants to end the curse he bears so he can lead men into the upcoming battle." Tessa's face was pale. "He'll come here soon, then. Before the Norwegian army arrives."

Madeline wrung her gnarled hands. "What can we do? The king requires Jeffrey to leave Brixton in order to help turn the Viking invasion away, yet Vikings threaten the lives of our children."

"I've been thinking about it since Jenna arrived," Jeffrey answered gravely. "If Arneson wants my sons dead, perhaps they must die."

Chapter Sixteen

Jessie

Though the warning to Tessa was on its way, Jessie couldn't make herself leave Glamis without knowing what had happened to Jenna. She wasn't with the Viking women. The men had delayed their journey and gone "hunting," which might mean Jenna had escaped them. How long would they delay their journey to search for her? Should she go home and hope her sister would be there, or stay in Glamis in case Jenna needed her? She'd watch until the Vikings sailed. If Jenna wasn't with them, she'd return home and hope to find her there.

There was the question, however, of what she'd do in a village full of strangers. Asking a group of women who sat carding wool with stiff combs and gossiping as they worked, she learned the present lord of Glamis, Menteith would not return from Scone for some time. "The thane's seldom here," one woman said.

"He claims to have business elsewhere," another added with a sly laugh, "but his lady doesn't mind. She too has business to see to."

"Viking business!" a third said, elbowing the woman beside her. "No need for the tall, handsome Northman to force himself on that one. She's willing enough!"

They all laughed, and Jessie moved away. If Lady Menteith was taken with Bjorn, she'd be unwilling to believe he'd wronged her family. And if she admitted to being Macbeth's kin, no one was likely to care what the Vikings had done to her.

Jessie wandered the village, watchful lest the Vikings return and see her. She was hungry, and she looked longingly at a fire outside a hut where a pot of stew boiled in a leather bag, scenting the air. The woman of the house stepped out and glared at her, and she moved on. Finding a place on the river edge, she sat down to watch men work on the boats there. The Madeline was gone, and she imagined it making its way to England. She said a prayer her message reached Brixton.

"Are you for hire, lass?" She looked up to see a sharp-faced man hovering over her, hands working nervously. When she didn't answer he added, "My mistress sent me to inquire, for she needs a girl."

A pigeon-breasted woman looked down her nose at Jessie from the pathway above. Despite attempts to appear disinterested, she shifted her feet impatiently.

Jessie considered. The woman appeared able to pay, and servants had to be fed. It would do no harm to hear the woman's proposal.

Keeping her eyes downcast and stopping well back so the woman could look her over, Jessie approached. Peeping from under her lashes, she took in what she could of her prospective employer: wide face, large, dark eyes, and clothing that was fine though not suited to her odd frame. The woman spoke in a loud, ringing voice. "Are you willing to work, girl?"

"Yes, my lady, if it pleases you." At home the servants weren't so formal, but she spoke as she recalled Alfred speaking to Donald and Meg.

The woman nodded, apparently satisfied with her demeanor. "I am Lady Menteith of Glamis Castle. Two maids of my household recently drowned, and I am receiving guests tomorrow evening." Her tone implied anger at the unfortunate young women who had died when she needed them to serve an important meal. "I have one day to teach what you must know, so you will pay attention and learn quickly."

"Yes, my lady." Jessie could hardly believe she was accepting employment as a servant. What would Meg say to Macbeth's niece working in their uncle's former castle?

The woman adjusted her coif, which stirred in the breeze. "I don't suppose you've been anywhere but this hole in the world."

Jessie might have admitted Glamis was the only town she'd ever seen, but she murmured, "No, my lady."

"Are there thieves in your family?"

"No, my lady."

"Are you in good health? Step up! Show me your teeth." As Jessie did so she remarked, "You walk oddly."

"I injured my hip, my lady. It will not hinder my work."

"Bad habits? Do you chew your fingers or snigger when you should not?"

"No, my lady." Jessie held out both hands to attest to her unbitten fingernails.

Leaning forward, Lady Menteith made a shortsighted examination and nodded satisfaction on that point. "Are you a Christian? Do you know your catechism?"

"We had no priest at home, but my sister taught me."

"Your sister?" One eye narrowed. "Are your parents drunkards?"

"No, my lady. They died. My sister raised us, and she is an honest woman."

The large bosom heaved once. "Very well. Go to the castle and wait. When I've finished my errands, I shall begin your training."

Retracing her steps to Glamis Castle, Jessie hoped she didn't meet the unkind man she'd spoken to earlier. The castle loomed over the village and the riverbank, nestling into the rocks behind it as if it were part of them, and she was seized with dread as she approached. Would they learn she'd misrepresented herself? Would they discover she was a macFindlaech? To her relief, her knock was answered by an elderly man who ushered her inside with shuffling steps. "You'll be serving Lady Menteith, then?" he asked when she explained her purpose for being there.

"I hope so, yes."

"She's a hard mistress but a fair one. Say 'Yes, lady' and do as she says in good time, and you'll get on."

"Thank you. I will."

And she did. Jessie listened and followed orders precisely. Lady Menteith seemed satisfied with the new girl's willingness, though she kept her approval to herself. Jessie went to bed the first night tired but pleased to have done well. When morning came she was up early, and preparations for the evening's banquet began. All day long she chopped vegetables, kneaded bread dough, and basted meats roasting in the oven, her face blasted by its heat. Her hip ached a little from moving about on the stone floors, but she ignored it. She'd always enjoyed being part of such preparations, though the meal at Glamis was more ambitious than she'd seen at home. She was shocked, however, when she learned who the visitors would be. "Vikings?"

"Aye," said a kitchen woman as she and Jessie polished pewter plates for the head table. Everyone else would get a trencher, a slab of bread that served as an edible plate. "They've been hunting in the hills, but they plan to leave Scotland on the morrow, so our lady invited them to a final supper. They're unusual folk, with a wise woman who is marvelous odd."

Jessie's mind raced ahead to the evening meal. She couldn't serve these guests. Most wouldn't look twice at a serving girl, but the sharp-eyed Aldis was sure to notice her.

Her solution was to stay in the kitchen when possible, loading serving dishes. When ordered to take a tray into the hall, she took it as far as the entry, waited until another servant came along, and traded the empty tray for the full one she carried. Since the others liked staying in the hall where the excitement was, no one objected.

At the end of the evening, Jessie carried a bucket of scraps outside for the animals. Though very tired, she was glad to know the Vikings would leave Glamis at daybreak. She'd succeeded in avoiding them.

Almost. As she re-entered the castle, a tall man was coming out on wobbly legs. He stopped, blocking the doorway, and Jessie's heart sank. "Well, well, lass," Bjorn said, "Were you looking for me?" He put his hands against the doorframe, steadying himself as he leaned toward her, and she caught the strong smell of liquor on his breath. A Viking. The worst of the Vikings. And worst of all, a drunken Viking.

Turning, Jessie ran. Unfamiliar with the castle yard, she had no idea where to go, but she had to try. Behind her Bjorn cursed as he stumbled against something.

She turned right, toward the darkest part of the yard, desperately hoping to find concealment. On her right, dogs began barking, and she almost tripped as a chicken brushed against her leg and scuttled off with a surprised squawk. A few steps along, she collided with something bigger—no, someone. She heard a grunt of surprise as she went sprawling onto the grass. Before she could rise again, Bjorn stood over her.

"You won't escape this time, pretty." He bent to grab Jessie's arm, but the person on the ground surprised them both, kicking Bjorn's legs out from under him. Bjorn landed on the ground with a surprised "woof!" and the other lunged at the Viking, landing atop him raining blows on his face. At first stunned, the big man recovered, rolled to his knees, and returned a blow of his own, knocking Jessie's would-be rescuer to the ground. As they both got to their feet, her defender's face showed in the dim light.

Alfred! A third shorter than the Viking, he'd squared off against him, hands raised aggressively.

With a chuckle of disbelief, Bjorn reached out a massive hand, grabbing for the gleeman. Alfred danced away, stepping in a moment later to deliver a buffet to Bjorn's ear before pulling back again. He managed the same trick again when Bjorn took a second swing at him. Though the Viking was bigger, drink had slowed his movements and his thinking. Alfred was quick, but if Bjorn managed to land a blow, he was sure to be hurt. Jessie looked around, seeking a weapon, but found nothing. The air whistled as Alfred narrowly avoided Bjorn's massive fist, ducking this time and delivering a blow to the big man's stomach before wheeling out of reach. Bjorn let out a growl of anger. How could she help Alfred?

Inspiration struck, and she removed her left boot, the one with the wooden block. Balancing on her right foot, she waited until Bjorn backed toward her then swung it smartly at his head, catching him behind the ear with a dull *thunk!* of wood on bone. He fell against a low stone wall, momentarily stunned.

Hopping on one foot, she put the boot back on. "Run!"

"This way." Alfred led her through the gate and into the

outer bailey. Deeper darkness there served them well, and they slowed, choosing stealth over speed. When they came to some outbuildings, he listened at the door of one then pulled her inside. The place smelled of hay and grain, and as they made their way to the farthest corner, Jessie hoped she wouldn't sneeze and betray them. A pile of harness lay on a rough table against the back wall, and they ducked under it, trying to quiet their ragged breathing.

No one came after them. No one called out for them to be caught. Other than singing in a distant cottage and the baying of the last few hounds, no sound reached them. When it seemed they were safe Jessie whispered, "How were you there when I needed you?"

"I was called upon to entertain the lady's guests. If I'd known they were that lot, I'd have left Glamis far behind me by now." He settled to a more comfortable position. "What are you doing here?"

Jessie shivered. "I took work as a maid so I could stay in Glamis and help Jenna."

He thought about that. "That's no longer possible."

"It might be. The Vikings will leave Scotland tomorrow."

"We must stay out of sight until then."

"Are we safe here?"

"When daylight comes, we'll be discovered, but I know a place."

Keeping to the shadows, they left the shed. Alfred led the way to an old, two-story house where light showed under the door and around the shutters. Above the door was a sign with a simple picture message, a mug of foaming ale and a bed. An alehouse and inn.

By-passing the front door, he led Jessie to the back,

where he opened a smaller door, beckoning Jessie to follow him inside. The room they entered was dark, and Jessie's fingers told her it was filled with kegs. There was a narrow passageway down the center, and Alfred moved along it to an inner door. Opening it, he peered into the next room, where there was a hum of conversation. Over his shoulder Jessie saw a rough counter, some tables where men sat drinking, and a woman moving about, serving ale and chatting with the customers. When she turned and saw Alfred, her face lit with joy. He put a finger to his lips to signal quiet, and she nodded. He closed the door and waited. Within a few minutes the woman came in, carrying a candle that sputtered and dripped as she moved.

She was pretty, with luxurious auburn hair and wide, clear eyes. Her bosom was fuller than Jessie's, her waist every bit as small. Her clothes, though plain, showed her charms to full advantage. "You came back!" Her voice revealed pleasure and something more. When the candle's light revealed Jessie behind him, however, her face froze. "What's this?" Jessie realized that while Alfred was welcome, she was not.

"My friend here was attacked by one of the Vikings from the ship anchored at the mouth of the river. We need a place to hide until they leave Glamis."

"You might have stayed as many nights as you liked," she said, her eyes flashing in the candlelight. "But you bring a 'friend' and ask me to help her?"

Alfred's face tensed. "I ask you to help us both."

She stared at him for a few seconds, her expression unreadable. "All right," she said. "You may stay for one night. Both of you." She turned and left, closing the door behind her with more force than necessary.

Alfred let out a breath in relief, but Jessie asked, "Can

we trust her?"

"I think so. She's been…kind to me other times when I visited Glamis."

"Oh."

"It wasn't…I mean, she isn't—" He stopped, shaking his head in frustration.

"It's all right, Alfred. You owe me no explanations." Jessie tried to keep her voice even. They hardly knew each other, yet she recalled him asking if he could visit her someday. How long had she stayed in his thoughts once they parted? Apparently not long.

Perhaps to hide his discomfort, Alfred went to work making a spot for Jessie to sleep. In a corner, he moved several kegs and laid out some empty sacks for a cushion. "There. Sleep if you can."

"What about you?"

"I'll be in the other corner. And lest you fret, Catherine will abide no lice here."

Nor uninvited women, if she has any say. Jessie kept that thought to herself. "Thank you, Alfred, for everything. Bjorn would have—" She stopped, unable to put it into words."

From his corner, Alfred chuckled. "I merely delayed him until you got your boot off."

Jessie giggled. "He called you the son of a moldy sheep when you struck him on the nose."

"An ancient Viking greeting, I trow." The tension of their near escape dispelled itself in bubbles of mirth, and they found themselves unable to stop laughing. Jessie laughed until her sides hurt. At last her spasms slowed to soft hums and quiet descended between them. Finally Alfred whispered, "Goodnight, Jessie."

"Goodnight." She lay on the hard-packed dirt floor, wondering what it would be like to have a man like Alfred to laugh with, talk with, and spend her days with forever.

The next morning when she woke, Jessie took a moment to recall where she was, why, and with whom. Alfred still slept; she could see his legs behind the barrels that separated them. Sitting up and stretching, she combed her hair with her fingers and braided it tightly, scrubbed her teeth with her sleeve, straightened her stockings, and put her boots on.

Finding a privy was the next necessity, and she hoped the hour was early enough that she wouldn't meet anyone during her search. Opening the door a slit, she peeped out. No sound, no movement. Locating the tiny building she started toward it, but as she neared, voices stopped her in her tracks. Listening, she heard a conversation between two Vikings who apparently shared a two-seat arrangement inside.

"Bjorn refuses to leave until he's hunted down the lying gleeman and slit his throat."

"He's only a singer of songs, Rothgar," the other said scornfully, "Bjorn should forget him."

"It's true we have much to do before our forces arrive. Lady Menteith says those we seek live in Jorvic, which she calls York."

"There's a bit of luck. Not far from our meeting place."

"You'll go with Leif to Jorvic and finish the blood feud while Bjorn and I will hunt down the singer and his lady love. We'll join you on the coast in good time, and wait for the arrival of our countrymen."

The second man lowered his voice a little. "Aldis says it's wrong to kill the girl."

"And Bjorn says Aldis has lost her power." The man named Rothgar sniffed angrily. "Leif's luck has worsened since we came here. He must cleanse his past so he's ready when the time comes to fight."

Sounds from inside the privy indicated the men were preparing to leave. Jessie stepped back against the alehouse, peeping around the corner.

The privy door opened and the men stepped out, stretching. The larger one gestured at the sky. "The weather is with you." He put a hand on the other man's shoulder. "Till we meet in Aingland, brother. It will be a glorious fight."

"When we defeat the Ainglish, we'll both be lairds." The man punched Rothgar's arm. "Kill the minstrel quickly, so you don't miss our day of glory."

Rothgar surveyed the area, and Jessie leaned back, out of sight. "They haven't left the village yet. Bjorn offered a gold coin to any who see them and report to him."

Jessie stood still as stone until they moved away, struggling to take in what she'd heard. Bjorn planned to kill Alfred. What he had in mind for her, she could guess.

Chapter Seventeen

Jenna

"Hurry, boys," Jeffrey called to the twins. The girls were already seated, Meg on Tessa's gentle palfrey and Eleanor behind Jeffrey on his huge black. Edward and Kenneth came running, carrying last-minute items essential for the trip, at least to the minds of boys. They mounted their ponies, joyful excitement showing in their faces. Jenna glanced at Tessa, whose expression revealed only worry.

Jeffrey was sending them to France to ensure their safety while he fulfilled his commitment to the king. "You'll stay with an old friend of mine, Giles Oldain."

"But won't that put him in danger?" Tessa had asked. "If this madman went into the mountains of Scotland to find us, a few miles of water won't stop him."

"That's the brilliant part of my plan," Jeffrey replied with a smile. "Word will be spread here that your ship sank. You, Jenna, and the children will be declared dead."

Though the women were stunned at his pronouncement, it neatly solved the problem. Leif's blood feud would be satisfied if all the macFindlaech males were dead

Jenna expressed a fear he'd return to the clan-hold and harm Meg and the others, but Jeffrey thought it unlikely. "The Viking invasion will come soon. He won't have time to return to Scotland." He added grimly, "With luck he'll be killed with the rest of the invaders."

Jenna recalled Aldis' comment about being ready when "they" came. No doubt Leif was expected to join the Norwegian armies once he'd completed his personal quest.

Tessa had been unhappy at the prospect of leaving her home and husband, but Jeffrey predicted things would be decided within a year. "It will benefit the children to see France, and Giles and Berthe will do all they can to make your stay pleasant."

"Without you?" Tessa's voice trembled, but she tightened her lips and crossed her arms. "I must speak with the servants. We have much to prepare." She'd left the room, and those left behind looked at their feet, knowing she'd gone somewhere private to shed her tears. They knew that once she'd had time to adjust, Tessa would face this trial bravely, as she'd faced so many others before.

The second sea voyage of Jenna's life was terrifying, not only for her but for everyone. As they boarded the little ship, dark clouds reached down at them like threatening fists. Jeffrey almost changed his mind about their leaving, but it was Tessa's turn to stand firm. "The captain makes this crossing many times each month. He won't sail if he can't outrace the storm."

Jenna cast a doubtful glance at the fellow under discussion. He seemed stalwart but hardly cautious, and a cautious seaman was what she preferred at the moment. "Besides," Tessa went on, "a storm will give credence to the story of a shipwreck."

Jeffrey bit his lower lip, and Jenna guessed what he was thinking. It was all too possible a shipwreck could become a reality in such conditions.

The little ship didn't sink, but Jenna had never been more miserable in her life. When they reached the Channel, choppy waves swelled under them, causing nausea and a feeling of dread. She sat very still on the deck at the center of the boat, hoping to control her stomach, but it was no use. When she moved to the ship's rail to be sick, both boys joined her. Tessa looked slightly green but didn't become ill. Her daughters suffered no seasickness, though their eyes were wide through the entire voyage.

When the crossing was complete, the little party descended the plank, glad to feel solid earth underfoot. Atop some barrels waiting on the dock lay a youth, body limp, mouth agape. Jenna heard him snoring as they passed, but moments later he called out, "My ladee, pleese! Art thou Madame Brossin?"

They turned at the sound of the name Jeffrey had invented, and the boy ran to catch up with them. He was about fourteen, his clothes dusty and disheveled. Lanky brown hair curled around his neck and brown eyes regarded Tessa anxiously.

"Brossin, yes."

Drawing himself erect, he made a formal bow. "Welcome to France. I am Henri, of Castle Oldain. My lord sends his compliments and begs you to allow me to make your journey as comfortable as possible." The pronunciation was garbled but comprehensible. Knowing no English, he'd learned the message by rote.

When Tessa spoke to him in French, he smiled broadly, relieved to communicate in his native language. "There is an inn my master recommends, the Poisson Jolie." Jenna, who'd begun learning French, strained to follow his words.

"*Nous sommes reconnaissants, Henri,*" Tessa said. Like an army decamping, the newly-invented Brossin family left the wharf for the inn called "The Pretty Fish."

The place was small, and they used up every available corner, but their overnight stay was pleasant enough. Supper was fish stew, thick with vegetables Jenna had never seen before. Afterward, some of the local men sang in the common room, and she hummed along, unable to understand the words but enjoying the melodies. It made her think of Jessie, who loved to sing. How she missed her! Not that Tessa wasn't good company, but like Meg, Tessa had forgotten much of what it felt like to be young.

The next day Tessa roused them early, urging speed. "With a day's hard travel we'll reach Oldain. Once there, we'll send word to Jeffrey that we're safe." Turning to Jenna she added, "And he can tell the world we're not."

Henri saw to the hiring of horses and carts for the trip. Giles had sent men to escort them, and when all was assembled, they set out for Oldain, a large fief near Amiens. "The land is called Normandy," Tessa said as they rode, "due to the Norsemen there."

"Norsemen?" Jenna was horrified. "We escaped one band of Vikings only to encounter another?"

"These Norsemen are quite civilized, Jeffrey says. They came to pillage the coast of France long ago, liked what they found, and ended up staying. Now they have adopted French manners and speech—" She chuckled, adding, "—and French airs, I'm told."

Jenna sniffed. "Silk can't civilize a Viking."

"Many Normans were honored guests at our late King Edward's court." Tessa frowned. "William, the Normans' duke, imagines himself Edward's heir, with rights to England's throne."

"Another madman who claims England? The Norwegian king claims he's the rightful heir, and you told me there were several candidates in England. Yet the English have already chosen their new king."

"Yes. The Witan named Harold Godwinson king of England in hopes of discouraging the others."

Jenna was reminded of their uncle, whose longing for kingship had cost him his life in the end. "I wonder why anyone wants to be a king, despite the power that accompanies it."

Tessa surveyed the land around them. "Modern kingship is very complicated. For example, our host, Giles, was given his fief by England's King Edward as a reward for military service. But since it is English land on French soil, Giles owes allegiance to the French king as well as the English one. I wonder if even Giles knows to whom he owes allegiance now that Edward is dead."

"Perhaps the English should have chosen a Scottish king," Jenna said facetiously. "They couldn't do worse than a Viking, even a tame one."

Chapter Eighteen

Jessie

When Jessie reported the Vikings' conversation to Alfred, he groaned. "What shall we do? We can't stay here another night, for some use the back door to reach the privy." Catherine came in just then, and he asked her, "Is there someone else who might take us in?"

Catherine thought for a moment. "Father Dominic," she said. "The church has room for guests, and he keeps his own counsel."

They asked her to approach Dominic, who agreed to protect them from the Vikings they'd angered. When darkness fell, Alfred and Jessie made their way to the church, so tightly wrapped in their cloaks they appeared to be moving rolls of fabric. Guided by the glow of candles inside and the steeple that stood out against the dark sky, they found the church and stepped inside.

The priest was in prayer, and they waited until he finished. When he turned to them, his eyes widened with surprise. "Jenna? What's happened to the ship?"

Jessie's heart leapt. "I'm Jenna's sister, Jessie. Do you know where she is?"

Getting to his feet with some difficulty, Dominic approached, staring in amazement. "You're very like her. Jenna sailed to England a few days ago on the *Madeline*."

It was Jessie's turn to be surprised. Jenna had gone south on the same ship that carried her letter. It was a relief to know she'd escaped the Vikings, and the message to Tessa was doubly done.

Alfred put a hand on her shoulder. "She's safely away. You can return home now."

It should have been a happy thought, but Jessie couldn't help but consider her future. What waited in the Cairngorms? Tending her sisters' babies and stirring the stewpot. Home would be different without Jenna, and besides, now that she'd begun exploring the outside world, she wanted to see more.

Telling herself not to wish for what couldn't be, Jessie returned her attention to the present. She and Dominic pooled what they knew of Jenna's story. Then she and Alfred told the priest what had happened to them. "What a wonder life is!" Dominic said happily. "When Catherine asked me to help two young people escape an angry Viking, I readily agreed. Now I'm rewarded with news that warms my heart, for your sister was much concerned for your welfare."

"We're not out of danger yet," Alfred warned. "Bjorn vows to stay until he finds us."

Dominic nodded in agreement. "I've heard he spreads gold like water on stone. Few could resist the promise of such wealth if they knew where you were."

His comment brought Catherine to mind. The woman obviously had hopes for Alfred's affection and saw Jessie as a threat. Was it because she couldn't separate the two that she'd helped them thus far?

"Could you go to the castle on our behalf?"

Dominic shook his head doubtfully. "The thane's wife is charmed by the Viking, Bjorn Bear-slayer. He claims you intended to rob her, and when he tried to stop you, Alfred hit him from behind in a cowardly attack."

"Well, someone did hit him from behind," Jessie admitted, "but it wasn't Alfred."

"And it's Jessie who was attacked!" Alfred added hotly.

"I believe you, my son, but Lady Menteith believes the worst of you."

"If we return to my home," Jessie said, "my kinfolk will protect us."

Dominic shook his head, causing his jowls to wobble. "Even shepherds on the hillside have been offered a reward if they report seeing you."

"Then we must go in disguise."

"I see no other choice." Alfred said with a sigh. Jessie realized he wished to be rid of her but was too kind to leave her behind while danger threatened.

Dominic chuckled. "I would have proposed the guise of a nun, for it is a good one, but I gave the robe to your sister. We must think of something else."

"Alfred and I might travel as father and daughter if he were made to look older and I younger," Jessie said. "We would seem to be wandering trade folk."

"Hmmm. Tinkers, perhaps?"

"Where would we get the tools of that trade?"

Dominic considered. "They would only be needed until you're out of Glamis. I will let you borrow a few pots and tools to hang from packs on your pony's sides. You can leave them somewhere outside the gates, and I'll bring them back a few at a time."

"My lute will be hard to disguise," Alfred said. "Its shape is easily identified."

"Blankets," Dominic said. "We'll wrap it in blankets you can then use for bedding as you travel." He gestured vaguely toward his sleeping quarters. "I have plenty, for the good women of the town have clever fingers and generous hearts."

Jessie gave him a grateful hug. "As do you, Father."

"We must be kind to those we meet, for we never know when we might entertain angels." Dominic chuckled. "I can't say if you are angels, but I'll wager the Vikings are not." He frowned as a thought occurred to him. "I have no clothing you might use, however, and if I ask, folk will wonder why a priest needs a skirt."

Alfred rubbed his chin. "Catherine might help us once more," he said. "Though I hate to ask her."

When they explained Jessie's plan to Catherine, she agreed to help, somewhat grudgingly. "Clothes I have, but she's lame. She'll need a beast to ride."

"I have a pony," Jessie said.

"I don't suppose she has money to pay for its keep." Catherine spoke as if Jessie weren't there.

"I'll pay the stableman," Alfred said with an edge in his voice. "No one will lose because of us."

Jessie almost smiled, hearing him speak as if they were a team. Then she saw the look of anger in Catherine's eyes, and the urge to smile disappeared. They must leave soon, before Catherine's fondness for Alfred was overcome by her dislike of Alfred's friend.

It took two days to prepare their escape from Glamis. Dominic fashioned two large bundles containing what he thought Alfred and Jessie would need for their sustenance. He attached various metal objects to the outsides, so their "trade" was obvious. Catherine did her part, bringing them plain but serviceable clothing. Alfred got a tunic and leggings of brown along with a battered hat he took outside and slapped against a wall to dislodge any "crawlies" in residence. Catherine also brought him a pair of gloves. "Your hands give away your youth. You must hide them, and I'll show you how to make your hair appear gray."

"Thank you, Catherine."

She rubbed something on Alfred's hair to dull it, teasing him gently as she worked. Jessie wondered again if his decision to help her had ruined a budding romance. If seemed so, and she felt even more guilty. She'd interfered with Alfred's schedule, his profession, and his romance. He must rue the day he met her.

When she finished, Catherine couldn't hide her satisfaction at the job she'd done. Alfred's hair was silvery, and he appeared to have a hump on his right shoulder. Using charcoal, she'd added the appearance of years to his face as well.

Jessie's costume was meant to hide her figure so she appeared childlike. She'd shortened the skirt Catherine gave her and bound her chest with cloth bands before pulling a shapeless tunic over her head. Wrapping her bright hair in a faded coif, she rubbed dirt on her face to dull her complexion. To casual eyes they'd pass for father and daughter.

To Jessie's surprise, Foot took to Alfred, calmly allowing him to load packs onto his back and feed him bits of carrot and turnip. "He's usually not so friendly," she remarked.

"Animals like me, though I've never had one of my own." Alfred patted Foot's neck, and the pony nuzzled his leg, leaving a streak of green. "Mayhap it isn't such a great thing to have a pony's affection," he said ruefully, wiping at the stain.

"Once you're away from here, you can decide what to do next," Dominic told them.

Jessie glanced toward home, and as if he'd read her thought, the priest tilted his head. "I advise you to avoid your home for a time, for they expect you to go there. I can send word that you're well without saying where you've gone."

Hugging him again, Jessie said, "I owe you more than I can ever repay, Father."

He waved away her gratitude. "I do what I do lest there be angels among us." Clasping her hands in his, he advised, "Make the best of things. See the sights of the world, at least those Alfred here can show you."

"I will, if you see that Meg doesn't worry." Few will even notice I'm gone, she thought.

That wasn't entirely true. There was Dougal, but Jessie knew now she wanted more from life than marriage to a man with no spark of life in him, no trace of imagination. Glancing at Alfred, she thought, He could never love me, but I'll be happier at his side than I've ever been before.

No one paid much attention to their departure from Glamis. Dominic walked with them to the gate, chatting to Jessie as if she were a darling child and matching his steps to Alfred's apparently aged gait. He stopped and called farewell, urging them to visit when their travels brought them north again. He joked with the guards, distracting them from taking a close look at the departing pair. With pounding hearts, Jessie and Alfred made their way through the meadow surrounding the village and into the woods.

Once they were out of sight, Alfred straightened and quickened the pace. They would go, he said, to Barl, a village he'd visited often and considered safe. After stopping to stow the tinker's equipment in a spot where Dominic could retrieve it, they went on. "What will we do in Barl, Alfred?"

"I don't know," he said honestly. "I can't sing there, lest someone should recognize me." Turning his gaze away he added, "I've little money left."

She guessed he'd paid Catherine, both in return for her help and to lessen the temptation she might feel to betray them. She'd seen him put coins in the donation box at the church as well, in gratitude for Dominic's help. "I'm sorry, Alfred. Once again I have cost you, though it was not my intent."

Looking back at the mountain she offered, "Help me cross the river, and I'll make my way home by some other path."

"No!" His tone was almost angry, but he softened it, finishing with, "Any other way up the mountain is too rough for you to climb. And as Dominic said, Bjorn's spies will be watching."

He was correct. If it were Jenna, she'd swim the river, climb the mountain, and reach her home through sheer determination. But then Jenna had no infirmities. She was not a cripple.

Alfred stopped and turned to face her. "Bjorn is hunting both of us, so we must stay together." Blushing, he added, "I promise I'll not...trouble you." Changing the subject, he went on, "But we need to earn our living."

"How?

His eyes lit with a glint of humor. "I have an idea."

Jessie's eyes narrowed. "From your tone, I don't think I'm going to like it."

The village of Barl welcomed a pair of musicians that night, an elderly man named Mark who played the lute, and his daughter Maureen, who sang. Some of the village women thought the girl too shy to give a good performance, but the men insisted she overcame her early weakness very well.

And besides, she was a pretty little thing, for all her dirty face and drab clothing.

"No!" Jessie had argued earlier. "I could never sing before a crowd of people!"

"You have a lovely voice, and the village is small, the perfect place to try my plan. They won't mind an unpolished performance, and they'll give us a meal and a place to sleep."

"But you're the singer."

"I *was* the singer. Now Bjorn is on the hunt for a young man who sings. He isn't looking for an old man who plays while his daughter sings."

That wasn't the end of the argument, but Alfred won, mostly because they had no other options. At their small campfire, Alfred instructed Jessie on how she should look at the audience, sing with confidence and animation, and bow prettily after each song.

His teaching served her well, but not at first. When the moment came and several dozen faces watched her expectantly, Jessie experienced every nervous manifestation possible: shaking legs, icy cold hands, difficulty breathing, red splotches on her neck, and an urgent desire to empty her bladder. Worst, though, was the inability to control her voice, which came out oddly high and constricted. Behind her Alfred reminded softly, "Deep breath in and out."

She inhaled, letting the air out slowly, as they'd practiced. Her chest muscles loosened, and her voice modulated to its normal soprano tone. He was right. It was possible to make herself relax. Recalling another bit advice he'd given, she stretched her lips in a smile and tried to look as if she were happy to be there. Almost without exception, the faces around her smiled back.

Alfred strummed the strings once more, and she began again, telling herself she'd do this for him. They needed a way to support themselves. Alfred believed she could be an entertainer, and she trusted him. Letting the familiar songs take over, she concentrated on reaching the audience, and nervousness disappeared. After she'd sung the pieces they'd planned, Jessie eagerly took up other songs by request.

At the end of the evening, when they were settled in a villager's loft and the residents were asleep, Jessie admitted she'd enjoyed herself. "They loved you," Alfred said exultantly. "In time you'll gain confidence."

"You mean we'll do this again?"

"Tomorrow evening and two days after that, if the weather is fine."

"You think we can continue this?"

"My disguise won't hold up well in daylight, but we're safe at night. They'll be looking at you, not at me."

Jessie made a dismissive noise, but she lay awake for some time, recalling the faces of the people she'd sung for. They had liked her. And when Alfred joined in with harmony on some of the songs, she'd felt something altogether new. She didn't know for sure what it was, but she wanted to feel it again and again.

Chapter Nineteen

Jenna

The ride to Oldain was a constant delight for Jenna. New sights, sounds, and smells assailed her as they journeyed, their pace slow to accommodate the luggage cart. France's countryside was less wooded and more inhabited than anything she'd seen before. Scotland was a wild tangle of moor and mountain, its people huddled together in small enclaves. England was a nation of villages, but they, too, were widely spread, with deep forests that separated them from each other. The continent was more open, more in use. Little of its land was enclosed, and hardy villagers left closely-built huddles of huts each morning to farm their allotted plots of land with brisk efficiency.

Even from a distance, Oldain was impressive, a large stone castle surrounded by a moat, or fosse, fifty feet wide. Inside the moat, a large mound with upright posts sunk into the earth formed a stockade wall. From the rise where they stopped they could see inside the stockade, where a veritable town existed. Central to it was the tower, where the seigneur and his family lived. Its walls were of crenellated stone, a huge donjon surrounded by wings added over time. With no danger imminent, the wide drawbridge was down, the foot-thick gates open. As they approached, shouts from the wall alerted those inside, and when they reached the entry, a small crowd had gathered to greet the English lady and her companions.

As they rode up the planked surface, a man strode toward them, his silvered hair glinting in the sunlight. He raised his arms long before he reached them, smiling broadly. "The Lady of Brisson, is it not?" he called out.

"Wife of your old friend, Compte D'Oldain," Tessa alit from her horse to bow gracefully, but he clasped her in an enthusiastic embrace.

"You must call me Giles. And is this your sister?"

Jenna dismounted, trying for the same grace Tessa managed so easily. It was difficult, since she'd never ridden so high off the ground before this. "Your Grace," she said, bowing low before looking up into the man's face. Integrity showed in his gaze, which explained why her brother-in-law had so much respect for Giles.

"He and Jeffrey campaigned together as young men," Tessa had told her on the way. "He's happy for Giles but regretful that the land he was granted for his service is so far away from Brixton."

"Jeffrey says you are the queen of his heart, and I've never seen a lovelier liege," Giles d'Oldain said now, bowing over Tessa's hand. "These are your children?"

The boys had dismounted and were helping their sisters dust off their skirts. Each child was introduced, and each gave a perfectly executed response. Giles declared himself relieved to have two more men to defend the castle, which brought a proud blush to the boys' cheeks. To the girls he shaded his eyes and said, "I must learn to look askance, so as not to be blinded by such beauty." They giggled at the compliment.

"You must have time to refresh yourselves before you grace this old man's table at dinner. My wife is seeing to it, as we had notice of your arrival from the shepherd boys." Giles led the way into the courtyard, pointing out where the servants could stable the animals and find refreshment for themselves.

Inside, Oldain seemed even larger than it had from a distance. The walls traveled up over knolls and down into depressions as they wound an amazing distance, shielding the buildings necessary to a community of its size. People worked at assigned tasks, acknowledging the visitors with a polite tug at their forelocks or a brief curtsey. The day was ending, and the smells in the air suggested the evening meal was fish of some sort.

Countess Berthe, a tall woman with an aristocratic nose and a high forehead, met them in the courtyard. Her fashionably pale skin contrasted starkly with her dark hair and eyes. Tessa greeted her in French, but she said proudly, "I have learned the Ainglish tongue, since Giles' friends often visit."

Despite the polite welcome the countess seemed reserved, and Jenna wondered what she thought of taking in six strangers and their retinue. Noble women were used to managing such things, but that didn't mean they had to like it.

As they entered the castle, Tessa politely asked about affairs at Oldain. "Things go well enough," Giles said. "The French king manages, no thanks to his fractious subjects."

"The Northmen?" Jenna asked, ready to hear the worst of men with Viking ancestry.

He nodded. "The Normans mix tolerably but not totally into our culture. My territory borders their holdings, so I'm aware of friction between them and the king." He tilted his head to the left and the right to mimic a balancing act. "I strive to remain at peace with my neighbors the Normans, my liege the king of England, and my host the king of France."

When Giles left them to his wife's care, pleading business, Tessa chatted with Berthe about the work of running a large estate, complimenting the lady's tapestries and discussing ways to monitor the work of household servants. Jenna fidgeted, unable to imagine that anyone enjoyed such banal conversation.

"I have a request, if it's not too bold," Tessa said candidly. "The French are known for their cooking, but my people, the Scots, depend largely on the grease used in frying to lend taste to their dishes." Jenna's anger rose at her sister's criticism of her homeland's food, but she remained quiet, trusting Tessa.

She saw the strategy when Berthe's face revealed the first sign of genuine pleasure. "My husband has learned to eat well," she said with a smile. "At first he complained, but now he enjoys the different flavors."

"I'm hoping you'll share recipes while we're here."

The lady's reply was animated. "Tonight's is simple enough. I take an onza of pepper, one of cinnamon, and one of ginger, a quarter onza of cloves, and a quarter of saffron. I sprinkle the saffron through my fingers to break it as I mix. This is delicious with fish of any kind."

"Jenna, will you write that down?" Tessa asked. "I must try it when I return home."

Berthe raised her eyebrows. "Your sister writes?"

"Our father taught us, though my sister had less time under his tutelage than I." Again Jenna saw purpose in Tessa's apparently casual comment. Jeffrey had told them Berthe was a woman of intelligence. Knowing the true story of Jenna and Tessa's visit, she'd no doubt expected a party of wild Scots, uncivilized and ignorant. Though willing to accommodate her husband's guests, she probably hadn't looked forward to it. When Tessa revealed some education and eagerness to try new things, the formality with which Berthe had first received them melted away. Pleased to comply with her sister's request, Jenna wrote the recipe down, repeating the ingredients as she worked.

"I'm hoping you'll enjoy some books I brought along," Tessa said. "Perhaps we might discuss them once you've had time to read them."

"I'd like that." Berthe's smile was warm this time, and Tessa had a new friend where a few minutes earlier she'd had only a dutiful hostess. That was good, since there was no telling how long they would have to stay in this foreign place. Besides, a friend was more likely to keep their secret than a grudging acquaintance.

Jenna liked Oldain. The people seemed content, the count and Berthe were amiable, and the weather was fine. Tessa worried about Jeffrey, preparing for battle with the Northmen, but they could do nothing about that.

"Giles sent a messenger to England," Berthe told them at breakfast. "In private he will give Jeffrey your letter, but in public he'll announce the sinking of your ship with all hands. To the English people, you will be dead." It was sad to allow Jeffrey's cousins, the people of Brixton, and their friends in London believe a lie, but Jeffrey had insisted the news must seem real.

Perhaps to change the subject Berthe told them, "You have arrived just in time for our fair." Jenna liked the sound of that. Where she came from fairs were rare, but in other places they were much-anticipated annual events, bringing new people, new products, and new ideas to the prosaic, uneventful lives of those on rural estates. Even Berthe seemed excited by the prospect. "For months we see the same faces, but during the week of the fair, acrobats, traders, inventors, and musicians visit our little corner of the world." She added drolly, "Even mountebanks and gypsies are entertaining if one does not trust them too far."

The celebration began the next day with an afternoon of

outdoor activities: games, entertainment, and contests of all kinds. As the children raced ahead, taking in the sights, Tessa, Jenna, and Berthe walked among the people, making small talk about the weather, prospects for the year's crops, and family events. Like a good chatelaine, Berthe knew the names of each serf's children, the condition of his elderly parents, and the likelihood of his having a complaint for Giles to settle.

A woman named Susan told them her son would soon leave Oldain to become a priest. "Last year was a good one, and I have the fee," she told them. Serfs were required to pay for the count's loss of a worker if a child went to college or to the church, but the woman's pride that her son would be devoted to God outweighed the cost to her. "My boy has a profession."

"Susan inherited her father's place on the manor, being his sole child," Berthe said as they walked on. "Wisely, she found a husband who helped her pay the death dues. With their combined farmland, they make enough to dedicate Rene to the church. He will be a fine priest someday."

They passed a crowd of people cheering and calling out advice. Two men stood in a fenced circle, each blindfolded and holding before him a cudgel. Inside the circle was a goose, which flailed wildly as the men tried to hit it with their sticks without striking each other. Jenna, who felt sorry for the "prize," turned her eyes away until the game was behind them.

Next they stopped at a cottage to visit a freeholder who'd been injured a few days before. He'd entered a stall where a bull was confined and been attacked, ending up with several broken bones. Berthe served as a sort of consultant in such cases, as the chatelaine of a large estate often did.

The freeholder, called Tom Freeman to distinguish him from all the other Toms on the estate, owned his piece of land, making him a step above the serfs. "He is truly Jupiter's child, well liked and industrious," Berthe said, "as they say those born under that sign will be."

The cottage was wooden with a turf roof. Inside, a fire-pit dominated the center of the single room. At one side was a kneading trough for bread and a table with a single bench beside it. On the opposite wall hung pots, pans, and other utensils for daily tasks.

On a straw-stuffed mattress in another corner lay Tom, both arms splinted and wrapped, and a blanket pulled up to keep him warm. Beside him sat his son, a boy of about twelve dressed in a loose cloth blouse, a handmade leather jacket, trousers, and high shoes made of felt. His father was urging him, "Go, lad. I'm all right. Enjoy the day before it's gone."

Berthe put a hand on the boy's shoulder. "I'll sit with your father. Go and see the games."

"You must accompany young Tom, ladies," she urged, settling herself on a stool. "I'll hear old Tom's story of his misfortunes with the bull."

Jenna and her sister wandered the fair site with Tom, Jenna asking questions in French to draw him out. His mother had died the year before. His respect was divided between Giles and his father, though his love centered on "old" Tom, who was, Jenna figured, at least twenty-nine, older even than Tessa.

As they stopped to watch a juggler, Tessa asked if Jenna had seen such things in Scotland. The boy's ears pricked up at the word. "I met a lady once who came from there," he told them. "Odd, she were, shrunken and knotted up. She told wondrous stories of a house that floated on a lake by some sort of magic."

"It did," Tessa said softly. "I saw it."

"Scots-land was not her real home," the boy went on. "She were an infidel that does not believe in the true God, but she was kind, and I pitied her, for she was ever in pain."

Tessa stared in amazement. "Why, I knew that lady many years ago. I heard she had gone back to her home in Spain."

Tom raised a finger. "That's where she was bound!"

"Her name is Miriam, and she is a Moor," Tessa explained. "Her God is the same as yours and mine, though our ways of worshipping Him are different."

"Infidels," he repeated.

With a wry look at Jenna, Tessa turned to talk of cocks and hens.

Chapter Twenty

Jessie

Jessie's enjoyment of her new life grew each day. She and Alfred traveled well together, and Foot was unfazed by the ups and downs of the Scottish countryside. When the weather was clear they slept outside, under the stars she'd always loved. When it was rainy, Alfred found them shelter at a farm or in a town. If that wasn't possible, he searched out a protected space: a cave, an outcropping, or even a stand of trees whose branches interwove enough to deflect the rain. She thought he disliked rain, however, for on nights when they shared those small spaces he was distracted and almost short with her.

By day as they traveled, they talked of things they'd seen and things they thought. Once when Father Dominic's name came up Jessie said, "He took you aside before we left. Did he speak of me, Alfred?"

There was a short silence. "He did."

"What did he say?"

Another silence. "He was, um, worried about you."

"Because of my leg."

"No." After a moment he said, "Not your leg."

"He promised to get word to my family, so it can't have been that." She recalled Alfred promising he wouldn't touch her. "Oh." Alfred examined the hills, avoiding her eyes. "He was afraid you and I would…sin?"

Looking away Alfred said, "I said it was not possible."

"I see." Was she so unattractive to him?

"I told him that when you return home, you are to marry

a man your family chose for you."

"Of course."

"Father Dominic was concerned that we might be…tempted as we travel together, but I told him we look upon each other as friends, nothing more."

She wanted to discuss it further, but Alfred had said all he intended to on the subject. "I see smoke," he said, pointing. "You won't sleep in a cave tonight, Jessie." He added in an undertone, "A blessing for us both."

When they arrived at the gate, a servant ran to get the seneschal, who appeared with an eager expression. "A gleeman who's a lass?" he said when Alfred introduced himself and his "daughter." He turned to Jessie. "Is your voice proper for singing?"

In answer Jessie sang a chorus of a familiar tune, and the man smiled. "You are welcome, for we've had no entertainment yet this summer."

He questioned them on events in the outside world, and Jessie, coached the night before by Alfred, gave a satisfactory account of politics, news, and fashion. Last he asked if she could teach them any new dances. "I am sorry," she answered. "I do not dance."

He waved a hand that looked too heavy for the arm that supported it. "No matter. With a voice like yours, we will be happy to sit and listen."

They were not the only entertainers in the place. An elderly bard, a wasted man with a hairless, shiny skull and a deeply-lined face, had retired there when he could no longer travel. He was gracious, suggesting they sing before dinner. "Later I will recite, but my voice is no longer suitable for singing. Afterward you can sing again, if you know the lilts folk want to hear."

When the time came, Martin the Storyteller took his place in the center of the room, head bowed, and waited for absolute quiet before beginning the saga he'd chosen for the evening. "Our king came in conquest to counter a crime," he began in the alliterative style of poetry. Folk in the audience smiled in recognition. It was the tale of Malcolm's rise to power and Macbeth's defeat.

Jessie looked around. No one here knew she was related to the late king, but all knew the stories that circulated after his death. Would what they heard be truth or lies? One thing was certain. Macbeth's version of the story couldn't be told. He was dead and gone.

The poet told first of Macbeth's rise to power. According to the account, he murdered the old king, Malcolm's father, in his castle at Glamis. Then, the bard said, he killed his friend Banquo, who suspected him of the regicide. After that came a part that made Jessie listen even more closely. "The fiend sent five to murder the fair mother and fine sons of Macduff, thane of Fife."

As the story went on, she found herself putting together things she'd heard over the last month. Leif claimed Macbeth had sent men to murder his family. Leif was a Scot, not a Viking. Was there a connection between Leif and the Macduffs? The poet said all Macduff's sons were killed that day along with their mother, but what if one of them had escaped? Could Leif be a son of Macduff returned to wreak vengeance, or was he a madman whose diseased mind had created a fantasy he now believed to be true?

As she waited for sleep, wrapped in a blanket on the hall's rush-strewn floor, Jessie wondered about her uncle. Had he been evil, as people now thought, or had the present Scottish king sullied Macbeth's reputation in order to justify the invasion and conquest of his own nation with the aid of English troops?

Her uncle's crimes, real or imagined, didn't matter, Jessie decided. It was over, and he was gone.

Still, what Leif believed mattered. Whether Macbeth was responsible for his misfortunes or not, Leif blamed him, and worse, he sought revenge on Macbeth's descendants. Looking across the room to where Alfred rested with the men of the castle, she said a prayer of thanks for his support. She hoped they'd escaped the danger, and things would go well for them from now on.

Chapter Twenty-one

Jenna

Jenna fell into a pattern of observing and learning the ways of a large estate. Though Tessa and Berthe were gentle teachers, they agreed she should know the duties of a proper chatelaine. "When this is over, you might decide to stay in England or even here in France," Tessa told her. "You're the niece of a king, and you should know how to behave like one."

Jenna snickered at Tessa's aspirations for her. "I'll never be a lady such as you are, Tess. My temper too often overrules my manners."

With her head tilted to one side, Tessa patted a spot beside her. "Come and sit here."

Jenna moved to a place on a tapestry-covered window seat, in the full sunshine of a French afternoon. "You think yourself an unsuitable prospect for chatelaine?"

Attempting a casual shrug, Jenna said, "When I am angry, I cannot control my tongue or my actions."

"What sorts of things bring on this anger?"

Jenna searched for examples. "When Con Balch took the baby's poppet and tore off its head, I hardly knew what I was doing until they pulled me off him." She chuckled despite herself. "His nose bled for an hour."

"I see. And another example?"

"When the travelling priest told Angus Reed his wife couldn't be buried in hallowed ground because she took her own life, I said in front of everyone he was wrong. The poor thing was out of her mind with pain."

"Your anger arises when someone is mistreated."

Jenna considered. "Yes, but I say and do things I should not."

Tessa touched her arm gently. "That isn't wrong, though it will benefit you to learn tact and timing."

"I am like our mother," Jenna said soberly. "All I recall of her is anger and unhappiness."

"I have the same memories," Tessa said, "but if your anger comes from injustice, you're like our Father, whose anger was never selfish, as our mother's was."

"But I have no control over it."

"That is a weakness," Tessa acknowledged, "but a lovely woman named Eleanor helped me understand that my weaknesses don't define me. They're only part of a whole."

Jenna considered that. If her temper was only a part of who she was, she might learn to control it in time. And if not, at least the bullies of the world had someone to face them down. She was pleased with Tessa's advice. Old age, she decided, might not be such a bad thing if one gleaned wisdom from it, as her sister had.

One morning Tessa and Jenna took the boys riding in order to explore the estate. Berthe had taken to the girls and often served as surrogate grandmother. They left her in the kitchen with her charges standing on stools beside the scrubbed slab table, wrapped in aprons much too big for them and rolling out fist-sized gobs of soft dough. "They'll learn the niceties of French cooking, and there will be a surprise for supper," Berthe said with an arched brow. Eleanor and Meg scarcely looked up as their mother left.

The day was fine, and the boys rode ahead, too grown up in their own minds to stay beside the women. Often they left the trail to investigate some sound or sight that intrigued them, so the adults had no trouble keeping up. The party wove first between the peasants' huts, which smelled strongly of onions and peat fires. Beyond them were neatly-planted fields. Finally they ascended a wooded hill above Giles' domain where they enjoyed an almost full-circle view.

Far to the west was blue water, which Jenna guessed was the ocean. To the southeast was the village of Oldain, with the castle behind and the river beyond that, wending its way across their line of sight. To the north were the lands of Duke William, the Norman neighbor who claimed rights to the throne of England.

A commotion in the trees caused Jenna's horse to start and shy. Calming the beast with a reassuring hand, she turned to see what had caused the noise. From the wood came a hound, running with the joy release from captivity brings. Behind it a panting boy with a coiled rope in hand. His chase was earnest, but the dog obviously considered it a game.

The animal stopped, looking challengingly at its pursuer. The boy, who saw no humor in the situation, marshaled his patience and spoke to the animal. "Come, now, Dite. You mustn't bother the ladies."

The dog regarded them, considering whether to make their acquaintance or not. Though approach might mean capture, curiosity got the better of her, and she stepped daintily up to Jenna's horse and sniffed at it, delighted with new scents to examine.

Jenna dismounted slowly, well acquainted with the frustration of trying to recapture an animal in such a situation. They often danced just out of reach, unwilling to be tethered. She let the dog sniff her hand, holding still until the beast lost its wary manner. Guessing her purpose, the boy stopped where he was and waited. The dog sat as she petted its ears, and once it relaxed, she took a firm grasp on the leather collar encircling its neck. Admitting defeat, the dog didn't resist as the boy approached and slipped the rope back into place.

"I thank you, miss," he said humbly. "My lady would be most displeased if her favorite hound was hurt running through the countryside."

Movement behind him signaled the approach of the lady he'd mentioned. She rode a magnificent horse, bigger than any Jenna had seen a woman ride before this. Though she was square-built, with large shoulders and a thick waist, the horse made her seem almost a dwarf. Pride showed in the set of her head and the flash of her eyes as she took in the situation before her. A lone escort behind her gauged the situation and took a relaxed but watchful position. A slight frown creased the newcomer's brow when she saw their faces. She'd probably expected Berthe, but she smiled politely.

"I apologize for my hound's bad manners, which caused me to stray from my own lands in pursuit." With practiced grace she dismounted, and Jenna tried to hide her surprise. Even Tessa was taller than this woman. The wriggling dog greeted her affectionately, almost knocking her down. "What a trial you are to me, Aphrodite." She glanced at them with a twinkle in her eye that indicated the dog would suffer no punishment for running away.

Certain she was loved, Aphrodite pushed her nose into her mistress' hand. "She has no shame," the woman said with a chuckle. "She led us all this way for sport and believes we should be glad for the entertainment."

Tessa dismounted and let the dog sniff her hand. "Worse than children, yet such good companions, are they not? I am Tessa Brisson, and this is my sister, Jenna. We are visitors at Castle Oldain."

"Giles' friends, I think. I hear the accent of the Anglish. I am Matilda, wife to the Duke of Normandy."

Jenna had heard much about their neighbors since coming to Oldain. Giles said Matilda was a force to be reckoned with, a woman who retained her husband's interest while holding strong opinions of her own. They were a love match, at first refused the church's permission to marry due to close blood ties. Now they stood strongly together, Matilda supporting the duke in all he did and managing his affairs when he went on campaign.

"And," Giles had said in conclusion, "William is often away, with his nose in everyone's business."

Tessa asked questions about the dog, commented on the beautiful weather, and introduced her sons, who returned dirty from investigating a fox's burrow. It was close to noon, and Edward asked, in the way of a hungry boy, if it was time to eat. Jenna flashed him a warning glance. Bringing up the subject meant they should invite Matilda to share their meal. Was the food Berthe had provided good enough for a duchess?

Taking her son's impulsiveness in stride Tessa said, "If you don't mind a simple repast, Your Grace, we will be pleased to share our meal with you. You've ridden far after this small miscreant," she indicated the dog, now resting beside her mistress as if she'd never leave. "It will be some time before you reach home."

Matilda showed her practical side as well as a natural friendliness. "That would be welcome. I thank you."

Opening the bag of food, Tessa smiled in relief. There was plenty for all: crusty bread, soft cheese, raisins, and mutton from last night's dinner. Taking choice portions, she put them on a cloth and handed it to Matilda, who thanked her. "I will enjoy the company as much as the food, for I am curious about England."

"England?"

"Yes. My husband will soon take the throne there, and I should learn what I can in order to be a good queen."

Jenna was thunderstruck. Could this woman really believe that William, the illegitimate son of a French-Viking nobleman, would take the throne of England? Tessa seemed at a loss as well, but she covered it by turning her attention to her sons, making certain they had equal shares and didn't quarrel about it.

When the boys went off, Tessa gave a portion of food to Jenna, took one herself, and handed the rest to the servants. "You say the duke will be king of England?"

"Why, yes," Matilda said with raised brows. "The old king named him to succeed."

"I had not heard that." Tessa's voice was neutral. "There is Harold Godwinson, and Edgar Atheling too."

"But Edward named William because he admired the Normans. Few support Atheling, since chaos follows a child king. And here in Normandy years ago, Harold Godwinson vowed he would not seek the throne."

Tessa nodded, her face impassive. "I hope we shall have a peaceful transition."

"We hope for that as well," Matilda said. "My husband cherishes friendship, but he is not a man to oppose."

Talk turned to other things, but Jenna's mind remained on what she'd heard. Would William of Normandy, sometimes known as William the Bastard because of his illegitimate birth, let ambition override humanity? If so, how many Englishmen would suffer?

Chapter Twenty-two

Jessie

A month after they left Glamis, the event Jessie dreaded occurred. They'd followed their usual pattern, traveling as far as the outer gate of a place then waiting for darkness. Alfred was more certain of his disguise these days, since he'd allowed his own beard to grow and no longer needed the false one Catherine had made for him. Still, his wrinkles and gray hair were artful additions of powdered chalk and charcoal, so daylight was always dangerous.

When the light began to wane, they entered the gate of Dun Castle and told the guards they offered an evening's entertainment in return for food and a place to sleep. Their news was welcome, since gleemen were a novelty in outlying regions. One guard said, "If you're skilled at your craft, I say you shall stay for a month. We're sick to death of Ralf's warbling."

The seneschal explained, "We have a singer here, but he's not inspired by angels. Your daughter's beauty will please the company as well."

Some places expected them to perform throughout supper, others afterward, and a few delayed the meal when there was special music. "You'll sing after the supper," the seneschal said. "See if Cook has a crust to tide you over, and tell him to save you some food."

"Eat when food's available; sleep when you can," was Alfred's motto. Thanking the seneschal, he led the way to the kitchens, where the odor of baking bread made Jessie sigh with contentment even as she winced at the metallic clatter of pots and pans. A friendly, rotund cook said they should help themselves to whatever they could find in the larder.

Jessie took the end of a loaf of bread, sliced it in two, smeared it with grease, and handed half to Alfred. He'd located some currants and a mug of cider, which they shared, standing in a corner to remain out of the way of ongoing preparations. People moved by in a constant stream, laden with fragrant trays, filled pitchers, and empty pots. When the meal began Alfred said, "I'll see how many are out there."

"Shall I come with you?"

"Stay here and rest. I'll judge their mood, and we'll decide on our song choices."

Jessie leaned against the kitchen wall, resting her hip. Despite Alfred's prediction this would be their biggest crowd thus far, she wasn't nervous. When she sang, she was no longer a crippled girl but an entertainer. People liked their music. They liked her.

She felt a jostle and Alfred was beside her, his voice urgent. "We have to go, Jessie. Now."

"What's wrong?"

"They're here. Bjorn and the other big one."

"No!"

"Hurry! We must go."

"Wait!" Her thoughts raced. "We need a reason to leave, or folk will speak of it."

"You're right." Without warning Alfred clutched his chest and slumped to the floor.

Startled, Jessie gasped, but she soon saw his intention. "Father!" She knelt beside him as several people rushed to help. Alfred gave a convincing performance, groaning and breathing with an alarming rasp. "Help me get him out of the heat and smoke." Willing hands carried Alfred outside and set him against the building wall.

"He will recover," Jessie told those gathered around. "He often has these spells, but our performance must be delayed until tomorrow."

Advice followed, and sympathy as well, but the servants had to return to their tasks. "Take him to the stable," a man advised. "He can rest there."

They did as he said, climbing into the loft and building themselves a nest in the hay piled in one corner. Once they were out of sight, Alfred told her of his close encounter with their enemies.

"I was making my way to the hall when I saw them. Fearing my disguise would not deceive one who knew my face, I slipped into a doorway and waited for them to go by. I heard Bjorn say, 'I'll have a look at the tweeter.'" Alfred's tone revealed outrage as he added, "He called me a tweeter!"

Jessie ignored his outrage. "I hoped they were gone."

"Here he threatens us; in England he threatens your sisters."

"I'm sure Tessa and Jeffrey have found a way to stop them by now."

"I hope so." His tone revealed frustration. "I thought we'd escaped. Perhaps we never will."

Jessie was thinking that if Alfred were alone, he could return to his home in Skye, where he'd be safe from the Vikings. He stayed with her because he felt obligated, and because he was a kind man. Kindness was all he felt for her. She must remember that.

Chapter Twenty-three

Jenna

A week after meeting the Duchess of Normandy, Jenna
entered their room to find Tessa kneeling on the floor, her
head bent over a chamber pot as she threw up her
breakfast. Alarmed, Jenna ran to her side. Although her face
was pale, Tessa smiled. "I know the signs. I will have a fifth
child in the spring."

Jenna didn't know whether this was happy news or not,
but Tessa seemed to think so. After a few days the nausea
abated, though she was careful about what she ate. With the
departure of morning sickness she settled into a demeanor
that was positively serene, so much so that she became a
poor companion. To Jenna's irritation, Tessa wanted to do
three things: make baby clothes, read to her children, and
nap.

Leaving Tessa behind, Jenna and the boys rode into the
countryside daily. Sometimes Giles accompanied them, but
if he could not, a stable groom went along. One day as they
rode near the river separating Giles' land from William's,
they saw Matilda on the opposite bank, recognizable due to
her diminutive figure. She and her ladies were picnicking,
and when she saw them she called, "If you cross the river I
will return your hospitality with food and company."

A few hundred feet downstream, the river widened and
went shallow, and they crossed there. Matilda met them as
they exited the water, her reddish hair plaited in a fat braid
down her back and a large straw hat tied over her coif to
keep the sun off her face. "Welcome to Normandy," she said
with a broad smile.

The meal was more elaborate than the one they'd
shared earlier, and much noisier too. The Norman ladies, a

colorful group, were introduced to Jenna and the boys. They made much of the twins, embarrassing them with comments on their physical similarity. They were given plates of cold chicken, salad, bread, and peas, with promises of sweetmeats and sugared nuts as dessert. Even the groom got a plate, and the three went off to enjoy manly conversation away from the noisy females.

That left Jenna alone with half a dozen women, all strangers. Her French was not up to the challenge, and she wished Tessa, who knew the proper manners, protocol, and language, had come along.

Despite this, the ladies were friendly. One indicated with gestures dishes she thought Jenna should try. They chattered among themselves, but she didn't feel left out, for they smiled to show they meant no insult.

When they'd finished eating, Matilda took her arm, saying, "Let us walk." Jenna fell in beside her and they traced the river's bank, enjoying the sunlight and the water's quiet mutter.

"I am pleased to see you today, for I meant to ask if you will visit us for a while."

Startled, Jenna was almost rude. "Me?"

Matilda laughed. "I am interested in England, as I told you before. I am the great-granddaughter of your king Alfred, often called the Great. You may teach me about your country, and I will help you learn our language."

Jenna had to be honest. "I'm no help in things English. Only a month ago I left my home in Scotland."

The small woman's eyes widened. "That is all the better. My husband will be interested, for he knows little of the lands he will rule in the north."

Jenna wondered whether she should say honestly that no Scotsman would consider William his king, whether he took the throne of England or not. She didn't need to answer, however, for Matilda went on, hardly aware her companion hadn't accepted her invitation. "I'm told your sister expects a child, but she won't need your help for some months. You might stay a fortnight with us, at least."

"I don't know," Jenna hedged, wondering how to refuse the determined little woman's plan. And how did she know Tessa was pregnant? It was hardly general news.

"You will find our court much livelier than Giles and Berthe's house," Matilda urged. "We have visitors from all over the world, and our cook sets a fine table. It will be more exciting for a young girl like you than Oldain, where the old couple lives almost in seclusion."

It was true there were few visitors at Oldain, no lavish dinners, and few entertainments. Giles and Berthe had had enough of all that, they claimed. She didn't want to desert her sister, but Matilda's court would be interesting, with new sights, sophisticated courtiers, and a chance to see the lifestyle of the wealthy and powerful. What girl of sixteen could say no to that?

"I'll speak to Tessa," she replied, "but I'm sure she will say yes."

Tessa seemed relieved when Jenna told her about the invitation. "I've been concerned about you. I should be helping you learn the ways of society, but this child demands I do naught but sleep," she confessed. "In a month I will have more energy than three women."

"You think I should go?"

"You'll learn much at a real court, and at the same time you can tell us what the Normans are up to." At Jenna's look of surprise she explained, "If William should succeed in becoming king, Jeffrey will want to know about him."

Jenna was indignant. "It's an ungrateful guest who tattles on her hosts."

"I'm not asking you to spy," Tessa said with an air of irritation. "I simply meant Jeffrey will want to know what sort of man seeks to be his king."

"What sort of man should he be?"

Tessa thought about that. "For many years, we've been a mix of languages, heritages, and allegiances. If my husband had his way, England would be ruled by a strong but just king who would unite Britain, prevent invasions, and encourage financial growth. He has little confidence in Harold Godwinson's ability to do any of those things. If William is such a man, and if Harold is deposed, Jeffrey might swear fealty to him as he swore it to Edward."

"And if others oppose a Norman king?"

Tessa frowned. "I don't know. But a Norman of strong character might be better than a weak Englishman."

"A Norman of strong character?" Jenna echoed. "William's ancestors were Norse. He is as lawless and violent as the rest of them. You may count on it."

Tessa smiled at her vehemence. "I once thought the same of Englishmen, but I discovered the English and the Scots, and the Vikings too, I think, have good and bad among them."

Jenna raised her brows at her sister's tolerance. If Tessa hadn't learned at her great age that Vikings were fiends, it was useless to argue. Though Matilda was likeable, she wasn't a Viking. Jenna already disliked William of Normandy, though she'd never seen him.

A few days later, Jenna set off for Falaise. Matilda sent a cart for her with two strong men to escort her. Berthe, anxious lest her houseguest lack what was needed to appear at a duchess' court, had busied herself gathering gowns, shoes, and feminine accoutrements. Jenna was grateful, because the dresses she'd been wearing, Tessa's own, were short in the arms and waist, despite the fact they'd let them out wherever possible.

Falaise stood at some distance from the sea on a steep, rocky hill that terminated on one side at the foot of the walls. On two other sides the ascent was too steep to be used by an enemy, and on the fourth side a gradual rise meant the inhabitants had plenty of warning when strangers approached. Farther down the road was a town defended by a ditch and draw-bridge with strong towers on each side of the gates. A stream, the lifeblood of any such place, meandered through the valley and disappeared into the rock of the hillside.

The castle was enclosed by stone walls of enormous thickness. As they entered the gateway, Jenna noted walls so thick that whole apartments were built into them. They passed several buildings, the largest a square tower several stories in height built of white stone. Beyond it was a chapel and various other structures. Amazed at the size of the place, Jenna soon realized that in addition to housing the family, their servants, and attendants, it also served as storage for munitions of war and as barracks for William's troops.

With that thought, she considered the castle's defenses. Towers along the walls had sentinels who watched for approaching danger. These men stared stoically at the broad expanse of richly-cultivated country, groves of trees, and the various colors presented by the changing vegetation, apparently unaware of the beauty that surrounded them.

The interior of the castle was abuzz with movement, and Jenna sensed urgency beyond normal life. Matilda was in the great room, giving orders with practiced efficiency. She looked up when Jenna entered. "You've come!" She embraced her visitor. "William has returned home, and he'll see what a lovely thing you are."

Jenna was taken aback. It was one thing to visit when the chatelaine was in residence. It was something else now that the duke was here with his soldiers.

Seeing her misgivings Matilda said, "You'll be popular, my dear, and you won't have to say a word. Our men are as susceptible to a pretty face as Ainglishmen are, by my troth."

Jenna was shown to a tiny room at the top of a winding stone stairway. Though dark and cramped, it was made comfortable with the addition of rugs, tapestries, and a basket of sweet-smelling herbs. In one corner was a pallet bed, beside it a basin of water and a scrap of cloth to wipe away the journey's dust.

When Jenna responded an hour later, as instructed, to a bell that chimed below, the scene before her crawled with life. People moved into the hall in twos and threes, heading to boards set on trestles and loaded with food. Servants brought more trays from the kitchens, wending their way through the throng of diners. Matilda, overseeing the whole, glanced up and saw her newest guest above. Motioning to a man standing with his back to Jenna, she turned him toward the stairs with a few words of command.

When the man turned to look, Jenna froze, as did he. It was Lukas, the Viking who weeks before had taken her captive on a Scottish mountainside.

He stared, apparently unsure what to do. Heat rose from Jenna's chest and into her neck. Her shoulders tensed. Below her was a crowd of people she didn't know. This man was at home with them, though not with the idea of approaching her.

How could he be? Lukas was Leif's man. Obeying the Viking's orders, he'd chased her and taken her captive. If he was here, it had to be for Leif's purposes. Lukas was spying on the Normans so the Vikings could conquer England before William claimed the throne.

Jenna had two possible courses of action. She could cry out against him, revealing his purpose to the whole assembly, or she could act as if he were a stranger to her. She wanted to do the former. He and his Viking band killed Ian, maybe Donald too. But if she spoke what she knew, would these people listen? Lukas was known to the Duke and his wife. She was someone William hadn't yet met, and female at that. Jenna decided to wait and see what the evening brought.

Lukas also chose his course, starting toward her with a blank expression. He, too, had decided to play a charade, pretending he didn't know her.

Jenna's hands formed involuntary fists. Could she tolerate his presence? Remembering Tessa's counsel that anger had its time, she calmed herself. *Tomorrow I'll go to Duke William and expose him. Tonight I will be silent.* Tessa would be proud of her.

Forcing herself to look at Lukas with neither fear nor anger, she watched as he threaded his way through the room. He glanced up at her once then lowered his eyes, ashamed, she hoped. When he arrived at the bottom of the stairs, she descended to meet him. People had turned to look, so she spoke evenly. "Are you sent to show me to my place?"

He bowed. "I have that honor."

She let him lead her through the crowded room, keeping her eyes lowered as the men of William's company examined the new female in their midst. Lukas seated her near Matilda's place, his eyes not once meeting hers. With a courtly bow, he returned to his own bench.

Dinner was a blur. There was conversation, and she answered as required but could not for the life of her make the charming replies a lady should. Her glance kept stealing to Lukas, who also seemed distracted. He failed to enter into the banter of those seated at his table and several times someone repeated a question before he answered it.

The room buzzed with talk, and a laugh or a shout for service occasionally rose above it. Jenna had learned basic table manners from Tessa. She knew how to carry meat to her mouth on her knife without dripping gravy on her clothing. Those who hadn't mastered that used their sleeves to blot up the excess, but Jenna knew better.

When her anger cooled somewhat and she could consider something besides attacking Lukas the Tracker with her fists, Jenna turned her attention to her host, William of Normandy. The duke was tall with a strong chin and a shock of brownish-red hair. His carriage and expression signaled a man of decision, one who might begin an argument with logic but move to violence when logic didn't work. She'd heard his early life had been hard due to his illegitimacy. He had persevered, and he had succeeded. What did it mean for England, and Scotland, too, if William was determined to be king in place of Harold?

Matilda spoke to her husband, nodding in Jenna's direction, and his gaze followed hers. After examining her with a good-humored expression, he said something to his wife that made her smile. He raised his mug toward Jenna in greeting, and she bowed in response. That was apparently the extent of the duke's interest in her.

William was no doubt a capable soldier. If he planned to conquer England, he'd have to be. Recalling Jeffrey's desire for a unifying king, she felt a stab of pity for the English people, who had only a boy, weak Harold Godwinson, and two Vikings as candidates for leadership. If she were English, she'd never submit to Vikings, neither those in Norway nor the Normans, still Vikings at heart.

That thought brought Lukas back to mind. William would be grateful to her for exposing the spy in his midst, and Lukas would be in trouble. She felt a flash of doubt, guessing he'd be put to death for his deception. Did she want him dead? Resolutely she put that thought aside. She'd tell the truth. What the duke did about it was none of her affair.

Matilda had said the duke was not a man one would want as an enemy, so Jenna would have to choose her words carefully. It had been wise to wait for a more private time, she thought when the duke put an arm around Lukas's shoulders as they left the table. The spy had convinced William he was a friend.

The next day was torture for Jenna, fearing every moment she'd meet Lukas face to face. She skulked about, avoiding groups of soldiers gathered in the courtyard and at the stables. Something was brewing, for they all looked busy, their conversations focused and serious. Plans were being made, but for what?

As she wondered, Jenna forgot to watch and paid for it. Lukas stepped out from the shadows and grasped her arm. "Jenna—"

She pulled free. "Don't touch me, Viking!"

"Why don't you believe me? I told Leif his quest was madness. When he wouldn't listen, I went to Scotland with him and tried to limit the harm he did." He leaned toward her. "I explained it—"

"My eyes give better evidence than my ears!" The words hissed from her tight lips. "You stood by as your friends murdered an old man."

"I wasn't—"

Ignoring his protest, she rushed on. "You kept me prisoner so your lunatic leader could kill me at his pleasure. Should I believe what you say, or what I have seen?" She stalked off, leaving Lukas stone-faced and silent.

He wasn't finished, though. A few minutes later as she started up the stairs to her room, a hand reached out and pulled her under the stairs. Lukas faced her again, this time less apologetic, less calm. "I will speak with you, and you will hear me."

"I won't! I'll scream!" She took breath to do it, but then he was kissing her. She felt the brush of his mustache on her lips, then the full press of the kiss. The feeling was warm, strong, and irresistible. While it lasted, Jenna was unable to think. Later she convinced herself he'd been too strong for her and she'd had no choice in the matter. In truth, the kiss was tolerated, enjoyed, even returned.

When he released her, Lukas said, "I am not your enemy." Then he was gone, leaving Jenna warm, this time not from anger, but from desire.

Chapter Twenty-four

Jessie

As evening fell, Jessie and Alfred approached yet another castle. Fife was hardly worthy of the name, merely a fortified house nestled into a hillside. Alfred said, "Ross, who is thane here, is a cipher. Though he welcomes gleemen into his home, he drinks so much that I often wonder if he remembers my visits afterward." He chuckled. "The place is unusual, but we'll have food and a warm place to sleep, as long as we can bear the noise and the laird's drunken company."

As he'd predicted, when they announced their trade they were ushered into Fife Castle and given drink to wash the dust from their throats. In the half hour or so between their arrival and the meal, dozens of people stuffed themselves into Ross' hall. The thane had seven children, Alfred explained, and the older ones had families of their own. With serving men, maids, and guests, the place grew noisy, and they abandoned attempts at conversation.

Sputtering pitch torches lined the walls, their smoke obscuring the faces of people across the room. At the center of the main table sat Ross and his lady, an ill-matched pair if ever Jessie had seen one. Somber-faced, the sallow, thin thane surveyed his hall gloomily, posture slumped and eyes cold. His wife was the largest woman Jessie had ever seen, with eyes almost buried in her plump cheeks. She spoke constantly to those around her, sometimes to no one at all. He said little. She took great interest in the meal, while her husband tasted only a few dishes, chewing with disinterest and finally pushing his plate away.

No one in the hall paid them much mind, and the meal proceeded with a raucous air. Children darted from place to place, teasing each other and pestering the adults. Though several made as if to swat them, no one actually did anything to stop their antics. Jessie had never seen such chaos at a meal. Smiling, Alfred raised his brows at her as if to say, "I warned you."

The food was good, however, and their place at the second table was close enough to the host that the platters were still half-full when they reached them. Ignoring the din as best she could, Jessie had a piece of meat, some pease, and a little of the gravy-soaked bread that served as her plate.

After the meal Jessie and Alfred took their places to begin the entertainment, but she'd hardly begun the second song when the thane started talking. At first it was soft, but his voice became louder and louder, until he almost drowned her out. It seemed to be nonsense, clumps of words that didn't connect to each other, and she thought he might be unaware he spoke aloud.

She glanced at Alfred, who shrugged and went on playing. Her audience ignored the thane's interference. She tried to keep singing, but it was maddening. Finally she let the song trail to a stop.

After a moment Ross, too, stopped. "Do ye know that story?" he asked. "Will ye recite it?"

"Which one, my lord?"

"The tale of this place—how a fiend destroyed a family!" He raised an arm in appeal to those gathered around. "It is a story that cannot be told enough."

There were half-hearted cries of agreement, and Jessie sensed the folk of Fife had heard all this before. She was struck dumb, but Alfred said in his old-man voice. "We do not know it, my lord. I'm sorry."

Ross squinted at them through the smoke, his

expression sad but somehow false, Jessie thought. "The lass is too young to know it, but she must hear it and learn what tragedy visited us here." Turning his gaze on Jessie he said, "The old king—" He spat the word "—sent men to this place in vengeance because our kinsman refused to bow to him. Macduff, my cousin, fled to England to escape, never dreaming his family would die as a result."

Voices sounded around the room "Villain!" and "Murderer!" The tale of Macbeth's cruelty was not simply a story here. It was a memory.

Jessie's cheeks burned, but she forced herself to listen as Ross recounted the story. He'd been present, so his account was vivid, alarmingly so. He'd told it many times, and his recital was almost as practiced as the scrope's had been.

The difference was in the eyewitness perspective. Returning from an errand, Ross had sensed something was wrong. Catching sight of a man with a bloody knife, he'd hidden in the root cellar.

"I heard them!" he said, his words slurred but still hurtful to Jessie. "They said the king would be pleased with their work. When they were gone, I found my cousin, Lady Macduff, stabbed in the back as she ran. Her sons we found in other parts of the castle, all killed where the heartless bastards found them." His voice turned tearful. "They murdered the servants, too, so none could tell who'd done the awful deed. If I had not sensed the danger," Ross ended, "I'd have died that day as well. Lord Christ was merciful to me that day."

But not to Macduff's family, Jessie thought. Alfred, ever tactful, made a pretty speech of appreciation for the tale, praising Ross' eloquence.

It had grown late, and the company began to drift away

to their beds. Taking advantage of the general movement, Jessie left the hall and hurried outside, where she pressed a hand against the castle wall, fighting back tears. Had her uncle indeed been such a monster? Everyone they met seemed to think so.

"Are you all right, child?" a voice asked, and Jessie quickly wiped her eyes and turned. Ross' wife bent solicitously toward her.

Thankful the darkness hid her tears, Jessie replied. "I am well, I thank you. The tale your husband told was sad, and I thought a few breaths of fresh air would revive my spirits."

"It was a terrible thing," the lady agreed. Leaning even closer she confided. "I myself might have been murdered with the rest."

"Oh, madam!"

"It's true. My husband insisted that morning that I take the children and visit my sister." She paused. "I recall it clearly, for I said 'My dear, I shall go on the morrow,' but he wouldn't hear of it." She shivered. "How could he know he was saving my life?"

"A lucky choice." But Jessie was thinking, *Did he know something evil would occur that day, something he did not want his own wife and children to suffer?*

Perhaps as a result of the lady's notice, Alfred and Jessie were given that most coveted of places for guests, a private room. It was tiny and served as a storeroom when food supplies increased, but it had a real door. The room was an indication of the esteem with which folk here regarded musicians, for seldom had they had such privacy. Even in a stable there were always others near. A pallet bed sat against the far wall, and beside it a bowl of water and a washing cloth. Elegant treatment for wandering musicians.

When the servant left them, Alfred seemed ill at ease, and his discomfort created a similar feeling for Jessie. They'd been together for weeks, but not in a room alone, removed from the view of others. The bed, the first they'd had in weeks, brought their true situation to mind: not father and daughter, but man and woman.

"I'll, uh, sleep there." Alfred indicated a corner.

"Nonsense. Since we have this luxury you must share the comfort the bed provides."

"Jessie, I—" The sentence hung unfinished, though she waited. They'd agreed to travel chastely together. What was so difficult about that?

She found out a few minutes later. As they lay side by side on the pallet, she felt the warmth of Alfred's body next to her. His scent too, a masculine one she'd noticed before, now seemed to affect her differently. She resisted the urge to reach out to him, to touch his face and his hair. To stop her thoughts she tried to think about something else.

"Alfred?"

"Yes?" His voice sounded odd, as if he were about to sneeze.

"Alfred, I don't trust our host."

"Why is that?"

"He says he hid in the root cellar, but Aldis told me the nurse and Leif hid there."

Alfred made a hum of understanding. "Surely they'd have seen each other."

"I think he knew what would happen that day. He might even have been part of it." She added, "A guilty past explains his drinking, too."

Alfred asked after a brief pause, "Do you see into the hearts of men, then, Jessie?"

She'd just been wishing she could see into his and know what he was thinking at that moment. Did he want to reach out to her, or was he as grumpy as he sounded?

When it was clear he would stay where he was, she answered his question. "No, I don't understand men. You are all a puzzle to me. Good night, Alfred."

"Goodnight." They lay awkwardly silent for some time, but finally Alfred turned his back. After a while, Jessie fell asleep, her hands clenched at her sides lest they pull him to her of their own volition.

Chapter Twenty-five

Jenna

Once she'd thought it through, Jenna became angry at Lukas the Viking all over again. He meant to win her silence by playing on her emotions. No doubt he considered himself so irresistible she'd forget his sins and keep silent after one kiss and a cryptic comment.

Evil could be attractive, and many a good woman was taken in by a handsome face, strong arms, and a pleasantly masculine smell. She'd seen it at home in the hills, though a Scot who drank too much or gambled away the family cow was not as bad as a murdering Viking. She promised herself there'd be no softening toward Lukas the Tracker.

What was she to do about his presence at Duke William's castle? If Lukas learned Tessa and her boys were nearby, he'd get word to Leif. She would expose him as a spy before he could make more mischief. She practiced her speech, making the words convincing. When she was ready, she went to find Duke William.

The hall was abuzz with activity, but she saw no one she recognized. Hearing footsteps on the stairs, she turned to see William descending, a woolen cloak in one hand and a pair of boots in the other. Calming her nerves, Jenna hurried to catch up with him. "My lord?"

"Yes?" His air said it was not the time for women's concerns. Matilda was his match, folk said, because she was not given to tears and emotional outbursts. At this important moment, Jenna must not appear vengeful or hysterical.

"I must speak with you about one of your men."

William moved his feet uneasily. "If you're with child, girl—"

She was shocked. "No, my lord, not that. He's a spy."

Now she had his attention. "A spy?"

"For the Vikings. He says his name is Lukas, but that could be a lie. All that he says is lies."

A strange expression came across the duke's face. "Come with me."

Gulping, Jenna followed the duke to the courtyard. Lukas, standing in a knot of men, looked up when William called to him. When he saw Jenna, his expression turned wary.

With a twitch of his lips William said, "This chit says you're a spy. How is it she knows you so well, my old friend?"

Lukas met Jenna's eyes. "She thinks Leif sent me here. She's the one I told you about."

William regarded Jenna. "You're the girl who is kin to Macbeth of Scotland?"

Her lips stiff, Jenna replied, "My father and he were brothers, my lord."

A smile spread across the duke's face. "And Lukas rescued you. Good lad!"

Jenna's face flushed with anger, and she forgot her resolve to speak calmly and reason logically. "He did not rescue me! This monster helped to capture me, not once but twice."

William looked to Lukas, who said, "Leif would have killed her and her whole clan. I tried to protect her."

Jenna looked from Lukas to the duke. "He is not spying on you?"

William laughed, enjoying her confusion. "He was spying *for* me. Knowing the scoundrel who now calls himself king of England, I guessed I'd be forced to take my throne by force. Knowing the Norwegian king might bid for the throne as well, I sent Lukas to discover what the Vikings are up to." He clapped Lukas' shoulder hard enough to make him wince. "Dangerous work, but he's returned in time to sail with me."

"You will attempt to conquer England?"

William frowned. "I *will* conquer it. Harold Godwinson will rue the day he tried to take what's mine." With that the duke strode away, leaving Lukas with Jenna.

Lukas looked at Jenna with one eyebrow raised. "You are wrong about me."

"I am not."

His expression turned sardonic. "I fear you are never wrong in your own mind."

She set her lips. "Not when it comes to sensing evil."

He touched her chin lightly. "One should be wary of always being right. It allows no room for new information, and much time is wasted that might be put to better use."

What was he talking about? "Even if you were in Scotland on the duke's behalf, it means little to me. You did nothing to stop Leif when he attacked us."

"I explained my purpose that night. You said you understood."

Confused, Jenna retreated into anger. "Leave me. I want nothing to do with you. Ever."

"As you wish." His lips curled in scorn. "I won't interfere with your prejudices again."

Jenna spent a fretful night, her thoughts making sleep an impossibility. What was she to think of Lukas? What did she think of him? Remembering the touch of his lips on hers, she blushed. He evoked something in her she'd never experienced before. Recalling his claim he'd explained earlier, she realized he'd told Jessie who he was. If she'd known he meant to help, would things have gone differently between them?

Before she'd solved all her questions, the dawn made a slice of light on the wall of her room. Rising, Jenna dressed and arranged her hair. The troops would leave Falaise soon. She wasn't sure why, but she needed to see Lukas again.

Looking out the window, she saw that preparations for departure were well under way. Hurrying downstairs into the bustle of activity in the courtyard, she found Duke William supervising the details of moving a large group of men from one place to another. "The winds favor us at last," he said to Matilda. "A full month I've waited and fretted."

"You needn't fret. God will see to it, husband."

The duke's expression said he'd grown tired of waiting for God to make up His mind.

Turning, he saw Jenna waiting hesitantly a few feet away. "Here's our guest. Lukas, a word!" He beckoned her over. "I've been thinking of you, young woman."

"Of me, my lord?" The man was off to conquer a nation.

"Lukas tells me you are the niece of the Scots' former king, Macbeth, as well as the sister-in-law of an English lord, Jeffrey Brixton. Your blood is noble, and your connections can be of some use to us."

Jenna hadn't thought much about her blood or her connections, and she couldn't see why Duke William was concerned with it now.

"A leader must always think ahead," he went on. "Having no doubt of my success, I've considered how my men will be rewarded for their service. They want land in the new territories, which will not be popular with the current owners."

Jenna's brows twisted. What had this to do with her?

"If my men marry with the women of Britain, it will create ties between us and we will quickly become one nation."

Jenna felt a stab of dread as he continued, "You and my young friend Lukas here are well matched, and you have some acquaintance with each other. Once the conquest is made I will send for you, and you shall be wed, setting my plan into action."

As Jenna stood, dumb with shock, the duke added what he must have thought was a strong incentive. "In this way, your sister may stay on the land her husband now claims, as long as he understands that Lukas is the true owner and his liege lord."

Overwhelmed, Jenna glanced at Lukas, who seemed as surprised as she. Not likely, but it didn't matter. William's word was law.

Jeffrey would lose Brixton, be reduced to a worker on the estate he'd maintained for years, his family's home for generations. Tessa would no longer be the chatelaine. That was what conquest meant. Victors did as they liked.

Despite her despair at Jeffrey's loss, hope was offered. If she wed Lukas, Jenna could save something for Tessa and her family. The duke's ends were served if an apparently happy couple demonstrated the advantages of conqueror marrying conquered. Would Jeffrey and Tessa be grateful to be able to continue to live at Brixton, or would they resent her being mistress of the estate that was rightfully theirs? Looking at William's confident figure and the well-trained, seasoned troops surrounding him, she thought, *What other choice will they have?*

Jenna turned to Lukas, whose expression was unreadable. What was he thinking? Matilda, supporting her husband as usual, said emphatically, "A fine idea. It will show the Ainglish we are willing to be fair."

"Precisely." William put a playful hand on Jenna's arm. "Folk enjoy romance, and any lack-wit can see the attraction 'twixt the two of you."

Jenna struggled to remain silent. When had she given any sign of being attracted to the Viking? She was sure she hadn't, though she admitted to herself she'd enjoyed his kiss. That meant nothing. A pleasant kiss didn't form the basis for a lifetime together.

William returned to his preparations, and Matilda hurried along beside him, her steps two to his one. Lukas stared after them. "I did not know this plan."

She steeled herself against her inclination to believe him. "You had no idea English lands would be taken from their rightful owners and handed out to you all as the prizes of war?"

He gestured vaguely. "It is the way of things, but I didn't realize—"

"There would be people on the land who'll be hurt?"

Lukas glanced at William, now busy elsewhere. "The duke will be fair."

"Jeffrey and Tessa are good stewards. What do you know about managing an estate?"

His jaw tensed. "Nothing."

"But you'll accept William's gift and take me as your wife

to get your share of the spoils?"

Lukas turned to face her. "Did you hear my lord ask if it was what I wanted?"

She was momentarily taken aback. Was he implying he had no choice, and further, that he'd have chosen otherwise if offered one? She recalled the night in the forest when he'd said he didn't need unwilling women. Surely he knew how unwilling Jenna would be.

If William's conquest succeeded, Lukas could marry her then ignore her completely. A decent bargain for him: an estate for the inconvenience of a wife. But she could bargain, too, and gain assurances to protect her sister.

"Neither of us chose what is forced upon us," she said. "Here then, Viking, is my proposal. I'll smile and say the words if you promise Jeffrey and Tessa will have as much control of the land as you can give them."

He stared hard at her for a second. "You would wed me to gain their security?"

"To keep a roof over my sister's head, yes." She hesitated, but honesty won out. "I'll play my part in the duke's plan, but I will always despise your kind: your murdering cousins in Norway, your arrogant William of Normandy, and you yourself, who'd take an unwilling wife to gain a fortune."

He smiled grimly. "Are there no unwilling wives in England now?"

"None more unwilling than I shall be."

His face flushed. "The land will be mine in any case."

"But your liege orders you to do it this way."

His voice wavered a little as he said, "Jenna, I would

help you if I can."

"You are vile, and I want none of your help."

Lukas made an angry gesture. "Will you never consider you might be wrong about me?"

She looked up, surprised at the almost pleading tone in his voice. "What have I seen from you? Murder. Kidnapping. Now war and conquest on my sister's people. Vikings take, without concern for anyone else. That is what I have seen, so I am not wrong."

Lukas stood rigid for some seconds. Taking a deep breath, he let it out slowly as if to calm himself. "You know best, with your vast knowledge of mankind and the ways of the world. Your brother-in-law will continue to manage the land, but I add one thing. Jenna macFindlaech, I'll never truly be your husband until you admit you're wrong about me and have been from the first. When you stop wasting time with hatred and suspicion, we'll be man and wife in the way God intends. Only then."

He turned and walked away, his posture so straight he seemed chiseled from adamant stone. As Jenna watched him go, a flicker of doubt passed through her, but she dismissed it. "Norman or Viking, no matter," she muttered. "There's no honor in any of them."

William and his men sailed on the 28th of September, a day that showed the onset of the harvest season at its finest. The fields were golden, the trees rustled with breezes, and the air warmed to just the right temperature for riding. Jenna rode to the top of a hill where she imagined she could see the fleet departing. There would be creaking ropes and shouted commands, cries of nervous horses and rumbles of shifting cargo. The ships would be crowded with men and animals, all tense at the notion of what was to come. She pictured Lukas, stalwart and calm, at least on the outside.

When would the battle be joined? King Harold Godwinson would resist the invaders with all his power, and his soldiers were among the world's finest. How would the Normans and their French allies fare against them? William was confident, and his archers, foot-soldiers, and cavalry seemed well-trained and ready.

Would Lukas return from the battle? When William announced their pending wedding to the company, men had slapped him on the back and turned to assess her with their gazes. Unsure how to respond, Jenna had looked down at her shoes. Soon they were gone.

An image crossed her mind: Lukas beset by English soldiers wielding their feared, double-edged battle-axes. It was only a few months since he'd fought the wolf. Was he fully recovered? She thought he was, but the disturbing image remained, and suddenly she tasted blood from where she'd bitten her lip.

If the Viking died, she wouldn't have to marry him. That would be good.

Or not. If Lukas died, William would no doubt give her to some other Norman, one who might demand that Jeffrey and Tessa leave their home. At least Lukas was not repulsive, and he'd given his word to be fair.

The days that followed were trying for everyone. Matilda was unusually quiet; Jenna felt nervous and sad. What was wrong with her? She had no cause to fret over the Northman's fate. A violent man might meet a violent end. Nothing she could do would change that. Of course she didn't want the Normans to defeat Jeffrey's people. Life was unfair, war meant unhappiness for many, and it was always worse to be on the losing side.

Word of Norman success came three weeks later. Though Matilda was tactful, her joy was evident. William was king of England, as she believed he should be.

"Was it a terrible battle?" Jenna asked.

"I suppose all battles are terrible," she replied. "The Ainglish took the high ground, so William was forced to attack uphill. He had archers and cavalry, however, which Harold did not. The Ainglish troops were fatigued, having recently battled and defeated the Norwegian king. When William's troops landed, the Ainglish had to march two hundred fifty miles in nine days to face them."

"An amazing feat."

"True, but God was on our side." Matilda's eyes closed briefly in a prayer of thanks. The battle was long, and someone started a rumor that William had been killed, and his men began to give ground. To prove it was untrue, he rode through the troops with his helmet raised." She shuddered. "The messenger says he had three horses killed under him."

Jenna shuddered too, imagining the blur of battle, the screams of dying men and horses, and the smells of blood and death. "But it was Harold who died."

"Yes. One of our archers shot him, and his two brothers also fell. That brought chaos, with Ainglish soldiers either fleeing the field or surrendering."

The next day's message brought more good news for the Normans. "William reached Dover and secured the Channel crossing," Matilda reported. "He's taken Canterbury and London. The Archbishop of York and the Ainglish earls met him there and made their peace."

"Will you join him now?"

The duchess looked around the comfortable room. "I will have to go to London, but I prefer to live here, where my children are. Once I am crowned, I will keep Normandy for William while he keeps England for me."

"You're a woman of many marvels." Jenna wondered what she should call Matilda now. My queen? Madam?

Matilda seemed uninterested in titles. Taking Jenna by the shoulders, she said, "My lord did not forget you, little Scot. I am to bring you to Angle-land so he can begin the joining of our nations. Once you and Lukas are wed, other Normans will choose Ainglish women as brides." Unaware of Jenna's lack of enthusiasm she added, "A beautiful bride and a handsome groom is the way to begin, my lord says. You must return to Oldain and prepare for our journey."

Jenna hadn't mentioned Lukas to Tessa, since their wedding depended on William's conquest of England. How should she explain it now that the plan had succeeded? I sold myself so you and your family might stay on your lands? She couldn't do that to Tessa. All the way back to Giles' house, she'd practiced, trying to make the marriage sound reasonable.

She found her sister in the garden with Berthe, cutting lavender for drying. The scent perfumed the air with sweetness, and Tessa glowed with well-being, as pregnant women often do. She'd recovered her energy, but her face betrayed concern as she ran to meet Jenna.

"I'm so glad you've returned," she said, hugging Jenna tightly. "I didn't want to send a messenger with bad news, but Jeffrey was wounded fighting the Norwegians at Stamford Bridge."

Jenna gasped, "No!"

"He's back at Brixton and says he is much improved." Tessa's eyes filled with tears. "I wish I could see for myself. He wouldn't want to worry me, but—"

"We must believe it," Berthe put in gently, "for the sake of your unborn child."

"Yes." Tessa turned to Jenna. "We're told England is conquered by the Normans. Is it so?"

"Yes. Matilda is preparing to join William for their coronation."

Tessa surrendered to a moment of bitterness. "Her husband will be king, while mine is—"

"Recovering from his wound," Berthe said firmly. "And that is an advantage."

Jenna frowned. "An advantage to be wounded?"

Berthe nodded. "Men speak of honor and fight to maintain it, but women are more practical. The Ainglish are now a defeated people, and it is a small blessing that Jeffrey missed the battle at Hastings. Those who fought against William are sure to lose their lands."

Tessa's eyes filled with tears. "All English lords have cause to worry. We are a conquered people."

Berthe touched her arm. "You could remain here."

"Jeffrey will stay at Brixton." At Jenna's announcement the others gasped in surprise. "I am to be married."

"Married?" The two women spoke together.

"William wants his men to marry English women in order to blend the two nations."

Tessa's face went still. "You'll marry a Norman, and Brixton will become his."

"Yes, but it will still be yours in most ways." She stepped toward her sister, hands raised in a plea for understanding. "Things will go on as before. You'll have a home, and—I made him promise, Tessa, and he made one in return." In spite of her efforts to maintain control, Jenna began to cry.

Tessa wrapped her arms around her little sister, and Jenna felt the slight bulge of the child she carried. "You mustn't do this, Jenna. Jeffrey and I had nothing once, and you cannot sacrifice your future for our benefit."

"I—I don't think I have a choice," she replied, sniffling. "William is king. If he says I will marry Lukas, I must."

"And who is Lukas?"

"He's—" Jenna stopped. If she told Tessa about Lukas' connection to Leif, any prospect of future peace between them was impossible. "He's one of William's most trusted men."

"Does he want to marry you?"

She was honest. "I don't think he had a choice either."

Tessa clicked her tongue. "The duke expects this scheme to bring peace? Only a man could think that."

Berthe injected a comment with the serenity maturity can provide. "I suppose you are afraid, being told who you will marry, but you may come to love this Lukas, as I did Giles. And since you have no choice, it is the sensible thing to do."

The sensible thing. Jenna considered the momentous changes her life had undergone in the last few months. If she'd stayed in the Cairngorms, Donald would have allowed her to choose a husband, though the pool of eligible men was small. Now she had no choice. "At least I know him a little," she told the older women. "He doesn't seem the type to beat me or go back on his word." Setting her face into a smile, she told herself the marriage was not repellant to her. That she was looking forward to being a bride.

Chapter Twenty-six

Jessie

Autumn came gently, and one could almost forget winter would soon send icy fingers to top the mountains and trace Scotland's hollows. Jessie and Alfred had a comfortable routine, traveling for a few days then staying a day or two at a castle, village, or town. Alfred played the rheumy old man, keeping his face buried deep in his hood. If anyone got too close, he'd go into a fit of coughing certain to send them scurrying away. Despite the father's apparently diseased lungs, the couple was welcome everywhere. Jessie's confidence increased each day, and Alfred remained in the background as much as possible.

Eventually their travels took them west again, and Jessie recognized the village names. The hills around them were familiar, too. She'd seen them from her clan-hold, but now she saw them from other viewpoints: in the distance, then closer and closer as they wove around and across them. She felt the incline in Foot's steps, but he seemed not to notice whether he went up or down. Jessie knew they'd spent the last few months heading in a large circle. Now the mists, the flowers, and the smell of pine combined to tell her they were getting close to her home.

Alfred usually went south in winter, a Scotsman being a novelty among the many English bards. That was how he'd come to know Tessa and Jeffrey. Jenna wanted to ask what his plans were for this year's winter, but at the same time she feared his answer. How much longer would they remain together?

At a castle a dozen miles from Glamis, they heard unwelcome news. "Two of the Vikings who roamed these hills last summer have returned," a traveling merchant told them at dinner. "They say little about what happened while they were gone, but sailors tell of a terrible battle in the south."

Questions followed, and Alfred's eyes met Jessie's as they listened. "The Norwegian king fancied he could conquer England," the merchant said. "His fleet of ships landed at York. Harold Godwinson had word of it, though, and his troops met them at a place called Stamford Bridge. Three hundred Viking ships arrived on England's shore. Only twenty returned to Norway."

"Why have these two come to Scotland?" someone asked. "Why didn't they go home with their companions?"

"One was wounded in the battle, and in the confusion they were left behind. Believing a lady near here would take them in, they paid a fishing boat captain to bring them north on his return trip."

Alfred glanced at Jessie but asked casually, "Where are the Vikings now?"

"In Glamis." The merchant grinned. "The thane is often away, and his lady enjoys the company of men."

"You said one of them is wounded?"

"He lost an eye, and his face will never again be thought handsome. Still, he's said to be mending, and he's vowed to take up a task he left unfinished."

"Which task?"

"Finding a criminal named Alfred the Singer."

"A criminal—!" Jessie began, but Alfred silenced her with an elbow to her ribs. She dug her nails into her palms, willing herself to stay calmly in place when she wanted to run from the room, dragging Alfred with her.

The danger hadn't passed. It had retreated briefly and

returned.

"Mayhap these men would pay to hear my daughter's singing. Are they still at Glamis?"

"They are." The man's grin became a leer. "Winter comes, and a lady's bed needs warming. It is the way of women." He looked at Jessie, who clenched her hands in her lap.

Leif and Bjorn had returned to take up their search for her and Alfred. Had the Vikings left Leif behind on purpose, blaming their defeat on his curse? If so, he would hate her family even more than before.

Glancing up, she saw Alfred's eyes on her. No doubt he was wishing he hadn't saddled himself with a girl who slowed him down, endangered his life, and attracted the attention of the very men he needed desperately to avoid. He raised his brows as if to say, *Who could have predicted this?*

Someone called for a song, and he settled his lute into position and struck the chord that gave her the key and her cue to begin.

Alfred was distant and silent as they traveled westward for two more days. When the land began to look familiar, Jessie reacted with surprise. Glamis was the last place she'd have thought they were going, but it was indeed their destination. A half mile from the village, Alfred stopped for the night. It had begun to rain, and they made camp in a copse as they'd done before, each taking on tasks suited to his abilities. Jessie set out a simple meal of cheese and bread while Alfred tended to Foot's needs and gathered what dry fuel he could find for the night's fire. Soon they sat under a tree, avoiding the worst of the rain and listening to its drip, drip, drip. Alfred spoke of the future.

"It's time for you to go home." His voice was rough,

unlike his usual mellow tenor. "Your clansmen can protect you."

"But we'll have to cross the river and then the open space at the foothills. We'll be seen."

He glanced to the right, at the mountain where her home lay. "That's true. Someone is bound to report us to earn the gold Bjorn has promised."

He sounded dejected, and Jessie's heart filled with sorrow. How he longed to be rid of her, to be able to go his own way! "Perhaps they'll leave Scotland if we wait a few days," she said hopefully.

"I can't believe it." Alfred looked in the direction of Glamis, though hills stood between them and the town. "Father Dominic would help, if we could reach him."

"If we hide your lute in the woods, we could pose as a man and his daughter come to consult him."

Alfred tilted his head and asked, "Shall we pack our things again? Night is best if I'm to play the part of your father." Jessie began putting their belongings back into their pack. Looking around, Alfred chose a tree with thick branches. "The lute will wait for us there," he said. "It will be safe enough in its case."

The town was dark and silent as they headed down the path and approached. When Foot huffed softly the sleepy guard came smartly to attention. "Who comes?"

"Martin Fitzmartin," Jessie said, her voice higher than usual, "and his daughter Mary. We've come to see your priest but were delayed along the way. My father is—" She paused as if embarrassed. "—not feeling well."

The guard peered at them. Alfred leaned against the pony as if he could barely stand, his head lolling to the side and his eyes unfocused. "Drunk, is he?"

"He met a friend on the road who had a full wineskin, sir. They finished it all." She let desperation creep into her voice. "I know we should wait until morning, but the rain has drenched us through and—" Letting her voice trail off, she wiped away an imaginary tear.

"Don't cry, little one," the guard said gruffly. "I can see you're no pair of raiders come to slay us in our beds. Take your father somewhere he can sleep off his revels, but don't wake up the village on the way."

"Thank you, sir. I'll keep him quiet."

Once they were away from the guard post, Alfred straightened and quickened the pace. He led Foot to the church, where the door stood open, inviting all inside. A row of candles burned on the altar, and they saw Dominic moving about inside. He spoke, listened, nodded, and spoke again. Jessie looked at Alfred, who shrugged once. He must be praying, though it seemed more like conversation than devotion.

As they stood outside, the priest disappeared and came back with a cup in his hand. Speaking to some invisible person—or perhaps to the angels—he moved out of view, then appeared again without the cup.

For some time they remained in the street, drenched by rain but unsure whether Father Dominic was alone or not. Finally Foot nickered, impatient with their indecision. Dominic squinted into the darkness, made a soft comment to someone out of sight, and stepped out. "Who's there?"

"We're sorry, Father," Jessie said. "We didn't mean to spy on you."

"Jessie?" He looked around to assure that no one heard them. "Alfred?"

"It's good to see you again, Father."

"And you." He hesitated. "There is danger here."

"We heard of it," Jessie said. "We plan to return to my home in the mountains."

Dominic considered the idea. "That's where you'll be safest, if you can get up the mountain without being seen. How can I help?"

"May we stay here until we can arrange things?" Alfred glanced inside the warm, dry church, obviously anxious to get out of the rain.

The priest hesitated, and Jessie wondered if it was from fear of the Vikings. Finally, though, he made a decision. "Tie your pony in the shed behind the church. You can sleep in the loft above, and I will bring you something to eat anon."

That surprised Jessie, since at her earlier visit she'd slept in a room within the church itself. Still, she was grateful Dominic was willing to help her a second time.

Alfred closed the shed's door behind them and gave Foot some grain from his pack. Climbing to the loft, they spread their blankets at opposite sides of the room and waited. In only a few minutes, Dominic appeared with two wooden bowls filled with steaming, aromatic soup. "Eat," he said, and they willingly obeyed. When they were finished he said, "Tell me your plans, and in the morning I will learn what I can of the Vikings."

They talked for some time. Alfred explained their adventures and how they'd learned of the Vikings' return. Dominic related what he knew of the battle at Stamford Bridge, adding to what they'd heard the night before. "When it was over, the Vikings departed in haste, with English troops harassing them at every step. Leif stayed behind, searching the field until he found Bjorn. He was badly hurt, and Leif saved him."

"Better if they'd both died," Alfred muttered.

Dominic made no comment on that. "The English troops had little time to seek stragglers, for they learned the Normans of France had invaded to the west. Once they were gone Leif bribed someone to carry Bjorn to a ship that would bring them north."

"Here."

"Yes."

"The wound is disfiguring?"

Dominic nodded a silent affirmation. "It would be a hard thing for any man to accept, but to one like Bjorn, it is doubly difficult." As the merchant had done, Dominic touched his cheekbone as if imagining such an injury. "He drinks overmuch and rails at those who appear to gaze too long at him. He beat one of the servants at the castle almost to death when she made some comment that offended him. Lady Menteith has made it clear they're no longer welcome in Glamis."

"So will they return to Norway?"

Dominic shook his head. "They insist there are things undone here."

"Killing me is one of them, I suppose." Alfred's tone was matter-of-fact.

"As soon as Bjorn was able, he and Leif began riding out each day. They call it 'hunting,' but I believe they search for you."

"Leif believes my family is responsible for his ill luck," Jessie said.

"He does." Dominic chewed briefly at his lip. "He's more

convinced than ever and less sane than before."

Jessie had hoped to hear differently, but it had been a small hope. She turned to Alfred. "We must go home. My people will protect us."

"Yes, you must go home." Alfred turned to the priest. "Where are the Vikings now?"

"A local thane offered them his hospitality for the winter. Bjorn told the laird that Alfred kidnapped you, and he wants to rescue you and return you to your family."

"A lie!" Jessie cried. "I'll tell the truth, and Bjorn will be revealed as the villain he is."

"You can't tell the truth if you're dead."

Jessie felt tears rise, and the priest put an arm around her shoulders. "Come now, daughter, we will prevail. Fife is some distance from here, so if we smuggle you out of the village, they'll never know you were here."

Alfred frowned. "It's the thane of Fife who invited those snakes into his bosom?"

"Ross. Do you know him?"

"We stopped there a while ago. Jessie said then that he wasn't to be trusted."

"You have a good sense of men," Dominic told her. "Ross is ever after his own good."

"He lied about the day Macduff's family died. Why would he do that?"

Dominic's bottom lip protruded. "Perhaps he is a coward who hid when the killers came."

"Or perhaps he sent the killers himself." Alfred said.

Dominic frowned in disbelief, but in the end he nodded. "When Macduff heard of his family's murders, he took vengeance on Macbeth. The new king rewarded Macduff with larger lands."

"And Ross became thane of Fife."

"If Macbeth had won, Macduff would have been banished from Scotland. Either way, Ross was likely to get Fife for his own."

"If Ross ordered the killing of his own kinswoman and her children," Jessie asked, "why would he welcome Macduff's son into his home now?"

"Perhaps to learn what Leif knows of the murders," Dominic replied, "and to convince him double of Macbeth's guilt by telling the story his own way."

"What does all this mean for us?" Jessie asked.

Alfred's expression turned grim. "It means we have another enemy. Ross will help the Vikings find us, hoping they'll return to Norway once we're dead."

"A man with much on his conscience," Dominic said. "I could see that much from the first, but I did not know the why of it."

"Ross has resources Leif and Bjorn could never hope for on their own," Alfred said. "We must get Jessie back to her people, for they can't claim to be rescuing a girl who's at home with her sisters."

"And what about you, Alfred?" Jessie asked.

"Once you're safe, I can make my way to somewhere I'm unknown." He smiled. "There's always a place for a singer of songs, whether his name be Alfred, Patrick, or Ethelbert."

Jessie tried to smile back, but she was thinking, *Whether*

I'm with you or with my family, Alfred, there will always be a place for you in my heart.

When the morning sun shone into the cracks between boards in Father Dominic's stable loft, Jessie woke. Alfred wasn't there. Telling herself he'd gone to the privy, she set about brushing the loose straw from her clothing and hair. Today they'd leave Glamis for her home, and though she was pleased at the prospect of seeing her family, she was also reluctant. The world Alfred had shown her was much to her liking, and though home would be safe, she'd miss the travel, the attention she'd received as an entertainer, and the time she and Alfred had spent together. He was so patient, so solicitous, so accepting. With his tutelage, she'd become a better-than-average entertainer, and she couldn't wait to sing a duet with him for her family. She imagined her voice blending with his and her family's surprise at the sound.

Of course, Alfred wouldn't stay. He was eager to be finished with having to protect her. For that reason, she'd told a small lie the night before, as they settled in their respective corners to sleep.

"Will you be glad to get back home?" he'd asked.

She'd been thinking how much she would miss traveling, but she said brightly, "Oh, yes! And Jenna's probably returned home by now."

"And the man who waits for you? What of him?"

She tried to picture Dougal's face, a blurry outline in her mind. "It will be good to see him."

"Will you marry, do you think?"

I could never marry him now. That was what she wanted to say, but how could she confess that Alfred had become so dear to her that no other man entered her mind? If he didn't return her affection, which she was sure he did not, he'd have to say so. And even if he did like her a little, she'd always be a liability to a man who traveled for his living. She forced herself to answer, "Yes, I suppose we will."

"That's good. I mean, that you'll be able to stay in the place you love."

"Yes."

She regretted that conversation when Dominic appeared at the loft trapdoor to tell her Alfred was gone. "I vowed to see you get home," he said. "And truly, it will be easier with only one."

Alfred had rid himself of her as soon as the chance arose. He hadn't even bothered to lie about how sad their parting would be for him.

There was more sorrow to come. Handing her a bowl of oatmeal, Dominic sat down beside her. "I have learned something you should know."

At his tone, dread seized her. "What is it?"

"Although Alfred lied to the Vikings about where your sister lived, they learned she was in England. The vitki tells me that she, Jenna, and the four children drowned in a storm as they tried to escape to France."

Jessie stared, unwilling to believe. "They're dead?"

"All of them. A worker on the estate heard it from the laird himself."

"Jeffrey." Jessie tried to picture the brother-in-law she'd never met. His grief must be as great as her own, to lose his wife and all his children in one tragedy. Leif's face appeared in her mind. Truly, it was enough to drive a person mad.

Jenna. Her sister, her twin, her other half. Had Jessie been so focused on her own affairs that she missed the stab of loss that should accompany Jenna's death? "I must think on this." She was unable to say more, and in fact, she was unable to think much at all.

Dominic backed toward the ladder, his head bowed. "I'll pray for you and for them."

When he was gone Jessie threw herself onto the straw, ignoring the dust and the sharp ends as she wept. She was in the same place, her face streaked with tears, when the priest returned some time later. Holding out his arms, the old man invited her in, and she stepped into his embrace. "I must decide what to do."

"You'll return home and take up your life again," he said. "You need to be among those you love."

It was the sensible thing to do, but home didn't beckon. There she was a cripple, the girl they coddled and loved but expected little from. With Jenna gone, there was only sadness there. "I don't want to go home."

The priest's bushy eyebrows rose. "But the Northmen seek you here."

"I'll leave Glamis. I'll find employment at one of the villages Alfred and I visited."

Dominic's expression turned thoughtful. "I have an idea that will provide time for you to decide what you want to do. At the same time, you can do a great service."

"What is that?"

He gestured toward the ladder. "Come into the church."

Jessie did as he asked, giving Foot a pat on the rump as she passed. Dominic led her to the small room behind the altar where she'd slept on her first visit. He stepped aside, allowing her to see a woman sitting on a nest of straw and blankets. She looked up, and her pale face lit with a smile. "Jessie!"

"Aldis?"

"It is I."

"But what—How did you come to be—Are you well?"

Aldis smiled thinly. "Well enough, since this good man gave me his protection."

"Leif?"

The smile turned to a look of pain. "He decided I am part of his curse."

"Because the Vikings lost their bid to conquer England?"

"Our losses were terrible." She looked down at her hands. "It took from Leif any humanity he had left."

Jessie heard the sadness in Aldis' voice. "I'm sorry."

"He hates me now as much as he hates your uncle. Some days I feared he would kill me." Her lips twisted. "Some days I feared he would not."

"Tush, now," Dominic soothed. "Terrible loss often brings madness, but in time he'll return to his senses. When he does, he'll see you are one who served him with faithfulness and love."

Aldis looked up at him. "I wish I could believe that."

"You must." Dominic turned to Jessie. "You and Aldis share a need. I propose you join forces and, with my help, set up housekeeping where you'll both be safe."

After a moment Aldis asked, "How should we do that?"

Dominic folded his hands over his ample stomach. "Aldis

has some items of value that can be sold to provide food and other necessities. However, she's alone in the world and can't live by herself."

"Where is your maidservant?" Jessie asked. "Hnossa?"

Aldis sniffed. "When word came the Viking armies were defeated, she left in the night."

"How could she? You are her countrywoman as well as her mistress."

Gesturing toward the priest Aldis replied, "This man, of another faith and another culture, cares more for me than Hnossa ever did."

"One never knows when he'll meet an angel," Dominic said modestly. "We must always keep it in mind."

Shifting his feet, he returned to his proposal. "A few miles from here stands a ruined castle. There is a small area within that's suitable for a simple existence."

"We'd be safe from discovery?"

"It is not a place anyone visits. Once each seven-night I'll bring supplies, using money from the sale of Aldis' jewelry."

"How will you explain such sales?"

"People often give baubles to the church, and I sell them to provide for the poor."

"And what will folk think of your trips outside Glamis?"

"They pay my travels little mind." He waved a hand. "I often tramp through the hills to find ingredients for my medicines. Jessie, your part will be to care for Aldis, keep her warm and well fed. Will you do that?"

Jessie considered. It wouldn't be easy, but she felt a debt to Aldis, who'd once protected her from Bjorn. Home would still be there in a month or even six months. "I will."

Dominic patted her arm. "Good. I'll begin preparations."

The two women spent the night in the tiny alcove, making plans. Before the next day dawned, Dominic lifted Aldis into a two-wheeled cart he'd borrowed from a villager. Jessie crawled in beside her, and the priest packed their belongings around them, covering them with tied bundles that trickled dust and dirt onto their faces and into their hair. He left the village leading Foot, who pulled the cart as if he'd been raised to do so. Hearing Dominic's cheerful greeting to the guards as he passed, Jessie tensed, but they didn't ask where he was going with his load of straw. Instead they joked about the length of Dominic's sermons. Wishing he'd hurry, Jessie prayed she wouldn't sneeze from the dust that clogged her nose and make it itch.

The day was damp and chilly, and she felt Aldis shiver. She snuggled closer, lending the tiny woman her body heat. How long before winter enveloped them? Could they cope with the cold? Could she care for Aldis while dealing with her own infirmity? She was determined to succeed, whatever the challenge.

Once they were out of sight of the village, Dominic stopped and helped her out, lessening the load Foot had to pull up the steep hillside. Brushing the hay from her hair, Jessie removed her cloak and spread it atop the one Aldis already wore. "I'll stay warm as I walk," she told the vitki.

Aldis' face was already pinched with the pain of the cart's jolting, but she smiled bravely. "I miss my Fire Horses, but I thank you."

The direction Dominic took was one Jessie had never traveled before, and the roughness of the path confirmed the priest's claim that few came this way. Two hours later, with legs aching from the climb and arms shaky from pushing the cart to help Foot, they came to a desolate tor where the ruined castle stood. She saw why the location had originally been chosen, for it commanded a wide view of the river, the surrounding land, and far in the distance, the North Sea. It was just as easy to see why the inhabitants had abandoned the place, for its position on the windswept cliff exposed it to the worst of Scotland's weather. The autumn winds howled around its walls, buffeting Jessie almost off her feet.

The castle was only a shell, its roof and much of its exterior battered away by wind and storms. Below it, the pilings of the wall lay askew, many missing, some on the ground, a few half-standing. Only one of the double doors at the front was in place, and it was missing several upright planks.

Jessie's spirits shrank as she surveyed the ruin, but Dominic stopped at the entry, tethered the pony out of the wind, and told Aldis they'd return for her soon. Leading the way, he climbed a winding stairway to the upper floor. Central to the place was the donjon, the last defense of a castle where a siege might be waited out. Its roof was intact, and there was an odd, round-topped door, too unusual to be useful anywhere else. It was meant to close with a stout bar, but a broken hinge had left it hanging at a severe angle. Dominic stepped through, and Jessie followed him into a small room with a second door on the opposite wall. Though empty, the room had a fire pit in the center and a smoke hole overhead. It was a small space, but anything larger would be difficult to keep warm.

Dominic looked around, taking in the broken door, the leaf-littered floor, and the open window slit. "If you think you can make it suitable, I'll fetch Aldis."

"I can," she declared, though the confidence in her voice came more from determination than optimism. Two women on their own, both crippled. Most of the work would be up to her.

"This place has an advantage you will find helpful." Dominic crossed to a second door, this one repaired with scraps of different woods. He knocked lightly, and a man opened it as if he'd been waiting to be summoned. He was hideous, with a cleft lip so extreme it made Jessie want to weep to look at him and a hump on his back that twisted his body to one side.

"This is Struan," the priest said. "He lives here with his mother, who has grown very feeble." Turning to Struan he said, "My son, these women need a safe place to spend the winter. We are counting on your Christian love and assistance."

Struan looked shyly at Jessie, no doubt fearing her reaction to his deformity. Used to the pitying looks of others, she looked for the man inside. In Struan's face she saw gentleness and sorrow, and her heart went out to him. "Will you allow us to stay here, Struan? We have food we'll gladly share with you and your mother."

He looked to Dominic, who nodded encouragement. "Aye." His voice was hoarse, as if not often used.

"The other woman cannot walk," Dominic said. "I will carry her up here if you will bring the other things."

Nodding twice as hard as was necessary to show his willingness, the young man started down the stairs. "Struan's brain is not strong," Dominic told Jessie, "but if you put what you want in simple words, he'll do his best to achieve it."

Dominic left and soon returned, carrying Aldis on his back. She was shivering, and Jessie once again took her cloak off and laid it on the stone floor. The priest left again, promising to return with wood for a fire. Jessie set about clearing the place. Lacking other tools, she used a piece of wood to scrape the leaves, dirt, and dead bugs into a corner.

"Here are yer things," Struan said, setting them in a corner. Jessie immediately took one of their blankets and hung it over the room's only window, an arrow slit about six inches wide and three feet high. The room darkened, but the cold wind lessened.

Bringing wood and tinder, Dominic began making a fire. Once the dry twigs popped and glowed, he added larger pieces. "Set me beside the fire and I will tend it," Aldis ordered. "It is something I can do to help." Jessie made her a bed of blankets within reach of the pit, and Aldis took over, adding fuel as Jessie cleared cobwebs from the corners. As she worked, Struan went to a nearby grove of trees and cut pine boughs for bedding. Disappearing down the stairs with a spade, Dominic returned several times with armfuls of moss, which he laid over the boughs to make comfortable beds.

Having done what he could for them, Dominic squeezed Jessie's hands and touched Aldis lightly on the shoulder in farewell. "I'll bring more food soon," he promised. "A bit of mutton, perhaps."

"Aldis eats no meat, and I need very little," Jessie said. "If we have barley and oats and the makings for bread and pottage, we'll fare well enough."

"Have a care for your supplies, for I cannot come often without raising suspicion."

"We'll be grateful for whatever you provide."

Struan was looking at Aldis with awe, as if he thought she might fly out the window and disappear at any moment. "Is there else I can do for ye?" he asked in his rough voice.

"I notice you most cleverly repaired the door to your own room. Can you do the same with this one?"

With a lop-sided smile the man turned to the task, testing

the door to see how he might make it swing correctly again. Jessie smiled to herself. Aldis had already won Struan's admiration.

"The locals know Struan and his mother live here, so your fire will cause no notice," Dominic said when he'd gone to get his tools. "He's happier away from society because of his deformity."

"And you give what solace you can," Jessie said.

"They, too, might be angels in disguise. One never knows, so—"

"—We must be good to everyone," she finished.

Dominic's expression sobered. "I fear Struan's mother is dying. I must think on what I can do to help him once he's left alone up here."

Jessie was struck by the goodness of this priest, who'd done his best to protect them and concerned himself with the poor and unfortunate wherever he met them. Surely any angels in this world and the next would find Dominic worthy of a place of honor in heaven.

Chapter Twenty-seven

Jenna

Jenna's wedding happened sooner than she'd imagined. The moment she and Matilda set foot on English soil, they met a delegation of Norman knights and English churchmen. "His majesty wants this matter knitted up soon," a chubby priest informed Jenna. "Is your sister with you?"

"No, sir. She cannot travel at present." In truth Jenna had insisted Tessa stay behind until she was certain of the situation in England. It had taken Matilda's intervention to convince her, but in the end Tessa had remained in France with her children.

"Send word when you can," Tessa had urged. "I must see Jeffrey's state for myself."

Dressed in a borrowed gown of blue, Jenna was flanked by Norman ladies as she entered an English chapel to join her life with that of Lukas Ladbroke. Embarrassed and nervous, she looked up to see her groom waiting for her at the altar, his face blank. As she neared, however, she saw something in his eyes. It was hard to tell what Lukas felt, but it didn't appear to be distaste.

Was it admiration? The dress Matilda had provided showed off Jenna's white complexion. Her thick, dark hair hung loose, and a cunningly woven net lay over it, scattered with bangles and beads. She'd been bathed in scented water and sprinkled with perfume until she smelled like a flower garden. Only her shoes were old, since none of the Norman ladies had feet as small as Jenna's. "Something old is part of the charm," Matilda commented. "And they won't be seen unless you dance too lively at your wedding feast."

"I won't dance at all," Jenna replied, and Matilda clucked like a disapproving hen.

As she'd promised, Jenna said the words the priest required. Lukas said them, too. Afterward William used the occasion to full advantage, giving a great feast for his men and those English lords willing to accept their lot and make the best of the Norman dominance. Jenna felt like a prize pony, trotted out for show and judged by her ability to breed. There was great merry-making, with revelers drinking toast after toast to the health of the new couple, the success of their marriage, and the future amity between their two cultures.

"I'm not even English," Jenna muttered at one point.

"And I am but half Norman," Lukas answered, though she hadn't spoken to him. "It is enough for the king that we become symbols of the future of England."

"I never wanted to be a symbol."

"Nor did I."

She wondered again what Lukas thought of their marriage. Would he change his mind about his vow to never be her husband? Well, he hadn't said "never." He'd said not until she admitted she was wrong about him. The same thing, because she was not wrong.

"Drink, my lady?" a boy asked. Jenna nodded, taking a drink as soon as the wine was poured. It was strong and fruity on her tongue, and she hoped it would still the flutter in her stomach and the tension in her spine.

What if lust or drink took over and Lukas decided to bed her tonight? She must bear it, she supposed. Many women married men they didn't love and suffered embraces they wouldn't have chosen. Once he got her with child, Lukas would leave her alone. And maybe it wouldn't be too bad. He was handsome, and the kiss they'd shared had been pleasant.

She was surprised, therefore, when Lukas showed no sign of lust when they were escorted to the bridal chamber. He closed the door on the group of rowdy folk offering all sorts of ribald advice. Standing uncertainly in the center of a room that contained nothing but a large bed, he bowed formally and said, "I paid a servant to give us a room with a window. In the morning I'll rejoin you, so none will know you spent your wedding night alone." With that he stepped to the casing, slid easily out the narrow expanse, and disappeared.

Running to the opening, she glimpsed her new husband's disappearing figure as he climbed nimbly down the castle wall, using whatever hand-holds he could find. When he reached the narrow space of ground that edged the moat, he looked up and made a second formal bow before disappearing into the night. Jenna didn't know whether to be relieved or disappointed, but in her heart she admitted that disappointment was the stronger emotion.

Chapter Twenty-eight

Jessie

As autumn faded, Jessie and Aldis fell into a routine that suited them. Jessie spent the mornings improving their living quarters, patching holes and cracks to seal out drafts, stacking fuel for the fire within Aldis' reach, and preparing simple meals. As he'd promised, Dominic came when he could, bringing necessities and sometimes treats that delighted the women: a pot of honey, a sack of turnips, a bundle of woolen fabric.

Struan served them to the best of his ability, doing tasks too heavy or far away for Jessie to do comfortably. He knew which native plants were edible, and soon they had a store of nuts in one corner and berries strung over their heads for drying. These added to the oatmeal and salted meat Dominic supplied.

In the long evenings the two women talked about things great and small. One night when Aldis mentioned Leif's name, Jessie explained her theory that he was the son of Thane Macduff, thought murdered long ago.

Aldis listened as she always did, unmoving but totally focused. "I never knew what his family name was, only that he was a Scot and once called Leith. He chose to be called Leif among us because it was close in sound to his birth name. It means' heir'."

Jessie sighed. "Why is Leif so certain his family's killers were sent by Macbeth?"

"Sigrid told him. She and Leif walked for days to reach her sister's home in England, where they stayed until Sigrid could arrange passage to Norway. Svenn Arneson, my uncle, took her in, because he'd once fought alongside her father."

"But why would Macbeth have killed a fellow Scot's family?"

"In revenge for his refusal to swear fealty to King Macbeth. Sigrid said he was known for such terrible deeds."

Though Jessie's mind argued, she kept silent.

Aldis went on, allowing her own doubts to creep in. "Sigrid was a strange woman. In her mind, Leif and the son she'd lost were confused. She loved him as if he were her own, yet she constantly reminded him of his place and all he lost that day." Aldis spoke the words Jessie had been thinking. "She set Leif upon his path."

In her mind Jessie added, *And if it was the wrong one, what can be done about it now?*

Chapter Twenty-nine

Jenna

William, now called "the Conqueror" by many, moved quickly to cement his success in England. He ordered castles built in the countryside, Norman structures with crenellated tops and stout defenses. Other invaders would find it daunting to attack the nation he now ruled.

The Norman system, a well-organized, formal sort of feudalism, was applied in England's patchwork hierarchy of land-holding. Lords, whether Norman or Anglo-Saxon, owed first loyalty to William, and they were made acutely aware of that fact. The new king sent out agents to list assets and liabilities all over the land. Plans were being made for the accounting to be placed in a great book so the information would be available for anyone's perusal.

Marriages between Normans and their former enemies continued. William approved those who followed Jenna and Lukas' example, and many English families were more than willing to ally themselves to the new regime. Joyful bells tolled daily as Norman knights wedded girls, sometimes tearful, sometimes not, who saved their parents' holdings and received their blessings.

After a month in London, Jenna got word Tessa was returning to Brixton. When Lukas came downstairs that morning she said, "My lord, I have a request."

He gave her a look of mock surprise. "'My lord'? I have been 'Viking' ere now."

Jenna looked at her feet. "You are my husband, and I owe you respect."

His smile was sardonic. "Very well, then, wife. What is your request?"

"I would like to return to Brixton. Tessa is on her way there, and I'm eager to see how things fare with Jeffrey and the rest of my family."

"And eager to see that our bargain is upheld, I trow." Lukas rubbed his chin absently. "You might go tomorrow, if it suits you. I must leave the city for a time."

Her eyes met his. "You won't come to see the lands that are now yours?"

Lukas chuckled dryly. "I'm sure the former owner is capable of tending the place."

"Where will you go?"

Lukas began his answer. "There's something I've been meaning to tell you. When I lived in Norway—"

"Learning to pillage and destroy—" The mere mention of Norway angered her, so much that she spoke in haste, without diplomacy.

A twitch of Lukas' lips showed she'd offended him. "As you say, but I also learned loyalty to my liege. The king requires my help with some Ainglish nobles who are not as amenable to reason as you were."

It was a barb, and she bristled at it. "I was given no choice, if I remember correctly."

"And you are always correct." He took up his cloak and gloves. "I might remind you I wasn't consulted either." At the door he stopped for a final word. "Perhaps you'll miss my company at dinner, wife, though not in your bed." Then he was gone, his boots sounding on the wooden floor like angry drumbeats. Jenna felt tears well in her eyes. What had she done to be yoked to a man who despised her?

Within minutes a carl came to say she'd be escorted to Brixton in the morning as early as she liked.

Before she left London Jenna took leave of Matilda, who was preparing to go back to Normandy. The parting was affectionate, and Jenna knew she'd miss the tiny woman who wore the title of Queen of England like a torc, pretty to look at but hardly something she couldn't live without. As usual, Matilda was the center of a hub of activity, with servants going in all directions to do her bidding. Wheels creaked, metal clanked on metal, and a mixture of scents rose from boxes and bags of English herbs and other items she would take home with her to France. Embracing her, Matilda asked, "I hope we have done well by you. Is Lukas a good husband?"

She had to answer that he was. Attentive in public, he'd left her alone in private. If one had to have a husband who was her enemy, she could ask for no more.

"Good," Matilda said, giving her another hug. "William is a canny judge of folk, and if he says you are well-matched, it is so. Still, I thought to see you smiling more of late."

"Other things concern me, which is why I will return to my sister's—to Brixton."

"Ah, yes, your Ainglish brother-in-law. I hope he is well, and your sister with her new babe still to come."

With that they parted. Jenna wondered if the queen would ever think of her again. England and its government were an aside to Matilda, who was happiest in her lands along the coast of France.

Jenna's trip was delayed at every turn, or so it seemed, and she feared the weather might prove difficult so late in the year. Her luck held, and her travel days, though cold, were clear. Even with lackadaisical horses and slow-moving attendants, she reached Brixton before Tessa and the children arrived from France. Aunt Madeline met her on the road, wrapping her in bony arms and the scent of evergreen.

"I hoped you'd return before winter," the old lady said in her ear. "It will be best if you are here when your sister arrives."

Jenna drew back. "Jeffrey isn't well?"

"Well enough," Madeline assured. They started for the house, arm in arm. "His injury was more serious than we thought wise to tell Tessa, so far away."

"I'm hard to kill, my past is evidence of that," said a voice from the doorway, and Jenna glimpsed Jeffrey in the shadows of the interior. Somewhat pale, he smiled bravely. One sleeve of his jacket hung empty, and his eyes searched Jenna's face, gauging her response. An omen, perhaps, of what his wife's reaction would be.

Having lived her whole life with Jessie, Jenna sensed Jeffrey wanted not sympathy, but a practical acceptance of his infirmity. A proud man, he'd want to know she didn't think him useless now. "I'm sorry to see your loss, Jeffrey. It will make your work more difficult as you manage the estate."

The tension in Jeffrey's shoulders relaxed a little. "I received a letter from your husband that was most cordial," he said. "What sort of man is he?"

"Stop it, you brute!" Madeline intervened. "Jenna's traveled all this way, and you start your questions before she's even removed her cloak." Shooing Jeffrey from the doorway, Madeline drew Jenna inside. "Come in, dear. I'll see you refreshed before I let this beast of mine interrogate you on the affairs of the world."

When Jenna was ensconced in the warmest spot in the room and provided with hot cider, Madeline ordered Jeffrey into the other chair. She hovered over him as Jeffrey said patiently that he had no pain at the moment, his seat was close enough to the fire but not too close, and he didn't require anything to drink.

"Have you had news of Tessa?" Jenna asked when Maddie was satisfied.

"Not of late." Jeffrey shifted in the chair, betraying nervousness. Whether it was worry for his family's safety or dread of their finding him maimed she couldn't tell. "We've told a story of a miraculous rescue to our servants, friends, and family."

"Is it wise for them to return?"

Jeffrey adjusted the empty sleeve of his jacket. "The Viking you warned us of was apparently killed in battle at Stamford Bridge. At least he was not among those who returned to Norway."

"I'm glad of it." If not for Leif Arneson, she'd be living peacefully in the Cairngorms, unaware of Lukas the Viking. But what would have become of Jeffrey and Tessa if events had not fallen out as they had? There was little doubt they'd be worse off than they were now.

Madeline prompted, "Jenna, we're eager to hear your news. How are Tessa and the little ones?"

"There will be a fifth in the spring."

Madeline clasped her hands in joy. Jeffrey swallowed, apparently unsure what this meant in his reduced circumstances.

Jenna hastened to reassure him. "My husband wants no changes at Brixton. You are to continue as you have, and your children will be provided for."

He looked relieved. "Tell us how you met and married Lukas Ladbroke."

Jenna found it easier now to tell the tale, but perhaps time had brought acceptance. She allowed her listeners to assume they'd met at Falaise, been attracted to each other, and agreed to William's proposal that they serve as examples of Norman-English amity.

When she'd finished, Jeffrey said, "And thus, Jenna, you saved us all."

She felt herself blush. "I hope you don't think I acted in my own interest."

"Of course not," Jeffrey said. "If this marriage is by your wish, you've done us a great service. The conquered do not often get consideration from the conquerors."

She chose to ignore the part about the marriage being her wish. "William's plan has quickly gained acceptance among the nobility of England."

"He won't win them all," Jeffrey said soberly. "I fear—"

A furious pounding sounded at the door, and they jumped. Madeline hurried to open it, and a familiar voice sounded. "I must speak with Jeffrey Brixton."

"Lukas?" Jenna moved to the entryway. "What is it?"

"Your sister's in danger. Leif Arneson and Bjorn Bear-Slayer live, and they know your nephews are on their way home."

"How?"

"That doesn't matter. Has she arrived?"

"No. They must still be on the road."

"I'll ride south and meet her."

Jeffrey stepped from behind Jenna, his expression determined. "I'm not whole, sir, but I will defend my wife and children to the death."

Lukas took in the empty sleeve and the air of

determination with one glance. "I'm sorry for your injury, sir. If you can ride and use a sword, you're welcome. In my haste I brought no men with me."

Jeffrey bowed slightly. "I'll make ready." Calling a servant to saddle his horse, he started up the stairs then turned to Lukas. "Will you require an oath of fealty before we go?"

Lukas didn't hesitate. "Your presence at my side will be enough."

Jeffrey bowed again, turned, and continued upstairs. Madeline went after him, anxiety evident in her posture. She was wise enough, however, to hold her arguments until they were out of the newcomer's hearing.

Lukas examined the room, apparently interested in each piece of furniture and decoration. Jenna suspected he was avoiding her rather than numbering his possessions. "What do you know, Lukas?"

"Too little, I'm afraid. A soldier from York arrived at court shortly after you left. Local women tell of two Vikings left on the shore when the Norwegians retreated. Leif's singular appearance and Bjorn's terrible wound created interest, but they disappeared a few days after the battle."

"You believe he'll resume the blood feud?"

"For Leif, the Vikings' defeat will be further proof of the curse. We must protect your nephews."

Footsteps sounded on the stairs, and Jeffrey returned with Madeline tripping at his heels. It was only two months since his terrible injury, but the old woman knew better than to attempt to keep him from this task. She folded her arms on her thin chest as if willing them not to reach out for her beloved nephew.

"I'm ready," he said, and Lukas moved ahead of him to the door, where horses' hooves clopped on the stone walkway. The women trailed the men outside and watched as they rode away. Were they enemies or allies? It was a question no one could answer. A conqueror and a madman forced them to work together. Jenna said a prayer for their success.

It was a nervous afternoon. Madeline kept mentioning things she should do but could set her mind to nothing. Jenna stood at the window, too worried to do anything but watch.

At dusk Madeline called her away, saying they must eat something. They were sitting at the table, pretending to eat what the serving girl had set before them, when the door burst open with a blast of cool autumn air. They hurried out to see Lukas in the doorway, his handsome face split in a wide grin. Stepping aside, he ushered in a small crowd: Tessa, Jeffrey, the children, and the servants, all safe.

"You found them!" Jenna ran to embrace her sister, whose cloak bulged with the child she carried. Ushering them to the fireside, Jenna began asking questions. Madeline added hers. Everyone began explaining and exclaiming, and soon there was chaos.

"Hold!" Jeffrey said with a laugh, and Jenna noted he already seemed more like the confident man she'd met months ago. The moment he'd dreaded was past, and his wife's reaction had apparently relieved his fears. Tessa had already begun to anticipate his needs and meet them with neither fuss nor pity. They were adjusting into an efficient unit, as they'd done for more than a decade.

For all Jenna's worry and Lukas' haste, Tessa's trip had been uneventful. If Leif had planned to waylay them, he'd been deterred.

"We must be watchful still," Lukas warned. "I doubt he'll

give up easily." Jenna noted the word we slipped out, as if he felt part of the family. And he was, she reminded herself, by marriage to her. And by William the Conqueror's decree.

After Tessa put the children to bed, the adults sat companionably around the fireside. It should have been an uncomfortable evening with their new overlord in their midst, but Lukas had put them at ease. Jeffrey even seemed to like him.

"Tell us about the man called Leif," Tessa said with a shiver. "Why does he hate us so?"

Lukas shook his head. "We were boys together, but when my mother died, I went to live with my father in Normandy. Until recently, I hadn't seen Leif for a decade."

"He came to Normandy?"

"No. I returned there to, um—" He glanced at Jenna. "—observe conditions. When I arrived, Leif was readying his men for a trip to Scotland. He said he had to end a blood feud, and he meant to do it before an important event took place. I guessed the event was the Norwegian invasion of England, and I guessed I could learn more about it if I traveled with Leif." Lukas' eyes met Jenna's. "I didn't know he'd hold a dead man's family responsible for his crimes."

"And who did our uncle supposedly murder?" Jenna heard anger in Tessa's voice. She'd faced stories of Macbeth's perfidy before and refused to believe them.

"It no longer matters. Whatever he believes to be true, Leif will have to leave England. William will not allow a Viking blood feud in his lands."

"Why did William send you to Norway?" Jenna asked.

Lukas hesitated, and she sensed he'd tell only part of the truth. "The duke hoped for a joining of forces, but the

Norwegian king wanted England for himself."

"And died attempting to take it." Jeffrey stood. "With your permission, I'll set guards outside."

Lukas seemed embarrassed. "I meant what I said in my letter, Brixton. Do as you see fit. I'll be gone in the morning."

"Won't you stay for one day?" Jenna heard herself ask.

Lukas turned to her, his face a polite mask. "Nothing would please me more than to spend time with my wife and her family. But the king has work for me, so I leave the estate in Jeffrey's very capable…care," He'd almost said 'hands'."

Madeline yawned discreetly, and Tessa said, "It's time we retire. This day has had a measure of excitement, but it ended well, thanks to our brother-in-law."

She smiled at Lukas, and Jenna thought, *She likes him.*

To Jenna's great embarrassment, Tessa offered the newlyweds the largest bedchamber. Lukas declined with a polite bow and a logical excuse. "You will need the space when your little one appears. Jenna and I will do well with any unoccupied room."

Accepting his reasoning, Tessa chose a room for them that overlooked the river. Recently used for storage, it smelled of drying herbs and grasses, but two maidservants cleared it out in a short time. They were making up a pallet bed of straw and blankets when Tessa ushered the couple in. "It's quite private," she whispered to her sister, and Jenna blushed. A bridal chamber was offered.

After a quick hug for Jenna and a little bow for Lukas, Tessa retreated, leaving Jenna nervous and unsure of herself. She'd begun to doubt her dislike of her husband, begun to wonder if she'd misjudged him. He seemed genuinely interested in Tessa and Jeffrey's well-being. His presence with the Viking band was explained, and truthfully, there was nothing he could have done to prevent what had happened. And he'd tried to keep her safe.

Was there hope for this marriage? She didn't relish a life without affection, shackled to a man who thought her cold and unyielding.

"Lukas?"

"Yes?" He was looking out the window, and his response was distracted.

"I want to say—"

He held up a warning hand. She moved to the window, but there was not enough room at the narrow slit for both of them to see below.

"What is it?"

"Stay here." In an instant he was gone. She heard no sound of his passage through the house, but soon she saw the front door open below. Stepping outside, Lukas stopped where Jeffrey's guard stood, speaking a few words before he disappeared into the darkness.

Quickly Jenna made a decision and headed down the twisting stairs after him, her slippered feet silent on the stone steps. The hall was dark, the dying fire the only light. A few forms huddled on the floor near it, still and at rest. She tiptoed past, taking two dark capes from a peg near the entry. Then she opened the door as little as possible, sliding out into the night.

"Who goes there?" The guard seemed eager to do his assigned duty to the best of his ability.

"It's Jenna."

"Yes, miss—um, madam. Your husband—" He stopped, unsure how much to admit.

"He often walks at night when he can't sleep."

"Just as he said, madam."

"I've brought him a cape, for it's cold tonight."

"It is, madam," the youth agreed.

Putting the shorter cape, which smelled faintly of cedar, over her shoulders, Jenna headed in the direction Lukas had gone. What was he up to? The sound of voices in a copse of trees alongside the river made her stop; she was closer than she'd thought.

"—over a month. Why haven't you found her?" Lukas was saying.

A voice answered, "We're doing our best."

"This woman is important to me."

"I understand," the other said. "When she's found, we'll bring her to you."

"Not here," Lukas said. "I'll arrange a place where she can live in comfort and visit her when I can."

Lukas had a mistress. Though she'd considered the possibility, facing the reality of it was jarring. Jenna clenched her teeth until her jaw hurt.

"You say the lady is beautiful. No doubt she'll be grateful for your protection." A snide note to the man's voice brought an angry response from Lukas.

"Her mood is none of your affair. You are charged with finding her, for she needs my protection."

"Yes, sir," the other said humbly. "I meant no harm."

"Go, then, before someone of the household sees you skulking about. Find her, and send word to me."

Realizing the meeting was about to end, Jenna turned and sprinted for the house. Passing the guard she hissed, "Say nothing of seeing me." Mouth agape, he nodded obediently.

When Lukas entered their room, she stood in the darkest corner, hiding her flushed and angry face.

"You're still awake?"

"I am."

"Of course," Lukas said. "You had something to tell me. What was it?"

Jenna recalled the words she might have said a short time ago: that she'd misjudged him and hoped their marriage could be a success. "I wanted you to remind me to thank Tessa for providing us a private room."

At her cold tone Lukas replied, "Yes. Your sister has been nothing but kind and gracious." The implication was that she'd been otherwise.

"I've said how I feel about you. Nothing has changed."

"No. I suppose not." Lukas' expression was grim. "We have a situation here, though. We must share this room, since the window is a mere slit.

"We must share the bed."

"As husband and wife should."

The husky tone of Lukas' voice sent a shiver down Jenna's spine. Was he reconsidering the vow he'd made at Falaise? If he had, should she submit to him after what she'd just heard? The thought flitted through her mind that if she became his wife in truth, she might win him from the mysterious woman he was paying men to search for.

"I'll take the inside." Turning away, Lukas unrolled a blanket and moved to the far side of the pallet bed. Wrapping himself in the woolen fabric, he lay down facing the wall.

Jenna stood still, unable to comprehend the difference between his earlier tone and the flat one of the last statement. Taking the other blanket, she wrapped it around herself and lay down on the straw-stuffed mattress. She waited, body tense, to see what Lukas would do. He was still and silent, as if asleep, but his breathing was shallow. She didn't think he went to sleep for a long time, but then, neither did she.

Chapter Thirty

Jessie

By the time winter came in earnest, Jessie and Struan had insulated the castle rooms with straw, moss, pine boughs, and whatever else they could find. Aldis spent her days wrapped in layers of fabric, feeding bits of fuel into the fire at regular intervals. They seldom heard Struan's mother, who slept much of the time and spoke only in whispers. Jessie offered to help nurse her, but Struan said, "Her's used t' my ways, ye ken."

"Of course," Jessie replied. "I'd feel the same."

Snow fell, collecting in the crevices between the rocks and drifting across the pathway. Sound was muffled, and the world went quiet, listening for spring. The trees sometimes drooped with the snow's weight, and Jessie delighted in watching as the wind jiggled the branches and sent puffs of white tumbling to the ground.

At least once each day she went outside, wrapping her feet in pieces of felt she'd fashioned into boot covers. She never went far, but walking gave her time to consider all that had happened since summer, some of it wonderful, some disastrous. She grieved for Jenna and Tessa, drowned in the crossing to France. She missed her other sisters and wondered where they thought she was. And her heart ached for Alfred, who was good and kind and gentle but did not love her as she loved him. It was a lot to think on.

Evenings they sat near the fire, talking of small things. One night Jessie asked, "How did you come to live with your uncle?"

"Svenn had no children of his own, so he opened his home to Lukas, Leif, and me."

"And you grew up together."

"Yes. I am the oldest, then Leif, then Lukas. Since I wasn't expected to live, those in my uncle's hall made a pet of me."

"And Lukas and Leif? What were they like as children?"

"They were both admired for their strength and skill, though Lukas was perhaps better liked."

"Leif was different," Jessie guessed.

Licking her lips, Aldis answered honestly, which Jessie guessed was difficult, given her feelings for the man. "Leif was an outsider. He and Sigrid were secretive and anxious, as if trouble were always at their heels."

"They were disliked?"

"Not disliked. Feared, perhaps. Sigrid was half-mad, and one never knew what to expect from her. And Leif had nightmares at first that would make a statue weep. He'd call out piteously and cry, 'They've killed them all!' As he grew older, he outgrew his fears and became a fierce fighter, which brought him much respect. When Lukas went to France, my uncle left his estate to Leif, asking that he give me a home for as long as I live."

"That was kind of him."

"Svenn was a good man. If not for the deaths of Leif's wife and children, he might have been like him, content to serve his people and live out his days in Norway."

"But the second tragedy, the death of his wife and children, destroyed his mind."

Aldis didn't answer, and Jessie guessed she couldn't admit to herself that Leif was mad. Seeing the love in Aldis' eyes, Jessie didn't say aloud what she was thinking.

Whatever his tragic past, it could not excuse what Leif had done, and what he intended to do.

Chapter Thirty-one

Jenna

When Jenna awoke, Lukas was gone. Hurrying downstairs, she found Jeffrey struggling to put on his boots and swearing in frustration. Embarrassed, Jenna turned to go, but he said with a sardonic grin, "I'll learn to do these things, but I must learn patience as well."

"It's a great difficulty," she said as he began again. Jenna put her hands behind her back, resisting the urge to help. "Things one took for granted must be done another way."

As she watched Jeffrey pull the boot on, Jessie came to mind. How was she coping without her twin? Who steadied her on steep trails so she didn't stumble? Who assured she wasn't distressed by spiders and wore mittens in the cold? She was so fragile. Was there someone watching out for her, as Jenna once had?

Completing his task with a sigh of satisfaction, Jeffrey said, "I'll manage. And you?"

"I, too, will manage." An unspoken message passed between them. A cheerful demeanor covered the heartaches of their situation, but they both understood that it was often difficult to maintain. Steps sounded on the stairs above them, and they said no more. Life at Brixton went on.

Jenna had no word of Lukas for two weeks, but, to her irritation, Jeffrey did. Two different times, a messenger came to consult with him on matters of the estate. Once as she came into the room, Jeffrey was telling Tessa, "Lukas says William will be pleased to hear we can provide a goodly amount of mancorn."

"Lukas was here?"

Jeffrey's expression became guarded. "Briefly."

"Where has he gone?"

"He didn't say." Jeffrey's tone reminded her it wasn't his place to ask.

"Is he on the king's business?"

Jeffrey shrugged. "We spoke of crops."

"Mancorn!" Jenna said, irritated. "What's so important about a few fields of grain?" She left the room, unaccountably unhappy. Why did she care if Lukas sought his lover and neglected her? It was best for them both if he stayed away, since she was determined not to let any affection grow between them. He was a Viking, despite pretty words and kindness to her family. She would not miss him. Would not.

Things settled into a routine. They sent a letter to Scotland, explaining to her family what had occurred since Jenna left the Cairngorms. "I hope someday to return," Jenna wrote, "but I have married a man I met in France, so my visit might be far in the future."

Looking at the words, she considered what she'd left out. It did no good to say she'd had no choice in her marriage or reveal her husband was one of the group that terrorized them. And of course, she didn't tell anyone her marriage was no marriage at all.

Though chatelaine by right, Jenna refused to let Tessa defer to her. "You must teach me as you were taught when you came to Brixton," she insisted. "It would be a disaster if I ordered your people about with my inexperience."

It was sometimes awkward, but Tessa's advancing pregnancy helped. She could legitimately claim fatigue and leave Jenna to finish preparations for a meal or some household task. Thus Jenna learned the ways of an English manor house, and she set herself to master everything she could. If Lukas were ever required to entertain his Norman friends at Brixton, she wanted him to be proud of his home. Berthe, Matilda, Tessa, and Madeline were excellent examples to follow.

Jeffrey regularly sent men into the countryside looking for Leif Arneson, but they found nothing. Still, there were plenty of places for desperate men to hide, so he kept guards around the house and patrolled the estate daily. The children were kept close to home, which irritated them, but Tessa and Jeffrey were adamant.

"I wish this were over," Tessa said to Jenna one night as they knitted by the fire. Jeffrey sat with a lap desk, a fat, dripping candle beside him to shed light on the accounts he kept. The wind howled outside, announcing that a November storm would soon follow. Hides had been fastened over the windows to keep out the worst of the draughts, but the cold insinuated itself into every stone of the house. Tessa was wrapped in a heavy woolen shawl, Jenna wore several layers, and Madeline seemed to have put on every article of clothing she owned. Bricks that had been warmed in the fireplace sat under each person's feet. A half dozen more rested on the hearth, ready to replace the originals when they cooled.

After a companionable silence Madeline said, almost to herself, "Why does this Viking not leave us and go back where he belongs?"

"He's a madman," Jenna replied. "There's no grasping how his mind works."

"He won't harm our children if I can prevent it," Jeffrey vowed. "And Lukas says the same."

"Lukas has other things on his mind," Jenna muttered.

Tessa regarded her for a moment. "Let's go up and see if the girls have crept from their beds again to spy on the servants," she said, rising and wrapping her shawl more closely around her.

Madeline yawned. "I'll be off to bed."

"I'll close the house and join you in a trice, wife." Jeffrey's eyes sent a message that made Tessa blush.

When they'd left the room Tessa asked, "Are things well with you and your husband, Jenna?"

Should she tell her sister the truth? No, she decided. A killer stalked Tessa's children, her husband had a grievous injury, and she'd soon have a new baby. She'd been demoted from chatelaine of Brixton to tenant at her brother-in-law's pleasure. She didn't need to hear that Jenna's hold on Lukas was no hold at all. "He's much concerned with the king's business. I'm pleased he trusts Jeffrey to manage things here."

"He's been more than kind to us." Tessa smoothed a lock of Jenna's hair that escaped her coif. "I hope you and he come to cherish each other, as husbands and wives often do as time goes on."

Jenna thought of the unknown woman Lukas might at this very moment be bedding. What chance did she have if his heart was already taken? "I'm sure we will." With that they parted and Jenna went to her empty chamber to face the night alone, without the comfort the other husband and wife of the household offered each other.

Chapter Thirty-two

Jessie

Dropping an armload of twigs near the fire, Jessie rubbed her hands to warm them. "The coldest day yet."

"And we must bear it for weeks more," Aldis observed. The room was dark and smoky with its window covered, and she was only a dim shape next to the fire. Noting the snowflakes that covered Jessie's head and shoulders she added, "It will be hard for you if the snow gets much deeper."

"I'll manage," Jessie replied. In truth, she found the more active she was, the less her hip plagued her.

A distinctive knock sounded. Struan, but he was somewhat early today. Aldis said he preferred Jessie's cooking to his own and therefore timed his visits close to the noonday meal.

Jessie opened the door to find Struan fairly bouncing with anxiety. "Twa men cooming," he reported. "Mayhap them ye told me t' watch for."

"Did they see you, Struan?"

"Nae. They're far doown th' trail, but ye said I should tell ye straight away if I saw such as them."

"You did well. Go down to meet them. If they ask about us, tell them you don't know where we are."

His brow puckered. "But lady, I ken where y' are. 'Tis a sin t' tell a lie."

Jessie looked to Aldis. How could they explain to this simple man their lives depended on him?

Aldis asked, "What if you didn't know for certain, Struan? If they ask and you don't know where we are at that moment, could you say that?"

He grinned as understanding dawned. "Ye'll gae somewhere, an' I won't ken where. When they coome, I will say tha', and twill be nae lie atall."

"Exactly."

His misshapen mouth split in a grin. "I can do tha'."

A few minutes of frantic activity followed. Struan went to his room to tell his mother what was happening while Jessie and Aldis began what became a grueling trek. Jessie helped Aldis into a small barrow Struan had found in an outbuilding and repaired for their use.

Open to the weather in places, the floor of the castle's upper level was icy in some spots and snow-covered in others. Jessie wheeled the barrow down the corridor, trying desperately not to lose her balance and tip Aldis onto the stones. For her part Aldis gripped the sides, jaw set, so she remained upright and didn't bump against the sides. Teetering and skidding along the slippery corridor, they imagined Leif and Bjorn's footsteps ascending the stairs at any moment.

In a corner of the old west tower, the roof was partly intact. Pushing the barrow into the most sheltered spot, Jessie left Aldis, promising to return as soon as possible. Hurrying back to their room, she hid everything that betrayed their presence.

"Remember," she told Struan. "You are here with only your mother." Struan nodded, but his brow knit with concern. "It's the truth," she assured him. "You will tell no lies if you say no more than that."

Taking a blanket from the bed, Jessie said a little prayer that Struan could manage the deception. As long as the questions weren't specific he'd manage, but what if the

Vikings asked him if he'd ever seen her or Aldis? He'd say he had, and where might that lead. Still, there was no time to coach him further.

As she gave the room a final glance, it occurred to Jessie that if Struan didn't know where they were hiding, he couldn't tell them when it was safe to return. It wouldn't do to have him shout for them and perhaps bring the Vikings back. "When the men are gone, Struan, go out and begin chopping wood. When we hear that, we'll know it's safe." With that she left, using a branch to sweep a skiff of snow over their tracks.

Aldis was already suffering from the cold, despite the heavy cloak she wore. Jessie debated whether she'd be better off on the blanket on the stone floor or in the barrow. In the end they sat on the blanket, huddled under the cloak, and shared their body heat. Though she tried to suppress them, Aldis' shivers shook Jessie as they waited in silent dread.

After what seemed like forever, they heard the sound of an axe on wood. Going to a window slit, Jessie peeped out. Struan was below, applying himself whole-heartedly to his task. Hurrying down the stairs, she touched his shoulder.

"Ah, there ye are, lady. They've gone."

"We must get Aldis to the fire."

"Poor thing," he said, unaware of his part in causing her distress. He followed Jessie inside and climbed with her to the ruined tower. "A wonderful hiding place!" he crowed. "I'd nae hae guessed ye were here." Aldis' face was grim as he lifted her into the barrow. "Ye must warm yerself, lady," he chided, as if sitting in the cold had been her idea.

When Aldis was as close to the fire as she could get without broiling herself, Struan told his story. "'Twas a loong time, an' I began t' wish I'd something t' do, because it was sae very loong. I whittled a bit, see th' wee bird I made? Is't not like a real one?"

"It is," Aldis agreed. "But the men?"

"Oh, aye. They coome, an' verra big they were. They pounded o' th' door as if I was deef." He paused again. "I am not deef, though Mother is almost sae."

"So you have told us," Aldis said patiently. "The men asked about me?"

"They asked aboot an odd woman wi' bones sae brittle she must be carried along. They wanted to help her, they sayed, an' asked if I ken where she'd be."

"And you said you did not."

"Exactly so," Struan said proudly. "I sayed I didn't ken where she was, because I didn't, did I?"

"You did not. Did they say anything else?"

"They asked why there's twa fires and twa rooms when 't wuld be easier t' warm one."

Aldis bit her lip. "And what did you tell them?"

"I sayed 'twasn't ma room."

A twitch of Aldis' lips revealed anxiety, but she said, "What else?"

Struan spoke earnestly. "I sayed 'twas where th' priest coomes t'see his ladies."

A second twitch revealed less anxiety, more amusement. "And what did they say to that?"

"One sayed t' th' other, 'It's some randy churchman's love nest.' He were angry, I trow."

"Possibly," Aldis said lightly. "Did they ask anything else?"

"Th' angry one sayed was I certain I didna ken where there was twa women. I sayed I couldna tell where twa such as that might be. Th' other sayed, 'They wouldna survive up here wi' only this lack-wit t' help them.'" Struan's expression turned angry. "He said right afore me I be a lack-wit!"

"But you're not," Aldis said soothingly. "You're very clever, for they didn't find us."

He grinned. "I might hae told 'em there are plenty o' places t' hide in an auld castle. I might hae sayed how could I ken where such women would choose t' hide, but they left." He frowned. "I didna think t' offer food and drink, which muther says we should aever do when we ha' guests."

Jessie met Aldis' gaze and rolled her eyes. They might have spent even longer in the frigid cold due to Struan's misguided sense of a host's duty.

"Did they say where they came from?"

He bit his lower lip in thought. "Not far, I trow, bu' the man wi' one eye sayed they'd hae t' hurry t' get back by nightfall."

"That is worrisome," Aldis said. "Still, they came here and found nothing. They have no reason to return."

"We owe you thanks, Struan, for the warning and your help," Jessie told him.

"'T were nothing," he said modestly. "Ye were clever aboot hiding yourselves. Tha's what go' th' best o' them twa, nae me."

Chapter Thirty-three

Jenna

As time passed, anxiety over Leif Arneson's reappearance waned, and the people of Brixton Manor decided he must have returned to Norway. As Jenna worried less each day about Leif, she became more concerned about Lukas' secretive behavior. Twice she caught him in falsehoods. Once he hid a letter under some other papers when she came into the room. Another time she saw him counting money into the hand of a stranger who came in a small boat and spoke to him on the riverbank. She'd never seen the man's face before, but she guessed he was the one hired to find Lukas' lover for him. His message made Lukas' head droop. They had not found her yet.

Whenever he visited Brixton, Lukas was a pleasant companion to all, teasing the girls, listening patiently to the boys' tales of rabbits snared and trees climbed, and joking easily with Tessa. He and Jeffrey had grown close, talking into the night about crops like matlin and mancorn. Jenna suspected he delayed coming to bed to give her time to settle in and go to sleep, but she never did. When he came in quietly and lay down beside her, she pretended to be asleep, but rest never came easily. The elaborate movements they made to maintain distance from each other might have been funny in other circumstances, but the whole thing made Jenna feel sad. It was almost a relief each time he rode off again. Almost.

On one visit Jenna had a gift for him, a green coat she'd made with Tessa's help. It suited him, emphasizing his wide shoulders and straight back, and Lukas seemed genuinely pleased with the coat and her efforts. He put it on the next morning, and she brushed a bit of lint from the front. The stirring in her core came when she touched him, as it always did. Lukas felt it too; she saw it in his eyes. His hand came toward her, as if to touch her hair, but he stopped it midway. She saw the effort it took in the taut line of his lips. Jenna held her breath. What would she do if he said what was in his heart?

To her great irritation, he spoke of agriculture. "Do you realize that Brixton has devised a way of mixing crops that helps to prevent disaster?"

"Really." The sarcasm in her voice was obvious, but he didn't seem to notice.

"He's mixed durham and rivet wheat, for example. Blight might strike one, but it will not kill off the other, so at least half the crop survives."

"I see." What she didn't see was what the excitement was about.

"William is very interested in his methods."

"The king cares about Jeffrey's fields?" She grimaced. "I mean your fields?"

Lukas shook his head at her lack of concern. "It's to William's benefit to pursue every means of making England safe from famine."

She had imagined it took only soldiers to create a kingdom, but she admitted William's approach was wise. Military might could hold power, but seeing to the everyday needs of the people would help them accept it. "So Jeffrey's crops make him an asset to the king?"

They do."

"And what is your role?"

"Having the king's ear, I make sure he knows the former lord of Brixton is worthy and intelligent."

To enhance your own status, Jenna thought, but it couldn't hurt to have word of Jeffrey's agricultural talents reach London. "It is good of you to commend us." The coolness in her tone made his grin fade, and Lukas moved on, leaving her alone on the stairway.

By day they were an amicable couple, working with Tessa and Jeffrey to keep the large estate running and its people content. At night they retired to their room, where Lukas was silent and cold, bidding her a brusque good night and turning his back to her. Jenna's attitude ranged from anger to longing, and at times she considered seducing her own husband. The thought of the other woman always stopped her, and she took refuge in resentment.

Lukas seemed unaware of her moods, and why should he take note? He hadn't chosen her for himself, so Jenna guessed he seldom thought of her at all.

One morning Lukas announced he would ride out for the day. "I might return by nightfall, but if not, surely by tomorrow." When Jeffrey offered to accompany him, Lukas said they shouldn't both be gone from the property. His face turned red as he said it. A lie.

When he was gone, Jenna hurriedly took up her cloak and boots. Taking up the box where Lukas kept his money, she removed a few coins. "I thought I might visit Cousin Mary today," she announced casually.

"But it's cold," Tessa objected. "Not a day for a pleasure outing."

"We were raised in the mountains, Tess. It's carrying a babe that makes you so tender these days."

Jenna surprised the groom in the stable by requesting a horse other than the gentle palfrey she usually rode. "Are you sure, my lady?"

"I rode every day in France." She glanced impatiently over his shoulder to where Lukas was disappearing from sight. "Please hurry."

Next Jenna insisted the groom did not accompany her. She felt a little sorry for the man, who'd be in trouble if anything happened. He could hardly refuse her direct order without support from Jeffrey or Lukas, and neither of them knew a thing about her outing.

Jenna left Brixton, following the eastern path Lukas had taken. The horse was restive, and it required all her skill to maintain control, but he was built for speed. Within an hour she spied Lukas on the trail ahead and slowed her pace. Holding back, she hid until he turned a corner or entered a wood then hurried to catch up. Twice she thought she'd lost him, but each time she caught a glimpse of his green coat and turned in the direction he'd taken.

By noon Jenna was beginning to worry. She'd never been so far from Brixton, and she'd have to turn back soon in order to find her way home before dark. Unwilling to give up quite yet, she spurred her horse ahead, catching a glimpse of Lukas as he disappeared over a hill. The next time she caught sight of him, he was descending toward a river along which lay a prosperous-looking town. York? It had to be.

Approaching the gates, Jenna pulled the hood of her cloak forward, hiding her hair and shadowing her face. The streets were busy with people, and she felt safe following Lukas in the crowd. When he left his horse at a stable and set off on foot, she stopped a boy and promised him a coin to watch over hers. He seemed willing, and she hoped, honest as well.

With hurried steps Jenna caught up with Lukas. His stride was twice hers, but his distinctive green coat stood out from the grays and browns of those around him. Several times he stopped to ask for directions but finally turned down a narrow street where the houses seemed to lean on one another, each more weary than the last. Two-thirds of the way down, he knocked at a door and was admitted by an old, tired-looking woman. Jenna hesitated, unsure what to do. Would Lukas keep his lover in such a place?

Twenty minutes later he left, lost in thought. That was good, since he passed quite near Jenna, who turned away and stepped into a narrow space between two buildings. Lukas disappeared, and she faced a choice: follow him or find out who was inside the house he'd visited. She chose the latter.

The woman seemed surprised at a second visitor in so short a time. Tall and gaunt, she had light hair and pale skin like the Viking seer Aldis but none of her beauty. Dirty and unkempt, she had open sores on her face, neck and arms. She peered at Jenna with milky eyes that revealed her sight was fading, perhaps almost gone. "Who is it?"

"The man in the green coat. Why did he come here?"

"It's nothing to you." There was no animosity in her tone, and Jenna guessed she'd tell what she knew if it was worth her while.

"I can pay."

After a moment the woman moved, tacitly inviting Jenna inside. The place was little more than a hovel, and a single cot and chair signaled she lived alone. The place smelled of rotting food, dirty clothing, and advancing illness. A month, perhaps two, and its tenant would be dead, her secrets hidden forever.

"Tell me what you can about the man who just left."

"I know nothing of your fine gentleman." Her tone was dismissive.

"What did he come for, then?"

She leaned toward Jenna in a conspiratorial manner. "He's searching for someone."

"Tell me what you told him."

The woman settled her back against the wall, finding a comfortable spot and running her tongue over rotting teeth. "You said you'd pay." When Jenna showed her a coin, the woman grasped her hand and pulled it close to see it better. Satisfied, she said, "Well, then. He seeks a young man with white hair like an aged one."

It was some comfort that Lukas had not asked about his woman. "You mean Leif Arneson."

"That is the name. I told him I know no such man."

"Why did he think Leif would come to you?"

The woman's head tilted to one side. "Long ago, when he stayed with us, we called him Leith."

Jenna was confused. Leif had been in England as a boy? "Tell me everything you know, starting from the beginning." She took a second coin from her pocket, letting the coins clink invitingly as she did. The woman smiled, perhaps as pleased to have two eager listeners in one day as she was anxious for the money.

"I am one of six daughters born in Olle, in Norway. As a girl, I married a fisherman and moved here to Jorvik with him." Her lips tightened. "A few years later, my sister Sigrid fell in love with a Scotsman who took her to the Highlands and after only a few months, left her pregnant and penniless. She found work as nurse to the children of a lord. She and her son lived with them for several years before tragedy struck."

"What was the name of the family?"

The woman waved a bruised, skeletal hand dismissively. "It's been too long, if I ever knew it."

Jenna sighed. "All right. What was the tragedy?"

Leaning so close Jenna caught the scent of her fetid breath, the woman told the story. "One night Sigrid came to our door with a boy at her side. She begged us to hide them, saying they'd be murdered else. My husband was a good-hearted man, and he let me take them in.

"It was a hard time for us. The boy spoke little all day and cried out in the night, keeping us all awake. Sigrid was like a madwoman, weeping for hours on end and almost fainting with fear each time someone came to the door." The woman squinted at Jenna, trying to find words to describe it. "Her heart was broke. Even when she calmed she was different, as if it healed askew." She glanced around the room, perhaps comparing the sister she'd once known with the one she'd last seen. "In the end, she sold some silver pieces she had rolled up into her bundle. With the money she bought passage to Norway for herself and the boy."

Jenna was trying to follow. "The boy was her son?"

The woman's gums worked. "She said he was, but they were odd, the two of 'em."

"What was odd?"

"Sigrid called the boy 'young master' sometimes when she forgot. And though the boy would have no one near him but her, he cried out for his mother in the night."

The boy Sigrid had taken to Norway was Leif. The Viking Jenna hated was not a Viking at all, but a Scot.

Jenna returned her attention to the woman. "Did you ever hear from your sister again?"

"Your man asked that too," she replied with a grin. "I'll

show you what I showed him." Taking a box from the floor beside her, she opened the lid to reveal a letter. "I cannot read it, and in truth she did not write it. But you may scan it if you can read."

The writing was the beautiful script of a trained copyist. Sadly, it was in a language Jenna didn't know. She handed it back to the woman, who cackled.

"I thought not. A woman who reads would be a rare thing." It seemed quite a joke to her, and she chuckled herself into silence. "I know what it says, though. I had it read to me many times, for it is the last word I ever got from her. It says: 'Dearest Ragnid: I took Leith to Norway, where our cousin Svenn Arneson welcomed us both. I will never let the boy forget what happened. He will become a true Viking, and one day he will avenge my lady and the children who died that day. He will repay Macbeth's crime.' She sighed with satisfaction at her perfect memory. "It is signed by my sister, Sigrid.'"

Jenna thanked the woman, pressing the second coin into her hand, and left the house. She rode homeward, pondering what she'd learned and watching to assure she didn't overtake Lukas. When she came over a hill and saw Brixton in the distance she turned, making a wide arc so she approached from the opposite side. When Lukas asked where she'd gone she answered, "East, along the river."

William of Normandy, known to his enemies as William the Bastard, announced he would be crowned king of England on Christmas Day, 1066, at Westminster Abbey. Lukas asked Jenna to accompany him to the ceremony. At first she demurred, but Tessa insisted it was an honor, and she must go to represent Brixton Manor. This meant preparation such as she had never imagined, including dresses being made or refitted from those available, dance lessons, and refinement of her knowledge of French. Lukas had bought her some fine fabric that felt like a whisper on her skin, and Tessa set about making a dress, working clumsily around her growing belly.

Dismal news arrived with the melting snow: a letter from Meg:

Dearest sisters and the Brixton household:

It was with great joy we received your letters, for we had greatly feared for your safety. We pray for your continued health and happiness, and rejoice in Jenna's news that she has married. Donald is much improved, though his progress is slow. He can walk and speak, but headaches plague him. He has no memory of that terrible night, but we praise God he is with us still.

Now for sad news. Your sister Jessie is missing. We were told she had taken employment at the castle in Glamis. But recently Dougal visited and learned she is gone from there. We hoped she had reached you in York, but since you did not mention her, it seems she did not. If you hear aught of her, we beg you to send word.

There was more about events at the clan-hold. Ailsa would have a child soon, about the same time as Tessa. The animals had fared well over the winter. Jenna hardly heard as she struggled to control her tears. Jessie! Her twin, the closest person on earth to her, was missing.

The others were concerned, but Jenna insisted she'd know if Jessie were dead. "I'd feel it," she insisted. "I'd know." They accepted that, or at least pretended they did, but no one could explain where Jessie might be if she wasn't at Brixton or home in Scotland.

On the day she was to depart for London, a light snow fell, turning the world white. As the horses came from the stables, their nostrils puffing clouds of steam, Jenna was surprised to see Lukas riding at the head of her escort. She almost waved but, remembering her dignity and his many unexplained absences, hid her hands inside her sheepskin muff instead. With nothing but pride to cling to, she told herself she must keep to her vow and never show softness toward him.

When he reached her, Lukas said with equal dignity, "Are you prepared, wife?"

"I am."

"Then we shall set off when my men are refreshed." Dismounting, he kissed her chastely on the cheek for the benefit of those watching. Jenna stood like a stone, but her skin warmed where his lips touched her. Turning to Tessa, Lukas embraced her with a teasing comment about her rounding shape.

An hour later they were on the way to London. Jenna chose to ride a horse rather than tolerate the jolting of the wooden-wheeled cart that held her finery. For the first half hour she was left alone as Lukas and Jeffrey, who rode with them to the edge of the estate, caught each other up on events. She heard their conversation, but they didn't seem to think she'd be interested, so she merely listened.

"How goes the king's plan for England?" Jeffrey asked.

"He's given lands to his allies, as you know, which doesn't endear him to the old nobility, but many are the estates of lords killed in the recent struggles. He will keep the shire courts and the hundred courts, so justice will continue as it has for many years. He also promised to uphold your ancient laws and keep the militia as well as the *fyrd*, the king's army."

"The common people will see little difference in their lives, then." Jeffrey sounded hopeful, and his horse jingled its harness as if in agreement.

"The two hundred Norman, Flemish, and French troops who fought for William are named tenants-in-chief. We may divide our lands among the knights, who will serve us but owe loyalty to the king."

"Again, not so different from the old system."

"William hopes to win the people with strong organization and laws that protect everyone. However, he's building castles in crucial places to prevent future rebellions and invasions."

"We would certainly benefit from fewer invasions," Jeffrey said with what Jenna imagined was a wry expression. It was a measure of the friendship that had arisen between them that he could discuss such topics with the man who had displaced him.

When Jeffrey turned back, wishing them a pleasant journey, Lukas clicked his tongue and spurred his horse forward. "Are you well, Jenna?" The use of her name, not the impersonal *wife,* was a good sign, and she nodded. "Shall we call a truce for the duration of our trip? It will be more pleasant for us both."

In truth, she'd been feeling nervous and alone. Only six months from the hills of Scotland, she'd take her place as the wife of a favored knight at the court of the king with no one to advise her. At least Lukas could tell her when to curtsey and to whom. "Very well."

They rode on in silence until Lukas said, "Jeffrey tells me

he and Tessa began as enemies and ended as husband and wife."

"Yes."

"Just as we did."

Despite her agreement to be civil, Jenna corrected him. "The difference is that Tessa chose to wed Jeffrey. No king ordered them to marry."

"But she didn't love him on first sight."

"Well, no."

"Then there is hope for us." Giving Jenna an impish smile, Lukas spurred his horse forward, leaving her confused and a little angry. Did he want her or not? And how dare he speak of hope for their marriage when by now he probably had his paramour hidden away in some house where he might visit her?

London was abuzz with preparation for the coronation ceremonies, and Jenna had to remind herself not to stare like a bumpkin at the many colorful platforms, artworks, and tributes on display. Despite the cold, the city rang with voices calling out in French, English, and several other languages Jenna didn't recognize.

Lukas had rented a house staffed with more servants than she knew what to do with, but it didn't matter. They were overseen by a tight-lipped Frenchwoman who made few concessions to her employers' dignity. Her brusque manner hinted that neither a Norman nor a Scot sat high in her estimation, but she was required to tolerate them, so she would.

Jenna was pleased to learn that Matilda was in London and wanted to see her. She rose a step in her housekeeper Mistress John's eyes when she announced the soon-to-be-crowned queen of England had invited her to visit. The woman herself arranged Jenna's hair for their meeting, scrutinizing every inch of her costume before allowing her to set out. Adding a sprig of lavender at the waist of Jenna's dress, she gave her a brief kiss. "For luck, Madame."

Matilda met Jenna in the great hall of the palace, rising to embrace her with great affection. In her ear she whispered, "It's good to see a friendly face. I'm stuck here with these resentful, cow-eyed women all day."

A fire blazed in the center of the hall, warming somewhat the winter's chill. Around it sat a dozen or so ladies wearing fine clothes in multiple layers and disdainful expressions. "This is Lady Ladbroke, wife of the king's great friend. She is friend to me as well. Jenna, come and meet the ladies of the court."

As she was introduced, Jenna saw jealousy, resentment, and distrust on many faces. Recalling Tessa's advice, she said as little as possible and smiled as much as possible. "They might think you a fool," Tessa had advised, "but it's better than saying the wrong thing and removing all doubt."

As she sat down, the woman on her right asked with a prune-like expression, "You are a Scot?"

Jenna's chin lifted involuntarily. "I am."

A second woman said, "How fortunate you were to be chosen by a man such as Lukas Ladbroke."

"Yes," Jenna replied. "Most fortunate."

A third woman leaned toward her. "Have you any news to give us?"

Jenna was confused. "News?"

They all leaned in, even Matilda. "It's been two months. Is there sign of a child?"

Jenna blushed furiously. Of course. Everyone awaited children from the marriages between the two former enemies, a sign that God had blessed the union. "No," she said, feeling her face burn. "Not yet."

A little sigh escaped the circle. It might have been disappointment, but no doubt some of them hoped to be the first to conceive the child who would symbolize Anglo-Norman unity. Jenna had a head start but nothing to show for it. If they only knew how little she had! No child, and not even a husband in the true sense of the word.

That evening she and Lukas attended a celebration. "Everyone wants a look at you," he commented.

"Why?"

"In the first place, we're the chosen couple. In the second place, you're quite lovely. They say you bewitched me, so short was our courtship."

"Some know it was the king's will that joined us."

"William likes the romance of it and claims I proposed the plan to him. Have you heard the story of his courtship of Matilda?"

"No."

"Apparently, when William's agents first approached her, she told them a descendant of Alfred the Great would never give herself to the bastard son of a Norman duke. Since he's ever sensitive to comments on his legitimacy, William rode to Bruges, found Matilda on the way to church, dragged her by her braids off the horse she rode, and argued in the strongest terms that she was throwing away a great opportunity."

"That's cruel!"

Lukas shrugged. "She agreed to the marriage."

Jenna waved disdainfully. "I don't believe a word of it."

Looking at the hand that had touched him for a moment, Lukas finally admitted, "I don't either, but it demonstrates William's determination when he sets his mind to something."

"He can order people to do his bidding," Jenna said, "but he can't force them to like it."

His eyes turned sad. "No. Love comes of its own will."

Jenna felt as if an invisible cord pulled her toward him, but she resisted it. Lukas was probably wishing he'd been allowed to marry the woman he loved, not the one chosen for him.

Taking a step back as if to break the imaginary cord Jenna asked, "You spy for William. You marry where he says. How did a Norman gain such power over a Viking?"

His eyes turned aside as he recalled the past. "I have told you my Norwegian mother married a Norman knight. My father traveled throughout Europe, and Mother remained in Norway, in her brother Svenn's home. When she died I was ten. My father came to Norway and took me with him to Normandy, where he'd become one of Duke William's men." Lukas smiled. "William was only a few years older than I, but his reign had been plagued with upheaval, and he depended on men like my father to help him gain control."

"So you became a Norman?"

"Yes. I was sad to leave—my Norwegian family, but I soon made friends among the Normans, and William took note of my skills in finding things: information, places, and people."

"I guessed from the first you were skilled at such things."

"I think as my quarry thinks, and it usually pays." He

smiled. "I'd have let you go that first night, but you blundered directly into Bjorn's path." With a frown he began a question. "How did you—?"

"You were telling me your history, husband," she said to forestall questions of how she got from the pool to the pathway without him seeing. "You missed your home in Norway. Is that why you returned?"

Lukas sighed. "William wanted an alliance, and he thought my uncle might advise the Norwegian king to accept it. My uncle had died, and Leif had inherited. With the deaths of his wife and sons, he was almost beyond reason." Lukas added with a shiver, "And all too susceptible to Bjorn's influence."

"Is Bjorn a relative?"

Lukas shook his head. "Merely another child Svenn took in, having no children of his own."

"And you have no other family?"

Lukas turned to her as if judging her mood. "A half-sister. I went to Norway partly to see if she still lived."

"And did you find her?"

"Yes."

"And she is well?"

"When last we met, yes." Something flashed in his eyes. "Jenna, I didn't know what Leif intended." He grasped her hand. "When I saw Bjorn's interest in you, I had to keep you with me. Even as a boy Bjorn enjoyed hurting people, especially women. As I told you that first night, I'd have found a way to help you escape once we reached Glamis and he could no longer spare the time to recapture you."

Jenna had never told Lukas it was Jessie he'd first met.

Since he kept secrets from her, it made her feel a little better to have one of her own. Would it have made a difference in their marriage if she'd heard all this that night? Would she have believed him?

A servant entered with a note. When he'd read it Lukas said, "Tell the boy to wait. I'll send a return message."

"What is it?"

"Nothing you need be concerned with." His eyes searched the room for writing materials but found none. "Shall we meet at the front door in an hour?"

"I'll be ready."

Lukas gestured for her to precede him as they left the room. The note lay on the table. A few steps down the hall, Jenna turned into a side room. Once Lukas was gone, she hurried back to the room they'd just left. Scanning the note she read, *Still no word of the woman. We continue our search, knowing the importance you place on this task.*

Jenna took special care with her toilette that evening, choosing a dress of deep red with a squared neckline that exposed a wide expanse of her white bosom. Back at Brixton when Tessa took it from storage and held it up, Jenna had pronounced it too daring. "Fill in the front with fabric, then" Tessa had advised. "We must use what we have that will fit you."

Jenna decided no scarf was necessary. She wanted a dress that got attention, and this one suited her coloring and her mood. The skirt draped nicely, the fabric was soft as rabbit's fur, and the long sleeves made an elegant effect. Leaving her thick, dark curls loose, she added a wispy veil and a simple gold torc as decoration. The maid said she was "most wondrous fair." Mistress Johns pursed her lips, perhaps approving, perhaps shocked. She went down early, in order to be waiting when Lukas came down the stairs.

He looked handsome in black leggings and a gray *tunica*, but he seemed preoccupied until he glanced into the entryway and saw Jenna standing there. He paused, his gaze taking in her costume, her face, and the smile she hoped was both brave and enticing. It took a moment before he stopped staring and came down to join her. Silence screamed between them for a few seconds before she said softly. "I am ready."

Lukas managed a thin smile. "In truth, you are." With that he offered his arm, and they moved forward together to where an openly admiring manservant opened the door to let them out.

The party was at the home of an elderly knight, one of William's closest friends. He welcomed Lukas with a clap on the back and leered at Jenna like a rabid hound. "Your lady wife is a lovely thing, Ladbroke."

Lukas stepped between Jenna and their host. "Well met, Rufus. Now we must locate your own lovely wife and make our greetings." Taking Jenna's arm, he led her away as the man's gaze followed hungrily. "Was it wise to dress so bewitchingly, wife? I'll have to fight off the males, and the females will despise you on sight."

Something in Lukas' grumbling tone pleased Jenna, but she kept her tone even. "I only meant to show your friends you haven't made a bad bargain."

His brow twitched—was it with humor? "Then you've made the point well. Shall I get you some wine? Rufus has sent for a fine selection from Normandy, and I think you'll like the sweetness of it."

The rest of the evening was an embarrassment. Jenna spoke with at least a dozen men whose gaze seldom rose to her face. Some were overt and some subtle, but most let her know that if she found Lukas unsuitable in any way, they'd be glad to comfort her.

Was it so obvious theirs was no love match? Jenna retreated into frosty politeness, but the barely concealed lust of several of the men shocked her. Judging from the set of Lukas' jaw, he was irritated.

That was good, wasn't it? Since he sought his lover all over England, he could at least have in the back of his mind the fear his wife might cuckold him in his absence. Not that she would, but it was satisfying to see him consider the prospect.

In the weeks that followed, Jenna and Lukas settled into an odd sort of companionship. Lukas went out of his way to be pleasant, though he never overstepped the boundary between them. Jenna had few people to talk to, since Matilda and her women were busy with coronation plans. The Saxon ladies showed little interest in her as they worked to ingratiate themselves with their Norman conquerors. Since Mistress Johns resented any interference with her routines, Jenna had nothing to do but attend parties. For one unused to being purposeless, the leisurely days began to pall.

She found herself arranging meetings with her husband each morning, apparently accidental, in hopes he'd include her in his activities. As soon as Lukas stirred in his sleeping chamber, she hurried to get downstairs before he left the house. Some days he made no invitation, but other times he seemed pleased to have her company. They toured London, finding its secrets together. They visited shops, explored winding alleys, and stopped at several churches, one with a priest who reminded her of Dominic.

The shops of London contained an amazing array of items, and Lukas seemed to enjoy finding new things to show her each time they went out. Sometimes black looks betrayed a proprietor's dislike of the Norman invaders, but for most business people, a sale was a sale. Lukas offered to buy Jenna things, but she was more likely to choose something to take home to her sister or one of the children. Finally he said in exasperation, "I would buy a gift for you, Jenna, not another bolt of cloth to be carted home to Brixton."

"So I should return to my sister draped in finery, reminding her I've taken her place as lady of the manor?" she said sharply. "You misjudge me, husband." That trip was abruptly shortened, and Lukas didn't ask her to accompany him the next day.

Toward the end of her stay, Jenna saw the hired searcher leaving the house. Lukas was distracted at the dinner they attended that evening, and she had to flirt outrageously with several men before he noticed and issued a terse command that they return home.

As they made their way he asked, "You find the company of Mark de Rhiems pleasant?"

Truthfully, Jenna couldn't have said which one was de Rhiems, but she liked the edge in Lukas' tone. "He's very entertaining."

After a second long silence he said, "I must leave London for a few days. Will you stay at the house, or shall I ask Matilda if you might visit her until I return?"

She sensed the question was important but didn't understand why. "The house, I think. Matilda needs no extra guests with the coronation only five days hence."

He said no more, and Jenna tried to decide what he was thinking. Did staying in the house mean she was happy there, or did he think she'd take the opportunity to invite lovers into her bed? Not with Mistress Johns on guard, even if she'd wanted to do so. The man she wanted walked beside her, but things in their past had destroyed any hope they would ever be lovers. It seemed now and probably forever, they were only man and wife.

The coronation was a solemn affair, and Jenna had a clear view, being both Matilda's friend and half of William's shining example of future unity.

Robed and wearing his crown, William was led into the church by two bishops, each of whom held him by the hand. Once inside, the king removed his crown and knelt at the altar while the notes of the "Te Deum" echoed across the church like angel voices. After the hymn of praise, the bishops helped the king to his feet. William then took his coronation oath, answering questions put to him by the archbishop. He promised in a clear voice to uphold common law, protect his people, and practice equity and mercy in all things. The archbishop offered prayers for the king and anointed him as a second hymn was sung. Finally, he placed a ring on William's finger, girded him with a sword, put the crown on his head once more, and pronounced a blessing. William was England's anointed king and God's representative on earth for the people.

A week after the ceremony, Jenna and Lukas arrived home at Brixton. Tessa waddled out to greet them, one hand resting on her belly in a pose common to expectant mothers. "You must tell us about your trip at supper," she said, hugging first Jenna then Lukas.

"My wife will be glad to," he replied, kissing her cheek. "My journey continues."

Jenna tried to hide her surprise. They'd become closer in some ways, but it seemed she still didn't share her husband's confidences. That was because another woman did.

Lukas stayed away much of the winter. Jenna busied her

hands with household tasks, but her mind refused to stay at the manor. She pictured Lukas' mistress a dozen different ways. Was she dark-haired and dark-eyed, or was she the type he was used to, fair and rosy-cheeked? Did she raise an arching eyebrow when they met or smile behind a coy hand? *Stop it,* she scolded herself. *Why do you care what he does, as long as Tessa can remain in her home?*

From time to time they received news from London. William's ambitious castle-building project was already underway, and motte-and-bailey structures, mounds of earth topped with a keep and surrounded by a strong wooden fence, were constructed all over the kingdom. Later he intended to convert them to stone fortresses like the ones in Europe, creating even stronger defenses. He also planned an abbey on the site of his defeat of the English. Remembering Lukas' view that the Normans shouldn't act like conquerors, Jenna wondered if calling it Battle Abbey was a wise idea on William's part.

In March, Lukas came home to confer with Jeffrey on the use of the land. The two worked companionably together, traversing the fields and pointing things out to each other. "Doesn't it bother Jeffrey that Lukas leaves him to do everything while he disappears for weeks at a time?" Jenna fumed. "He's no help on the estate."

Tessa sat in a comfortable chair close to the fire, resting her slightly swollen feet. "I think he's embarrassed at being Jeffrey's overlord. His absence lets Jeffrey act the part of master."

"Still, he could take more interest in things here."

"Like his wife?" Jenna turned to find her sister's gaze on her, and she blushed. "Things are not as they should be between you two. Is there something I can do to help?"

"It will take time, that's all," Jenna said, attempting a

casual tone. "We didn't choose this path, and we aren't yet able to agree on how to travel it."

"It will come," Tessa said. "I have seen you together, and there is a spark between you that will someday start a flame."

Jenna nodded, unwilling to admit to Tessa that Lukas had a lover, someone he'd have married had William not interfered. She knew she could fall in love with her husband if she let herself, but another woman had a prior claim on Lukas' heart. Jenna was unwilling to accept only part of him.

Chapter Thirty-four

Jessie

"Tell me more about your young man," Aldis said one evening as she and Jessie listened to the wind howl outside. Winter was upon them in earnest, and she spent most of the time in a state near hibernation, lying or sitting very still and staring into the fire. Though she brooded on her sadness at times, she never let it lead to anger or tears. To Jessie she was a good companion, and Struan considered her a goddess. This was the first time she'd asked directly about events between their first meeting and their second.

"Alfred isn't mine," Jessie replied, as she always did. "He only let me travel with him to keep me safe."

Jessie and Aldis often talked about the past, since they no longer had reason to keep secrets from each other. She enjoyed reliving her time with Alfred, singing for crowds of people and seeing the enjoyment on their faces. As she talked about the feeling of accomplishment performing gave, Aldis murmured agreement. "I know what you mean. All your life you're pitied, but suddenly you can make a contribution."

"That's it," Jessie said, seeing the similarity between entertaining folk and enlightening them. When she revealed the magic of the bones, Aldis wasn't the woman who couldn't stand alone. She was the voice of the gods. It must have been a source of great pride for her to do things that made people gasp in wonder.

Aldis returned to the topic of Alfred. "You are fond of this young man."

Jessie knew the vitki understood impossible love. "He is the man I'd choose, were I one who had a choice."

"Those who have such choices are indeed fortunate."

"Have you always been in love with Leif?"

Aldis showed no surprise at the question. "I think so. When we were children and I was learning to accept being a prisoner of this helpless body, I watched Leif and admired him. He was strong physically, yet so sad, so silent. I wanted to comfort him, but what could I do?"

Jessie looked up from darning a hole in her stocking in a spot where her boot rubbed. "Perhaps there is no comfort when the pain is so deep."

Aldis smiled wistfully. "Leif was always kind to me, though I am only half a woman."

"No," Jessie corrected. "You are a whole woman who happens to have an infirm body."

Aldis didn't argue, though her expression said she disagreed. "Leif treated me well, as did Lukas."

"But Lukas left Norway."

"I missed him very much. Seeing my loneliness, Leif tried to comfort me. That was when I began imagining impossible things."

Jessie had imagined those same impossibilities. "That you and he would marry."

"It was only a dream, a wish to escape pain, my abnormality, and the cruelty of others."

"You were mistreated?"

Aldis' face set in hard lines. "There are those whose cruelty is so subtle that only the victim knows of it."

Jessie thought about who would abuse a girl already plagued with such misery, and the answer came easily to mind. "Bjorn?"

Aldis' eyes answered the question before her words did. "Beautiful on the outside but black at heart. If he could find me alone, without Lukas or Leif to defend me…" Her voice trailed off.

"How did he come to be in your uncle's household?"

"Bjorn is the son of Svenn's boat-builder, and his mother was a thrall. Bjorn was born free, but he hated being the son of a slave. He resented Leif and Lukas, and when Lukas left Norway, he tried to move into his place. He ordered me to urge Svenn to adopt him, though Svenn had already settled on Leif as his heir." She touched a scar on her left arm. "He was very angry when I refused."

"Did no one else notice Bjorn's ugly temperament?"

"I'm sure the slaves did, especially the young women. My uncle grew more and more forgetful due to a blow he took in battle that cleaved his helm in two. After Lukas left, he made Leif his steward and paid little mind to affairs in the house." She paused as if hesitant to say more but then went on. "It was with great difficulty that I persuaded him not to give me to Bjorn in marriage."

"Bjorn wanted to wed you?"

Aldis' smile was bitter. "He told my uncle he'd take care of me, but I knew he wanted half of Svenn's lands. When I pleaded with my uncle to let me remain as I was, he refused Bjorn's request."

Jessie shuddered. "Bjorn was angry, I suppose."

"I paid in small ways every day." Staring into the fire, Aldis said, "It was Bjorn who suggested I come with them to Scotland. I suppose he hoped the trip would kill me and Leif would have no one but him for counsel." She huffed in disgust. "He has what he wanted, for Leif believes now that I worked against him from the start."

"I'm sorry," Jessie said. "I was pitied, but Jenna never let anyone mistreat me." She chuckled. "In fact, she seldom let anyone outside our family near me, so I can't say if they'd have been cruel or not."

"You miss her very much."

"I do." And yet..." Aldis waited, apparently hearing the hesitation in her voice. "I've learned to survive on my own. A few months ago, I couldn't have imagined myself going anywhere. Now I've traveled the Highlands and met many people, some good, some bad. And you and I manage well here, do we not? We have few comforts, but neither do we suffer."

"I feel blessed to have met you, despite the circumstances. Leif would have killed me if you and Father Dominic hadn't helped me escape him."

That brought a frown to Jessie's face. "I'm sorry Leif turned against you. Alfred doesn't love me, but if he wanted me dead..." Her voice trailed off.

"It isn't all Leif's fault. I started him on this mad quest, and Bjorn encouraged it." She swallowed hard. "The gods punish us for such things."

Though Aldis excused Leif's behavior, Jessie found it hard to do. "Does he know you love him?"

"No." Aldis' smile was brave. "When he came to tell me he would marry Cella, I expressed joy even as my heart broke." She touched her eye, drying a tear that had formed. "At the birth of his children, I made blessings for them, wishing with all my being they'd been mine. And when they died, I grieved for them all."

Laying a piece of wood on the fire, Aldis continued. "Leif asked me to tell him what he'd done to anger the gods. When I looked at the signs, I told him not what I saw, but what I wanted. I said he must turn his mind to those who love him and see they were not neglected." Her eyes brimmed with tears. "I thought he'd see me and the devotion he'd missed all these years."

"But he interpreted the message differently."

"Leif took it to mean he should avenge the murder of his Scots family. That is what brought us to this place." Aldis touched her heart. "Jessie, I'm so sorry for my part in this evil."

"You've done what good you could in the midst of a great wrong."

"I thought I could soften Leif, change his plan, but I couldn't." Her expression hardened again. "Bjorn was always there to pour poison into his ear."

"What does Bjorn hope to gain in all this?"

"Now that Leif has no sons, he has named Bjorn his heir. With the madness upon him, he barely eats, and his strength wanes a little each day. Bjorn only has to wait, and he can return to Norway and take over Leif's lands and his wealth."

Jessie shivered. "I knew from the first he was evil. In his eyes is the desire to hurt."

Aldis turned back to watching the flames. "For Bjorn, hurting others is the highest art."

Chapter Thirty-five

Jenna

"I am ordered to Scotland, Jenna. Would you like to accompany me?" Lukas watched her, humor lighting his eyes. Home! Of course she wanted to go.

"How? When? Where?" Questions burst from her lips before she could stop them and her feet thumped on the wooden floor in a little dance of joy.

"I will tell if you'll let me," he said with a chuckle. "William wants me to meet with King Malcolm and some of the thanes."

"So you won't be—" She hesitated, unsure she could keep her opinions to herself if Lukas was sent to scout the possibilities of an invasion of her people.

Lukas raised a hand. "I'm not sent to spy. William has too much to do in England. I'm to let the Scots know we're no threat to their way of life." With a sidewise glance he added, "I thought you might visit your sisters in the Cairngorms while I conduct some business I have in the area."

"I'd like that very much." She hesitated again. "Will you come with me?"

He raised a brow. "I'll have much to occupy my time, and isn't it best if you don't bring your Viking husband home to the macFindlaech clan-hold with you?"

"Well, if you'll be busy, I can go alone," she said, neither confirming nor denying his last statement.

Did Lukas have his own reasons for wanting to go to Scotland? It was useless to wonder. It was enough she would see Meg and all those dear to her.

"I shall be quite jealous," Tessa said jokingly when they told her of the proposed trip, "but I have plenty to do here." She glanced lovingly at her newest child, sleeping peacefully in his cradle beside her. Just three weeks old, he'd arrived as the days warmed and the rains began their annual reawakening of the earth.

It was still raining a week later when Lukas and Jenna embarked for Scotland. The trip was miserable, and they arrived in Scotland with every item of clothing they owned damp and mildewed. Lukas kept his even-tempered outlook, and Jenna remained cheerful in anticipation of seeing home. He said no more about his reasons for choosing to stay in Glamis, far from King Malcolm's court in Scone. Jenna hoped it meant he wanted her to see her family again at the first opportunity. She didn't let herself think about what other reason he might have.

Chapter Thirty-six

Jessie

As winter began to loosen its hold on the land, Jessie realized it had been some time since Father Dominic visited. She counted the tick marks she'd scratched on the stone wall in order to apportion their food. "It's been a fortnight." She examined their stores anxiously. Spring was coming, but it would be a while before the land yielded anything edible.

"He'll come today," Aldis said. "Tomorrow at the latest."

But the priest didn't come, and their food supply dwindled. Struan accepted life as it came each day without complaint, and he knew nothing of Dominic's schedule. His mother grew less and less aware of anything as her life leached into the floor where she lay. Jessie did what she could for her with what Meg had taught her of physic, but they all knew the death angel waited in their room, stepping closer each day.

"Will you go to Glamis and buy food?" Jessie asked.

Struan's eyes widened with fear. "I dinna go there, lady. They're feared o' my face, and t' say truth, I like not theirs, neither." She understood his reluctance, but it was clear he didn't understand their predicament.

"That's all right. I'll go." Aldis' brows rose, but Jessie's glance signaled silence. When Struan was gone, she said, "What else can we do, Aldis? We need food, and I'll see what's happened to Father Dominic."

Aldis' eyes revealed worry. "You must take care."

"Depend on it," Jessie replied grimly. "I have no desire to meet your old friends—any of them."

With her hooded cloak covering her hair and shadowing her face, Jessie entered Glamis. She'd used tricks learned from Alfred's friend Catherine, drawing lines between her brows and along the sides of her mouth with half-burnt sticks to simulate age. She'd also covered her teeth with pine pitch so her smile was "a great deal less beautiful," as Aldis put it.

Her first stop was the church, but it was empty. She went on to a shop where she traded one of Aldis' gold earrings for the supplies they needed. If Father Dominic were sick or injured, they'd have to live on what she and Foot could carry back with them.

Laden with dried fruit, oat flour, and other necessities, she returned to the church. There was still no one there; in fact, the air of emptiness made her shiver. Who'd know where the priest might be?

Catherine. Stowing the supplies and her pony in the church's outbuilding, Jessie went to the inn.

It might be a mistake, she told herself as she walked. Without Alfred present, Catherine might betray her and collect the gold Bjorn offered. Her gain would be double: the money itself and the chance to dispose of a rival for Alfred's affections.

As Jessie stood outside the inn, considering her options, the door opened with a shuddering scrape and a man came out. She turned aside, sensing a familiarity about him that signaled danger. Peeping out from under her hood, she affirmed her first impression. The man was a Viking. Hugging the wall of the inn, she prayed he wouldn't look in her direction.

Stopping on the street, the Viking called to a boy who staggered under the weight of a sack almost as large as he was. "Have you seen a woman who cannot walk, lad? She rides about on a shield borne by four blond men." The child looked at him as if he didn't understand. "She was with some Northmen, but she remained behind when they left." The boy still stared, apparently afraid to speak to one so grand. After a moment the man muttered, "Never mind. I'll find her."

He walked away, and Jessie let out the breath she'd been holding. No time to speak to Catherine. She had to leave Glamis before the Viking saw her.

As she hurried away, Jessie tried to remember the Northman's name. She recalled that he had showed her some kindness, and briefly she wondered if he might have come to help Aldis. She couldn't take the chance. She and Aldis had survived with only each other this far. It was best if they continued that way.

Chapter Thirty-seven

Jenna

When they arrived in Glamis, Lukas left Jenna on the dock with their baggage while he went to find lodging. He returned to report, "There's an inn with three rooms. I took them all."

The inn he found was a tavern with sleeping quarters in a half-loft, sure to be both smoky and noisy. The smell of food made up for that, since the aromas promised a delicious meal. As they entered, the proprietress frowned at Jenna. "Is it you, then?"

"The lady is my wife." At Lukas' formal tone, the woman recovered her manners.

"I beg pardon, sir. She looks very much like someone I once knew." Pointing to a ladder that served as a staircase she said, "The upper story is yours alone, as you ordered. Call for Catherine if there is aught you need. Supper is almost ready, and it's best you eat it before the crowd comes in. Your lady will not enjoy the rough company."

Jenna almost said she was not above such folk, but she realized with chagrin that she now looked like a lady with her fine gown, maid, and pile of luggage.

"Thank you, Catherine," Lukas said. As they ascended the stairs, he whispered, "Is she someone you know?"

"No." Turning back, she saw that Catherine was staring after her, a puzzled frown on her pretty face.

Lukas chuckled as she reached the loft. "Someone who looks like you has made an impression."

Someone who looked like her? Jenna needed to have a word alone with Catherine.

Their baggage settled, they went down to supper, a stew of mutton and vegetables that rose above ordinary inn fare. Catherine also cut them each a generous slice of crusty oat bread recently taken from the brick oven at the back of the room.

Lukas complimented Catherine's cooking so nicely that she warmed to them and even smiled once. When he went outside to arrange transport for the next day, Jenna sent her maid upstairs. Alone with Catherine she said, "You said I look like someone you knew."

"So like it is uncanny."

"Please, tell me her name."

Catherine thought about it then shook her head. "If I ever heard it, I've forgotten. She stayed for a time in my storeroom, hiding."

"Hiding?"

"From them Vikings. The one with white hair and the handsome one." She added almost under her breath. "Though he's not so handsome now."

"And you helped this woman?"

Catherine's expression soured, and she took up a cloth and began wiping the table clean of crumbs and spills. "A friend asked me to. Alfred."

That meant nothing to Jenna. "Where is she now?"

"They left together." The terse comment hinted that had made her unhappy.

"And you have had no word of them since?"

"None." Catherine tossed the cloth into a bucket, splashing water onto the hearth, where it hissed into steam. "They dare not come back here, because the Vikings have returned."

"They're here?"

"At Fife, guests of Thane Ross." Catherine eyed Jenna speculatively. "Is she kin to you?"

"I think so, and I would give much to know if she is well."

The innkeeper sighed. "The priest might have told you something, but he's dead."

"Father Dominic? Dead?"

"You knew him?"

Jenna recalled his kind face. "He helped me once."

"He was at the altar. 'Tis said his heart give out."

Crossing herself, Jenna said a brief prayer. "Does anyone else in Glamis know where my sister went?"

"I doubt it. The Northmen seek them everywhere."

"The Northmen—Tell me what you know of them."

Catherine took up a spoon and stirred the pot hanging over the fire. "There are two of them. Bjorn was once handsome, but he lost an eye in a terrible battle in some foreign land. His companion looks like he's already dead, but it's his mind that's sick, not his body."

"Still, they keep searching?"

"I've not seen men so determined ere now." She shuddered. "And Bjorn is not a man I'd want after me."

Jenna couldn't keep from looking around to assure herself that the man wasn't coming in the door at that moment. "When did you see him last?"

"Four or five days back." She gave Jenna an appraising

look. "I'd be careful, were I you. He might mistake you for her, as I did."

Jenna heard steps outside and looked up to see Lukas approaching. "It would make no difference to Bjorn which of us he caught. One sister is as good as another for his purposes."

Once they were upstairs and alone, Jenna told Lukas what she'd learned, leaving out references to Jessie. "We're in danger here. Leif wants me dead, and he knows by now you're more Norman than Northman."

"I'll send you to your family in the morning," he said. "With an escort, you'll reach the clan-hold safely."

"Where are you going?"

"There is something I must do."

Her safety was secondary to the "something" he had to do. Did that mean the woman he sought was here, in Scotland? Is that why he'd been unable to find her all these months? Anger flared, and Jenna's chest tightened. "As you say, husband."

"Stay with your folk until I send word. All will be well."

"Yes."

"Jenna."

Distracted by her thoughts, she didn't turn to look at him. "Hmm?"

"Jenna." Something in his voice got her attention. "You will come when I send for you?"

It was both a question and a plea.

Until that moment, she hadn't realized it was a matter of trust for him to let her return to her family. She might tell them everything, appeal to their pride, and refuse to return to England. They were outside William's sphere now, and she had the power to resist him and re-take her freedom.

Oddly, she'd never considered it. She belonged with Lukas. Though they weren't really husband and wife, she'd return to England with him. If her head didn't understand why, her heart did.

"Lukas, I'll come back. I promise." Her heart warmed at the smile that brought to his lips.

They set out midmorning, after the fog had dissipated and the air warmed somewhat. As they approached the bridge, Jenna smiled to herself, thinking those wanting Bjorn's reward would hardly see her as the mountain girl he sought.

Lukas accompanied her for a way then turned northward, leaving her in the care of her maid Lilly and two stout Scots with grim faces and thick cudgels. Though she felt tempted to offer a tender goodbye, Lukas had given no hint of what his business would be in her absence. Secrets. Always secrets! She lifted a casual hand in farewell and turned her back to him, looking up at the mountain she'd once called home.

They climbed for several hours, and Jenna reveled in the landscape. The trees, the rocks, even the mosses that cushioned her steps were familiar. Her escort, a stern pair of Scots, made no conversation. Her maid, used to gentle English hills, kept looking backward, terrified of the height they scaled. Jenna didn't mind the tightness in her calves. It was good to feel Scottish earth beneath her feet, no matter how steeply it tilted.

Just before the sun reached its zenith, they saw a figure descending the path. At first he was just a shape, but as he came closer, Jenna stopped in surprise.

"You!" It was the gleeman she'd last seen the night of her sister's abduction.

"Jenna!" He hurried to her, his expression anxious. "Do you know where Jessie is?"

"No. I hoped she might have returned home by now."

"I've been there." He glanced up the hillside. "They've neither seen nor heard from her." The gleeman's manner was almost frantic. "When she wasn't there I told myself she'd gone to England to find you." His eyes searched the hills. "Where else could she be?"

"Tell me what you know," Jenna ordered. "Then we can decide what to do next."

It took some time for the gleeman, whose name was Alfred, to tell his story. She couldn't help but smile at his sing-song style, suited to long nights in a castle hall.

"You're the man the woman at the inn spoke of, the one who took Jessie away?"

Alfred blushed. "I made a vow to treat her with respect at all times, and I kept it."

Despite that, Jenna sensed Alfred cared for her sister. In fact, he cared very much.

Alfred ended with his decision to send Jessie home as winter approached. "I didn't tell her I was going on without her because I couldn't bear to," he said. "I thought she'd be safe at home, that she'd marry and forget me." His voice rose. "But she's disappeared!"

Jenna was amazed. Her sister had set out alone, made difficult decisions, and become an accomplished and admired entertainer. None of that sounded like a girl in need of protection, though Jenna thought Alfred longed to do just that.

She told him a brief version of her own story, ending with the fact that she was married. "Lukas was with the Vikings that night, but he's not like the rest of them."

"I must take you at your word," Alfred said with a humorless smile. "I remember only Bjorn and Leif, since I've had much to do with them since."

Jenna's expression turned thoughtful. "If I accompany you back to Glamis, we can look for Jessie together. Since you hold more sway with a certain innkeeper than I do, she might tell you things she didn't tell me."

To get them out of her way, Jenna sent her escort and her maid on up the mountain. The maid was horrified at the idea of facing a clan of wild Scots alone, but Jenna explained she could distribute the gifts they'd brought along, which would make her a very popular visitor. The two men Lukas had hired as her escort took a little more convincing, but she argued he'd hired them to guard the luggage, not his wife. Not fully understanding the situation, they finally continued up the path, defending sweets, fabric, and hair ribbons.

As they made their way back down the mountain, Alfred explained he'd found a place where the river could be crossed in secret. "We can avoid the sentries, but the water is deep and very cold."

Jenna thought of the night she'd dived into the icy waters of the mountain pool to escape Lukas. "If you can do it, I can."

The spot was rocky, the river fast-flowing. Jenna's skirts immediately pulled at her, tugging her downstream. Using her hands, she fought to keep moving toward the opposite bank. When the rushing water deepened in the middle and her feet could no longer touch bottom, Jenna feared she'd be swept downstream, but Alfred gave her a strong push forward. Soon she found a foothold again and went on.

Daylight was fading as they waded from the frigid water. Alfred built a fire using materials from a pack he'd left hidden along the bank. They huddled over it, shivering.

"Your fine dress is ruined," he said.

"My husband will buy me another," she replied through chattering teeth.

Setting another twig on the fire he asked, "How did you come to marry the Viking who kidnapped you?"

Alfred seemed genuinely interested, and Jenna found herself confiding in him, even revealing her belief that Lukas had come to Scotland in search of a woman he loved. "He sought her in England but never found her. I suspect he found her here, since he wouldn't tell me where he was going today."

"And you know nothing of this woman?"

Jenna's voice quavered. "Only that he must love her well, to spend so much time in this search."

Alfred touched her arm. "I'm sorry, for I think you care for him."

"I tried to hate him for being a Viking, and for forcing me into marriage against my will, but in truth, none of it was his fault. He's kind to me despite my behavior toward him. He has become...dear to me."

Even to the sympathetic Alfred she didn't admit to the fire that kindled in her core when she and Lukas touched. Swallowing her tears she said, "He loved her before he met me. I must accept that."

"Then again, I'm sorry, for you deserve better." That was all there was to say, and they returned to their own thoughts, staring into the fire as their clothing slowly dried, tightening around them like bands of care.

The next morning Alfred spied out the situation at the inn and returned to where Jenna crouched along the village wall. "Your husband told the stableman he'd be gone overnight."

"This is our chance." Together they hurried to the inn, pulling their hoods around their faces. Catherine was alone except for one elderly customer dozing in a sunlit corner. "Well, well," she said when Alfred pulled back his hood. "You've traded sisters, then?"

"I need to find Jessie, Catherine."

Alfred's tone was so earnest that her face softened. "I told the lady here everything I know."

"Wait for me." Leaving Alfred with Catherine, Jenna returned to the room she and Lukas occupied. Pulling his bag out from under the bed, she did a quick search. At the bottom was a letter in a hand strange to her, but she recognized the signature at the bottom. After scanning the letter, she hurried downstairs. "My husband has a letter from Father Dominic."

Alfred rubbed his jaw. "That's what brought him here."

"The priest says a woman Lukas knows asked that he write to tell him she's hunted by two Vikings. Dominic found her a hiding place, but in the letter he urges Lukas to come as soon as he can." She turned to Catherine. "Where might the priest have hidden her?"

"All the hill cottages are occupied." Her brow cleared as another thought occurred to her. "Dominic often went up the high path to find herbs for his medicines." Catherine pointed to the mountain that rose behind the village. "At the top is the old castle, ruined now."

Jenna slapped the table smartly. "That's where she is." Handing Catherine a coin she asked, "Don't tell my husband I returned here. And thank you for your help."

Outside she said, "Alfred, we must find that old castle."

Alfred looked up the rugged path. "You think Jessie's up there?"

Jenna's mind was reeling. Could Lukas have been looking for her sister all this time? She'd thought he didn't know there were two of them, but—"I think my husband is looking for her, but we must find her first. I want—I need to know if Lukas and Jessie are lovers."

Alfred shook his head as if to argue but said instead, "We have a place to start. He doesn't."

Together they traced the little-used path Catherine had described. Even for those used to hills, the way was steep. Alfred was solicitous, asking often if Jenna needed to rest. She refused, eager to reach their destination. Somewhere inside she felt certain they would find her sister today.

When she found Jessie, would she also find Lukas' true love? She refused to think about that. She'd face that when it came, though it hurt in a place inside that she could not ignore.

"Jessie isn't the one," Alfred said suddenly.

They had stopped, both a little out of breath, and he turned to Jenna earnestly. "I know that's what you fear, but it isn't so." He touched his chest as he explained. "I knew in my heart Jessie would be mine if I but had the courage to ask. It's why I came back for her."

That might be true, Jenna thought, *but even if Jessie didn't pine for Lukas, he could still pine for her.*

A light rain began as they continued their uphill journey,

and Jenna pulled her cloak closer about her face and neck to try to stay dry. At midday they saw the castle ahead of them, its defenses fallen into uselessness. The stout palisades that had once surrounded it had crumbled, and they entered the courtyard without effort. The outbuildings were in shambles, some burned in a long-ago fire while others lacked doors or had caved-in roofs. The main building was solid, with no aesthetic appeal, built only for function.

Smoke rose from the center of the ruin, in what had been the keep. Someone had made a home there. Could it be her twin? As the question arose, the door opened and Jessie stepped out. Glancing at the sky, she disappeared behind the ruin.

Jenna looked at Alfred, noting the joyful expression on his face. He was smitten, that was clear. "It seems safe. Shall we let her know we're here?"

Alfred's expression turned anxious. "Perhaps you should go first."

Jenna thought a man who loved a woman should be more confident, but she said, "Very well. I'll call for you when I've spoken to her."

At the level spot where the ruin stood, Jenna followed her sister's path. Rounding the wall, she found Jessie and a young man standing beside a freshly-dug grave. She had her hand on his shoulder as they looked into the hole. Jenna waited, unwilling to interrupt the solemn moment.

Finally Jessie patted the man's shoulder and stepped back. Picking up a spade lodged in the soil from the hole, he began filling in the grave. Jessie turned away, and, squinting through the rain, saw Jenna standing near the castle wall. Next instant she was coming toward her, arms outstretched.

"Jenna! Jenna, Jenna!" Even in her joy Jenna noticed

Jessie moved more easily than she'd ever seen her. There was no pain on her face as she almost ran across the castle yard.

They collided at some speed, almost knocking themselves off their feet, but the joyful embrace kept them upright. Tears streamed down their cheeks as each cried, "I thought you were dead!"

The man with the shovel turned toward them. "This is a friend, Struan," Jessie said, giving Jenna a chance to adjust to his deformities. "His mother died last night."

"I'm sorry to hear it, Struan," Jenna said. "Jessie and I lost our parents too, so we know what a grief it is."

"I'd know ye're sisters," he replied, "for ye're very like." With that he returned to his task.

Jessie led Jenna away. "He's cared for her a long time. We'll leave him to do this last thing for her. When Father Dominic comes next, we'll—" She noticed Jenna's expression and asked, "What?"

"Dead," Jenna replied. "In his church, while he prayed."

Jessie's eyes filled with tears. "When the angels came, they knew where to find him."

Once Jessie had recovered from her grief a little, they moved away from Struan and shared their joy at finding each other. "I heard you were lost at sea," Jessie said.

"A lie told to cover our escape to France. We little knew you'd hear it in Scotland."

Jessie hugged her again. "I'm so glad it isn't true."

"We had a letter from Meg saying you were missing and feared dead. I told them it wasn't true, for I'd know it. Alfred and I have been looking everywhere for you."

"Alfred?"

Jenna grinned. Raising her voice, she called, "Come, Sir Minstrel, and greet my sister."

Alfred appeared in an instant, his eyes searching Jessie's face for a sign of her reaction. Jenna too, looked at her with interest, but Jessie's expression revealed nothing. "Alfred." Jenna sensed a change in her sister over the year they'd been apart. She was more confident, and her mood, which Jenna once could have read in a heartbeat, was covered as if she'd thrown a blanket over her feelings.

"I have much to tell you, Jessie," Alfred said.

"Then it seems I have much to hear."

Though puzzled by the cold exchange, Jenna focused on the matter at hand. "We must leave this place."

Alfred shook off his doubt. "We must get you to safety."

"I can't leave."

"Why not? The Vikings are determined to kill us all."

"Come inside." Turning, Jessie led the way.

The place was a shell, but Jessie went up a winding stair to a small room in the inner keep where a fire burned. Beside the fire pit, atop a mound of blankets, sat Aldis, pale and disheveled.

"Jenna, is it not?" she said with a smile. "And might you be Alfred, Jessie's minstrel?"

"Not mine," Jessie said, "but he is Alfred."

Aldis' brows rose sardonically. "Welcome to our home."

Aldis, Jenna thought. It's Aldis he's been searching for all these months. She recalled the tenderness they'd shown each other on the trail, the concern for each other's welfare. She'd assumed—stupidly, she saw now—that love couldn't bloom between a man and a woman so afflicted. But she'd been wrong. Lukas married her because the woman he loved couldn't be a true wife. Despite that, he'd come all the way to Scotland to find her.

Jenna shook off the sorrow that engulfed her. No reason to blame the vitki for her own pain, and no way to help Jessie without including Aldis. "We've come to take you away."

"I see." Aldis touched the plank floor lightly as if unsure she wanted to leave.

"Leif now includes Aldis in the count of those he blames for his ill luck," Jessie said. "Father Dominic suggested we might help each other."

"Leif was mad before," Aldis said sadly. "Now he is beyond madness."

"And Bjorn hunts us all," Alfred put in. "Pride will not allow him to let us live."

"I remember him," Jenna said. "An evil man if ever there was one."

"If we leave here, what will we do?" Jessie asked.

"We'll go to Brixton."

"But how?"

"My husband will take us." Glancing at Aldis Jenna added, "It's why he came to Scotland."

"Your husband?" Jessie asked, but Alfred interrupted.

"We must go. If we found you here, our enemies can, too." He was at the window, and he pushed aside the stretched hide. It scraped against the stone wall as he peered down the mountainside.

"He's right," Jenna said, "but how will Aldis travel?"

"Dominic borrowed a hay cart to bring her here, but he returned it." Jessie bit her lip. "We have a barrow, but it will never hold together on the rough path."

"Then you and Alfred must fetch the cart." Jenna took a ring Lukas had given her from her finger. "This will serve as payment." Taking one from another finger, she offered it to Jessie. "I kept this one for you."

"Father's ring! I thought it was gone forever!"

Jenna hugged her tightly. "And I feared I might never be able to return it. Now go with Alfred, and hurry."

Jessie nodded, though the glance she gave him signaled reluctance. He ignored the look, or at least appeared to, and announced he'd wait for her outside. When he was gone, Jessie fussed, making sure Aldis was comfortable. At the door she whispered to Jenna, "Her pain has grown worse over the winter, and traveling in the cart will be hard for her. We must do what we can to cushion the jarring she must endure."

Smoothing Jessie's tangled hair Jenna said, "You're fond of her."

"She is not so cold as she first appears," Jessie replied, "and her courage is admirable. I suppose I pity her as well, for which of us would trade places with her?"

"Not I," Jenna admitted, "but to serve a man like Leif?"

"Don't you see she loved him?" she asked. "I believe she loves him still, despite his mad insistence she's somehow deepened his curse with her magic."

How ironic that Jenna loved Lukas, who was in love with

Aldis, while Aldis loved Leif, who wanted her dead. Hugging her sister in temporary farewell, she noted the thinness of the cloak she wore. "Take mine," she urged. "It's warmer. I'll stay by your fire, so I won't miss it."

"Thank you." Jessie replaced her cloak with Jenna's. "I'll tell Struan our plan. If he hadn't been digging his mother's grave, we'd have had notice of your coming."

"What will he do now?"

Jessie frowned. "I'll ask him to come to Glamis with us, but I doubt he will."

"He'll remain up here all alone?"

Jessie shrugged. "Better that than have folk stare and mimic him behind his back."

Jenna glanced around them, where spring was staking its claim with flowers, leaves, and soft smells. Though stark, the place had its own beauty, and Struan was comfortable here. It was no surprise he chose peaceful solitude over the cruelties society inflicted on him.

"Perhaps someone would visit from time to time, if we arranged payment."

That pleased Jessie. "There's an innkeeper—"

"Catherine," Jenna said. "She will do it, or at least she'll know someone who will."

Jessie hugged her sister again. "It's good of you to concern yourself with Struan."

With a tight smile Jenna said, "We must be kind to all, for we never know when we might meet an angel."

After Jessie and Alfred left, Jenna gathered items to make the cart comfortable for Aldis. Once she'd done that there was little else to do, and she paced the room. "I wonder how long it will take them to return."

Aldis refused to guess, staying instead, "Your sister loves the gleeman."

"It didn't seem so from the cold way she looked at him."

Aldis smiled thinly. "We cripples learn to hide how we feel, to spare ourselves the pity of those we love."

"But Alfred is afraid to speak of his love for her."

"How sad humans are! There is so little real love in the world, yet when we have a chance, we fail to take it."

Because we know the hurt that might follow, Jenna thought, but she asked, "Why didn't Leif go back to Norway when the Vikings were defeated?"

"I begged him to do so," Aldis replied. "He still has his lands. He could start a new life." She looked away. "But Bjorn said that only by killing the Scotti girl and her lover could they find a brighter future."

"And you as well."

"I didn't realize that at first, but yes." Aldis swallowed hard. "I'd misread the signs, giving them false hope of success, he said. I'd done it so Lukas and his Norman friends could win England."

"How could you have known what would happen?"

Meeting Jenna's eyes Aldis replied, "A vitki is supposed to know. It's our purpose." She returned her gaze to the fire. "Bjorn said my heart turned from the Vikings' cause because my brother is a Norman."

"Your brother." As her thoughts came together, Jenna cried out, "Lukas is your brother!"

Aldis looked surprised. "He never told you?"

Jenna struggled to organize the thoughts that flooded her mind. Aldis' uncle had taken her in when her father rejected her. She hadn't made the connection, though she should have. Lukas and Aldis had the same mother, Svenn Arneson's sister.

Why hadn't Lukas told her? She'd been cold to him for months, believing he sought a lover, when he'd been looking for the sister who desperately needed his help.

Which meant Lukas didn't have a lover.

Did that mean he might care for her, as he sometimes seemed to?

Trying to slow her spinning brain, Jenna asked Aldis, "Leif blames Lukas too?"

"Bjorn calls Lukas a traitor. They'll kill him if they can." With a sigh Aldis added, "I thought I could win him back in time, but he thought me treacherous and worse."

"And yet you love him."

"Still." Aldis' voice turned bitter.

"How did you escape them, if they were both determined you should die?"

She flashed a grim smile. "Bjorn is superstitious, and I threatened to curse him if he came near. Though Leif's heart had turned from me, a spark of affection remained. He was reluctant to finish it, but I knew the day would come. I had no hope but escape."

"Someone must have helped you."

"The priest, Dominic, heard Bjorn boasting that Leif would soon be done with me. While they were out searching for Jessie, he carried me away on his back."

Jenna smiled. "He ever looked for ways to do good in

the world."

Aldis grimaced. "It was hard for me to believe a Christian priest would rescue a pagan, and a pagan magician at that. He wasn't sure what to do with me until Jessie arrived. Then he suggested we should stay up here until he could get a message to Lukas."

"A desperate move, to winter in such a place."

"They watch the path to your clan-hold, and everyone else I ever cared about had rejected me."

"But you knew Lukas would come for you."

Aldis' smile was thin. "He tried to convince me to go with him to Normandy. He said I was foolish to cast my lot with Leif's, but—" Her voice held a plea for understanding. "—I told myself someday he'd recover and be himself again." As if it cost her to say the words she added, "I thought if I helped, he'd see that I love him. Lukas said he'd grow worse, but I wouldn't listen."

Again Jenna chastised herself for missing the signs. At the Viking camp, Aldis had shown concern for Lukas. When he'd hired the man to find her, Lukas told him the woman needed care. Jenna even remembered a time when he'd tried to tell her about it. When she'd dismissed all Vikings as cruel and evil, Lukas had dropped the subject. All this time he'd been trying to locate his sister, whose heart was as broken as her body. Jenna's anger had kept her from seeing the truth, but now she admitted she'd been wrong about him from the first. When she found him, she would tell him so.

Chapter Thirty-eight

Jessie

Alfred said nothing for a time after they left Jenna and Aldis at the old castle. Jessie refused to ride Foot, claiming he'd need his strength for the strenuous walk back uphill pulling the cart. When the path turned and they were out of sight, Alfred stopped and faced her, his expression earnest. "Jessie, I'm sorry I left without telling you. I—I couldn't bear to say goodbye."

"I understand. You needed to forget about me." She said it calmly, but her voice trembled at the end.

"I could never forget you." Taking her in his arms, he pulled her to him, the first time he'd touched her voluntarily in all the months they'd spent together. Every part of her reacted: her body, her mind, her spirit. She understood that Alfred's passion had been the cause of his dour moods. Her response matched his, though she'd never seen it, never acknowledged it.

"Jessie," he said miserably. "I love you. I've loved you from the first time I saw you. If it were possible I'd marry you, though I know that can't be."

"Why not?" She stopped, a little embarrassed to be so bold but wanting to know.

Stepping away, Alfred said, "First, you are promised to someone else."

"But I don't love Dougal. I doubt I'd have wed him even if you hadn't come along."

"Jessie, your uncle was a king. I'm a gleeman who owns nothing but what I carry with me. I travel nine months of each year. You would find such a life difficult."

"I wouldn't!" she objected. "I'd love seeing the places you see, castles and other lands."

"Back doors of castles and cheap alehouses full of drunken folk? It's no life for a girl like you."

"If you mean my leg would hold us back, it won't, I promise. Foot will do whatever I ask." Jessie realized with a jolt that she was trying to convince Alfred he should marry her. "I'm sorry. I didn't mean to sound..." She paused in embarrassment.

"Willing?" There was gentle humor in his tone. "Jessie, if you knew how happy it makes me to hear your arguments. I have made them in my head a hundred times since we met on the mountain. I never dreamed we'd have the chance to get to know each other, much less—" Now he stopped, unable to speak of her loving him. "If you'll have me, I'll do everything I can to make the way easier. We'll travel only in good weather. We'll avoid the worst places and settle somewhere each year when winter comes. A thane near Dundee would welcome us, for he enjoys my songs and stories."

"You would have a wife like me?"

He laughed aloud. "A wife like you, my dearest Jessie, is the thing that will make me most happy. For you I'd even give up travel and earn a living some other way."

"Maybe in a decade, when we're very old. Oh, Alfred, I loved you from the first too. I just didn't think—" Before she could finish he was kissing her, pushing the hood from her hair and burying his hands in the heavy waves. Time slowed as Jessie responded. For a few moments nothing mattered except Alfred. Nothing.

When they separated, the world returned slowly to her consciousness. Gradually she became aware of the soft sounds around them. Her eyes began to see again. Alfred said nothing, holding her as she felt his breath and his strong heartbeat.

A bell sounded far away. "We must go," he whispered. "Others need us."

The world and its threats returned. "We must hurry."

As they walked on, Alfred wondered aloud, "Do you think Glamis will get a new priest soon?"

"Why?"

He smiled down at her. "Could his first rite be a wedding, do you think?"

Chapter Thirty-nine

Jenna

Jenna needed to get away, to be alone and let what she'd learned settle in. Telling Aldis she meant to watch for Alfred and Jessie's return, she left the room, wrapped in Jessie's inadequate cloak. The best view of the path to Glamis was from the inner wall of the keep, where lookouts once had been posted. Parts of the stairway were open to the air, and the last segment was accessible only by a ladder that seemed fairly sturdy, with only one cross-piece missing.

When she cleared the protection of the wall, Jenna felt the slap of wind. A storm was brewing. Once she'd braced herself against the stiff breeze, she suspended worry and let the view take over. Below were the buildings of the ruined manor, beyond them the path to Glamis. To the west she could see a tiny slice of the village, with the river running alongside it. Beyond that on the right were the mountains of home, and to the east the sea, crashing against the rocky shore in endless, pounding movement. Although her hair whipped about her face, she reveled in the peaceful scene, so different from the chaos of her thoughts.

They were in danger, and the man who might have stood between her and that danger was unaware of it. She'd lied to Lukas, abused his patience, and rejected his attempts at kindness. And she'd been wrong. It was not Vikings who were her enemies, but two cruel and misguided men. She recalled Father Dominic saying that all races and cultures contained both good people and bad. Jenna said it aloud. "I was wrong."

Lukas had protected her from a multitude of evils, had saved Tessa from losing her home, and brought her to Scotland though he feared she might not return with him. He'd searched ceaselessly for his half-sister, afraid to tell

Jenna about her and admit a connection to the people she hated. She'd been a fool. From his first touch, Jenna's heart had told her Lukas was the man she was born to love.

Turning her gaze to the trail, she sought the cart they needed to take Aldis back to Glamis. She hoped Alfred and Jessie could find one. When they got to Glamis, she would find Lukas and tell him everything. She would—

Movement flickered at the far end of the tree line, and she caught sight of Jessie and Alfred, leading Foot, who pulled a sturdy two-wheeled cart. They moved at a goodly pace, and even from a distance it was easy to tell the coolness between them was gone. Alfred spoke animatedly, telling Jessie something that made her laugh. When they reached a flat spot on the path, he stopped and pulled Jessie to him to kiss her. Jessie participated fully in the kiss. "Well, well, Jessie," Jenna said with a smile. "And well done, Alfred."

Something to her left caught her eye, and Jenna turned toward it. Just inside the tree line a man stood, watching the lovers kiss. His face was hidden, but he stood frozen, as if unable to believe what he was seeing. When Jessie and Alfred continued on their way, the man watched them go, dejection in every line of his body. As he turned toward her, following their passage, Jenna recognized him and almost fell from her perch. "Lukas!"

He didn't hear, since the wind took her voice in the opposite direction. His face was as dark as the clouds overhead. What was he doing here? And what conclusions had he drawn, seeing a woman who looked like his wife and wearing her cloak, locked in a passionate kiss?

Hurrying down the ladder and then the stairs, she careened out the door, desperate to catch him. Lukas would conclude she had a lover. *Lukas, Lukas!* Jenna thought as she raced down the path. *How could you think there is anyone in my heart but you?*

Brushing past the surprised couple, she ran until she could run no more, but he was gone. Surrendering to tears, Jenna turned back to the ruined castle. She'd believed Lukas was unfaithful, and now he thought the same of her. She could explain, but would he give her the chance? Thinking as he did, he might leave Scotland, and he'd proved already that he knew how to stay out of her life.

Returning to where Jessie and Alfred stood looking after her in surprise, she said, "Hurry! We must get Aldis and go." As they climbed to the ruined castle, she told them why.

Chapter Forty

Jessie and Jenna

Storm clouds continued to gather, and the day darkened though it was not yet night. Jenna chafed at the delay, but the others convinced her they had to wait until morning to start down the mountainside. "The path will be slippery and the way dark," Alfred said.

Aldis argued, "Lukas can't leave until he's done what the king sent him here to do."

"We'll set out at dawn," Jessie said, "and we'll find him. Pray for a fine day tomorrow."

Alfred went out and brought the cart, pony and all, into the ruin, closing the one rickety door and stacking rocks across the remaining gap. Unhooking the cart, he gave the pony some straw and joined the women as Jessie handed out a simple meal of cheese and bread. Struan ate with them, listening to their talk but contributing little. As Jessie had predicted, he insisted he would stay where he was.

"'Tis ma home," he said stoutly. "Ma friends are th' creatures hereabout, and I am content wi' them and nae eather."

Jenna meant to argue, but Jessie caught her eye and shook her head. Struan wouldn't be convinced to leave. They would help him in some other way.

Hollow ticks sounded as drops of rain hit the roof. Within moments, it poured down. Although their living space was dry, there wasn't much room. They huddled together, waiting out the night.

Aldis stared into the fire, and Jessie guessed she was thinking of the burden she'd be on the morrow. Jenna seemed worried and unhappy. To distract them Jessie said,

"Tell us about your husband, Jenna."

She decided to be honest. "Lukas was with the Viking band that attacked our people, but—"

"You married my brother?" Aldis' voice was a croak.

"He never told me you were siblings, I suppose because I kept repeating that all Vikings are evil. I didn't know who he's been seeking all these months or why." Turning to Alfred Jenna said, "I told you my husband was not to be trusted. I was wrong. He came to Scotland to find his sister and assure her safety."

Alfred whistled, looking to Jessie in confusion. Equally confused, Jessie shrugged.

Jenna knelt beside Aldis, taking her hand gently. "We'll never abandon you, Aldis, first, because Jessie loves you, second, because Alfred is a good man, and third, because you are my sister-in-law. If it is within my power, I will take you to Lukas, who will, I pray, forgive me and help us all."

Aldis looked at Jessie, and a single tear ran down her pale cheek. "I've been feared, pitied, and reviled. But I've known love and devotion. Jessie, I'll always be grateful for your kindness and care."

Kneeling beside her, Jessie touched Aldis' arm. Jenna caught Alfred's eye, and a look of understanding passed between them. They must head into danger in order to escape it. The delicate Aldis made escape more difficult. Jenna prayed they might all survive.

The storm had abated by morning, and as Alfred hitched the pony to the cart, a pale sun rose over the decaying wall. Bird songs heralded the end of the storm, as they spread their wings out to dry in the trees above. Aldis was awake early, or perhaps she hadn't slept. She'd combed her blond hair with a pine branch and plaited it neatly. When all was ready, she wrapped herself in her woolen cloak, fastening it with the pin Jenna had noticed when they first met, a metal disc with an array of tools attached to it with sturdy chains.

Struan carried Aldis to the cart, setting her gently on blankets Alfred had thrown over the hay. When she was as comfortable as her condition allowed, they said goodbye to him and began their trip to Glamis.

The day was gray but not rainy, warm but not hot. Jenna and Alfred walked beside the cart, steering the pony around the worst of the bumps in the road. They were soon wet to the knees from passing through wet grass. Jessie walked beside Aldis, who allowed no sound to escape her lips, though they were tight and ashen.

Jenna was anxious, rehearsing what she'd say to Lukas when she found him. Jessie watched Aldis' pinched face while Alfred watched Jessie, fearful the pace might be too much for her. They were all distracted, or they would have noticed the silence ahead of them as the birds stopped singing. As they came around a turn in the path, three grim-faced men stepped from a copse of birch and alder. Jenna's heart seemed to drop in her chest.

Alfred tensed, but two more men stepped out behind them, each taking one of his arms. One man reached out and stopped the pony. Then, in a nightmarish repeat of their first meeting, Leif stepped from the woods and approached, his demeanor serene, as if he didn't have murder in his heart.

Behind him came Bjorn, his bearing as prideful as ever but his face horribly changed. One eye was gone and the cheekbone below it caved in, so his face had an unfinished look, as if a sculptor had abandoned a piece half done. The eyelid drooped over the empty cavity. The impression was of two faces, one alive and human, one dead and bestial.

"Did you think you'd steal into Glamis without our knowing?" Bjorn asked. "Gold is a great persuader."

Leif looked from Jenna to Jessie in wonder. "Twins! It is a sign, for my youngest brothers were twins. I will put their souls to rest." Stepping past them, he went to the back of the cart to face Aldis. "Well met, Witch. First you denied me the fullness of your magic. Then you left me with none. I will defeat you nonetheless, for my will is stronger than yours."

Aldis returned his stare, but her voice shook a little as she said, "Leif, listen to me. None of these people means you harm, nor do I."

"You lie!" His calm manner evaporated, and he pointed at his companion's ruined face. "Do you see this? You should have prevented it! Do you recall my sons, each as beautiful as a flower of Valhalla? They lie in their graves, and their mother, too. Why? Because Macbeth's seed lives!" He gestured widely. "Now you will pay the price my beloved wife paid!"

The hard-faced men shifted their feet, ready for action but uncomfortable with Leif's ravings. "Guard them," he commanded. "I must prepare myself for the vengeance I will exact." Leif gestured to Bjorn. "Come with me."

Bjorn looked as if he might refuse but in the end did as Leif ordered. The two went down the trail a short distance and knelt among the wet plants, Leif devoutly, Bjorn looking unhappy at the idea of soiling his clothing.

The Vikings' henchmen stood waiting, uncertainty showing on their faces. One by one they looked to a man who seemed to be their leader. He lifted his chin, tacitly ordering patience.

Jessie stepped toward him. "I know you." To Alfred she said, "Do you remember?"

Alfred nodded. "Ross. The thane of Fife."

The man's smile had all the warmth of an adder, and the smell of stale wine hung about him like a mist. "You seemed an old man and a girl-child that night at my hearth," he said after studying their faces. "That was well done, but you'll pay now."

"You mustn't believe what Bjorn tells you."

Ross glanced toward the spot where Leif prayed. "Do you think I care what you did or did not do? Once this Viking kills the lot of you, he'll go back to Norway and leave me in peace."

"Leif is Macduff's son," Jessie said for the benefit of Jenna and the others. "Ross fears he will lose the fief he gained through lies and murder." To him she said, "We know what really happened that day."

The smile Ross gave in response to her words was frightening. "Clever, lass. Too clever, perhaps." Setting a hand on his sword hilt, he said in a conversational tone, "We need not wait for Leif to finish his prayers. You will try to escape, and my men will be forced to kill you all." He signaled the rough-looking men, who moved grimly toward them.

Jessie and Jenna clung to each other. Separately they'd eluded death for months, but now that they'd found each other again, it seemed there was no way they would not die here together.

Pounding hooves sounded on the path below, and they all turned to look. In seconds two destriers, trained warhorses that were fearsome weapons in themselves, hurtled toward them. On the lead horse was Lukas, sword already drawn and jaw set. Close behind him was Jeffrey.

Jenna pulled Jessie to the back of the cart, where they

took what cover they could. Leif's men moved into defensive positions, and Bjorn and Leif hurried to join them. They formed a wedge, swords ready, protecting each other as the horses neared.

While their opponents were distracted by the newcomers, Alfred took action. Stealing up behind the man nearest them, he grasped the head of an axe-like sparthe that hung from his belt. Sliding it quickly from its loop, Alfred swung it at the man's head before he could turn and stop him. When he fell to the ground, stunned, Alfred backed away and took a stance between the women and their attackers. Though he was no trained fighter, he brandished the sparthe menacingly, prepared to do what he could.

Chaos reigned for a time as the two men on horseback engaged the six on the ground. The women huddled together, avoiding sword thrusts and charging horses. Grunts of exertion sounded as Jeffrey and Lukas surged forward then wheeled aside as their opponents sliced at them. In response, the usually placid Foot squealed and reared in terror, sending Aldis sliding against the boards.

As Jenna helped Aldis sit upright again, Jessie hurried to quiet Foot, holding his head and speaking softly in his ear. Alfred acquitted himself well with his pilfered weapon, delivering blows with the axe whenever one of their enemies got close enough.

The man Alfred struck rose and returned to the fray. Jenna scanned the ground around them, looking for something she might use as a weapon. She saw nothing she could reach without getting trampled by men or horses.

Seeing her intent, Jessie pointed at the cart, where a pitchfork hung lashed to the outer wall. Pulling it from its place, Jenna used it on the skull of the nearest enemy, who reeled away and fell to the ground, bleeding. As she waited for another opportunity, she noticed that the man Jessie had identified as the thane of Fife stood back, apparently waiting to see how the battle went.

Lukas fought Bjorn and one other, using both the horse and his sword as weapons. Jenna cried out when Bjorn gave the horse a vicious blow, causing it to stagger wildly. Busy with the other man, Lukas was unprepared when the animal went down, but he rolled free and regained his feet quickly. He'd lost his advantage, however, and now faced two determined enemies.

Controlling his own mount with his knees, Jeffrey brandished a sword with his single hand, keeping Leif and the remaining attacker at bay so they could neither go to Bjorn's aid nor reach the women. Man and horse worked together, advancing and retreating in the movements each knew well.

The man Jenna had stunned began to recover, shaking his head and rolling onto one hip in an attempt to rise. Crawling under the cart and out the other side, Jenna came up behind him, took his metal-rimmed helmet from the ground where it had fallen, and smacked him with its edge. His eyes rolled back, and he collapsed, either unconscious or dead.

A burly man with bare arms made a move to get past Jeffrey and reach the cart where Jessie stood next to Aldis. Signaling his horse with a twist of his body, Jeffrey wheeled abruptly, sending the man stumbling backward. When his head connected with a sturdy tree trunk there was a sickening sound, and he dropped to the ground and lay still.

A scream sounded, and one of Lukas' opponents fell, blood gushing from his neck. His death signaled an end to Ross' alliance with Bjorn and Leif. The thane whistled once, turned, and melted into the trees. His remaining men backed away, holding each other up and tacitly sending a message that for them, the battle was over.

Alfred followed the retreating men for a short distance, brandishing his axe. When he returned to the cart, Jessie saw that he had a long cut on his arm.

"You're hurt!"

He seemed unaware of it and said merely, "I will almost certainly live."

The retreat of Ross' men left two men still engaged: Lukas and Bjorn. Jeffrey managed to kick Leif's sword from his hand, and he maneuvered him backward until he bumped against a huge rock. As he held him there, Jenna ran up, retrieved the dropped sword, and tossed it into the trees.

Leif clearly wanted to go to his friend's aid, but Jeffrey and the horse easily prevented it. An old soldier himself, Jeffrey must have sensed there was a matter to be settled between the two men. Unlike Jenna, he didn't know how long their animosity had smoldered, but he, along with everyone present, knew it had burst into a flame that would burn out only when one of them was dead.

The two paused briefly, measuring each other's remaining strength. Both men panted with exertion, and Lukas murmured something Jenna couldn't hear. Bjorn grimaced in response, his face pulling oddly to one side. Without further word, they raised their swords again.

The opening moves were tentative. The two knew each other well and knew each other's strengths. Neither assumed the fight would be easy. Physically Bjorn was taller and heavier than Lukas, his reach longer. In addition, Lukas had a sense of fair play, while Bjorn had none: no decency, Jenna reminded herself. No boundaries and no honor.

After a few tentative feints, the blows quickened. Bjorn advanced, pressing Lukas with his long arms and strong legs. Lukas parried but had to step back each time. He ducked and sidestepped, looking for an opportunity to attack, but he was so busy avoiding Bjorn's flashing sword that he had no chance to attack.

A ringing blow from Bjorn's strong arms sent Lukas sword spinning from his hands. Reacting quickly, Lukas evaded the return swing, meant to finish him off. Bjorn smiled, knowing he had the advantage, "You are done, Outsider."

Jenna whimpered, both in fear and in anger at herself for tossing aside a weapon Lukas now needed.

Jeffrey called out, "Here, brother!" and tossed his own sword to Lukas.

Catching the weapon deftly, Lukas once more turned to Bjorn. "Not yet, Bjorn. Not yet."

A scream echoed across the clearing, and they turned to see Leif pulling Aldis roughly from the cart. Taking advantage of Jeffrey's distraction, he'd chosen the weakest member of the group as his prey.

Jessie fell on him, beating his back with her fists, but a casual blow sent her staggering backward, her lip bloody. When Jenna tore her gaze from the duel and saw what was happening, she ran toward them, but she was too late. Leif held Aldis before him like a rag doll, his dagger against her neck. Jenna stopped, terrified and furious.

Aldis' misshapen legs splayed at odd angles on the rocky ground. After the first cry, she made no further sound. Leif called in a commanding voice, "Hold, or I'll kill her."

Lukas froze with sword raised to defend against Bjorn's next blow. Jeffrey swore an oath so vile it surprised Jenna to hear her gentle brother-in-law speak it. Wiping blood from her lip, Jessie begged, "Don't hurt her, Leif!"

The madman spoke calmly. "I will do what must be done." To Lukas he said, "You know it. You know what I have endured."

"Leif. Brother." Lukas lowered his sword. "Macbeth is dead. No one here has hurt you."

Leif's eyes were haunted by images only he could see. "We could not even stay to bury them." His pale eyes flashed. "Each day Sigrid reminded me. Macbeth. Macbeth. Macbeth!"

"It was not our uncle!" Jessie said boldly. "Ross killed your family and blamed Macbeth for his crimes!"

"Treacherous, like all of them," Bjorn's breath rasped from exertion. "She defends the man all know was a murdering fiend."

"It's true," Aldis said, but her voice was weak and breathy. "Leif, listen to me!"

"You listened to her before." Bjorn pointed to his empty eye socket. "See where it has brought us! She must die! They all must!" With a growl of pure hatred he lunged toward Lukas, sword raised.

The blow came within a hair's breadth of taking Lukas' head off, and only his natural quickness saved him. He ducked, avoiding the blade, and raised his own in instinctive defense. The mighty swing Bjorn had taken carried him forward, and Lukas' sword point slipped under his leather vest. His own impetus drove it into his heart, and with a single, strangled roar of outrage, Bjorn Bear-slayer fell dead.

Silence followed. What would Leif do now?

"Bjorn!" The shout ended in a cry of pain. "Friend!"

"Not your friend, Leif," Lukas said. "He only played that role, hoping to share in your wealth."

303

"Liar!" Leif bent over Aldis, sword at her neck. "He stood by me, unlike this one." His eyes met Lukas', anger and madness glittering within them. "You care for her, and she for you. Now you will know how it feels to lose what you love."

The vitki seemed unconscious, slumped limply in the Viking's grasp, but her hand moved upward as Leif spoke, seeking something at her shoulder.

Aldis' hand closed on the scissors from her housewife's kit. Blindly she raised her arm, accompanying it with a scream that might have signaled pain, sorrow, or victory. The blades slashed at Leif's neck, and he recoiled in shock. Aldis fell to the ground with a sickening crunch. Clutching at the scissors protruding from his throat, Leif tried to pull them out, but his hands would not obey. It would have made no difference. Blood gushed from the wound, and Leif made strangling sounds. His face paled. His hand released the sword. Finally he slumped to his knees then fell face-first onto the ground.

Jenna and Jessie rushed to Aldis. Lukas made certain Bjorn was dead while Jeffrey dismounted and examined Leif. Alfred moved to Jessie, putting a comforting hand on her shoulder as she knelt beside Aldis, whose frail body looked like a jumble of sticks. Opening her eyes, Aldis sought Jessie's face.

"Is he dead?"

"Yes."

"I had to do it."

"You saved us." Tears streamed down Jessie's face. "I don't want to lose you, Aldis. We'd have made a home for you, Alfred and I."

Aldis chuckled, but it ended in a gurgle. "You—were

always soft-hearted, Jessie. It is—how I knew there were two of you, for your sister is less forgiving."

Jenna was stung. "I was grateful for your help."

Aldis smiled. "But you blamed me for Leif's madness, and perhaps you—were right. I hope you can—forgive me." Jenna nodded, tears making it impossible to speak, but Aldis was looking beyond her to where Lukas stood. "Forgive me, brother. I should have—listened to you."

"There is nothing to forgive," Lukas said hoarsely, bending near. "I love you."

Aldis smiled weakly. "When he said he needed me, my foolish mind heard 'love' instead. You must see to his funeral. Leif died in battle and might yet reach the joys of Valhalla."

"We will."

A rattling sigh came from her throat, and Aldis died. Jessie wept, turning to Alfred for comfort. Lukas turned away, putting an arm around Jenna. Jeffrey stood back, not understanding most of it but keeping his sword ready in case their attackers returned.

"How did you know?" Jenna asked.

His chest still heaving from exertion, Lukas found his sword and replaced it in its leather baldric with an efficient movement. "I went to Fife, having heard Leif and Bjorn were there, but the servants said they'd gone hunting. On the way back to Glamis I saw a track up this path that looked newly traveled."

"The Tracker," Jenna said. "It's what I called you in my mind before I knew your name."

"As I climbed I came upon two people—" He stopped, and Jenna smiled.

"Jessie and Alfred."

"I wish I'd known." He fidgeted a little. "I retraced my steps, and I must admit that my heart was heavy. When I arrived back at the inn, Jeffrey was there."

Jeffrey took up the story. "Almost as soon as your boat left, I heard that the two Vikings were in Scotland, looking for you. I took the next available boat and arrived not far behind you. I've had some dealings with the thane of Glamis, so I went to him first, and he loaned me the horses." He patted the dark animal beside him. "Though the climb was hard, they served us well."

"Jeffrey told me things I should have known long ago, of twin sisters and such," Lukas said. Turning to Jeffrey he added with a grin, "I thank you, brother, for the sword and for your strong right arm."

Jenna winced at the joke, but Jeffrey seemed to enjoy it. Turning to Jessie, he said. "I am your sister Tessa's husband."

Jessie embraced Jeffrey then turned to Lukas. "You are the Viking who protected me from Bjorn. You said you'd help me escape, but then Jenna came."

Lukas again looked aggrieved. "We might have been saved much trouble if I'd known from the first there were two of you. I never understood why my promise was ignored." Lukas met Jenna's gaze. "It seems my wife has kept secrets from me."

"You didn't tell me Aldis was your sister," Jenna retorted. "I thought you had a—"

His eyebrows rose in surprise. "A lover?"

"Yes." She felt her face warm, even in the cold mountain air.

Lukas chuckled grimly. "When I saw Jessie with this fellow, I thought the same of you."

"This fellow will soon be my husband," Jessie said, moving into Alfred's arms. "We have agreed on it. I love the life of an entertainer, and I love Alfred."

After a moment of surprised silence, Jeffrey said, "Perhaps your reunion with family will include a wedding, then." At the idea of visiting the clan-hold Lukas looked doubtful, but Jeffrey added, "You'll be welcome as Jenna's husband and the lord of—What is the place again?"

"Charleton." As Jenna turned to him, a question in her gaze, Lukas explained, "I'm sorry to tell you, wife, that you're no longer Lady Brixton. That title has been returned to its former holder."

"But—"

Lukas and Jeffrey grinned as if they had no wits at all. "William, King of England, is pleased with my crop-growing methods," Jeffrey said. "He restored my lands with the stipulation I teach others to do as I do."

"I am his first pupil," Lukas added. "Our new holding is north of Brixton. The former lord was among those who rose against William and died in the attempt."

"I see."

Jessie looked confused. "It seems you have much to tell me, Jenna."

"I do."

"What about Ross?" Alfred asked.

Lukas shrugged. "I'll inform your king of his wickedness, and the Scots may punish him if they will. We've all seen the harm a blood feud can cause."

The silence that followed indicated no one was willing to stir up more trouble.

"And Aldis?" Jessie knelt beside her friend. "We can't leave her here."

Lukas looked at his sister's crushed body, and his face softened. "It is tradition for the Northmen to burn their dead. She and Leif will be together at the end."

"And they'll wake in the morning in Valhalla, whole and strong, isn't that the belief?" Jenna asked.

"Yes."

Jessie nodded. "It would be good if, free of this world, Aldis could be happy in the next."

Jeffrey, Alfred, and Lukas gathered fuel and stacked it in the center of the flat expanse of rock. Jenna and Jessie straightened Aldis' broken limbs as best they could, combed her white-blond hair, and smoothed her clothing. The men laid her and Leif together at the center of the pyre then added the other bodies. Alfred used his tinderbox to light the flames, and they all stood back, respectfully quiet, as the fire took hold.

It was both terrible and beautiful, the Viking death. Jenna thought about the unhappiness in lives now ended: a hopeless love, overflowing greed, and a misdirected purpose had combined to make toil and trouble for them and for those who now watched their final rite. Still, Jessie had found love that was tested and proven true. And Jenna had found Lukas, a man she thought she hated but who stood beside her, holding her as she dried her tears. Loyal to those he loved, ceaselessly kind and patient, Lukas was the only man she'd ever love. It was time to say so.

"I was wrong," she said, looking up into his face. "I blamed you for Leif's deeds, and later I blamed you for

William's. In my heart I knew you intended harm to no one, but I couldn't admit I was wrong."

She waited for Lukas to say he'd told her so, but he didn't. His arm tightened around her, and his voice in her ear was so soft that she hardly heard the words when he said, "Then we must hurry home, wife, for we have much lost time to make up for."

Macbeth

In Shakespeare's *Macbeth*, the ambitious thane kills to gain access to the throne, not realizing that shedding blood will lead to more and more violence. Macbeth is so fearful his crimes will be found out that he has his best friend Banquo murdered. When a fellow thane, Macduff, opposes his claim to the throne, Macbeth sends men to kill his whole family. That's the incident this story takes as its kernel.

There isn't much truth to any of it.

The real Macbeth was a decent Scottish king who ruled for thirteen years. His wife never urged him to do murderous deeds—that was a queen who lived a full century earlier. And Macduff, if he really did go to England to raise troops to defeat Macbeth, was probably not popular with his fellow Scots, who'd have regarded English troops on Scottish soil with horror.

Shakespeare was a playwright, not a historian. His life's work was writing for the stage, so he took old stories and made them suit his purposes. Many "histories" in his day made little attempt to be factually accurate, and often picked up gossip or included magical elements in their supposedly historical accounts. King James I actually believed he'd been pursued at sea by two witches, possibly sailing in a sieve. He had them executed.

I picture Shakespeare smiling as he wove the docu-drama we know as *Macbeth*. It wasn't accurate, but why should he care, as long as people were willing to pay the price of admission?

Recap of *Macbeth's Niece*

My earlier book, *Macbeth's Niece,* concerns the adventures of Tessa macFindlaech, the second-oldest of five fictitious sisters born to Macbeth's brother Kenneth. Tessa appears in this book as a married mother of four, but she had plenty of adventures in the original story.

Tessa is sent to her uncle's castle to be taught proper manners and how to keep a rein on her tongue. On the way she meets three weird women who tell her she'll travel to England, marry two men she doesn't love, and find her true love only among the dead. Tessa doesn't believe a word of it.

At Thane Macbeth's castle she meets Englishman Jeffrey Brixton, who irritates her to the point that she speaks out boldly to put him in his place. Later she hears Brixton plotting against the Scottish king. When he discovers her presence, Brixton has no choice but to take her back to England with him.

Their stormy relationship means that neither will admit the attraction they feel toward the other. When Jeffrey goes missing and is presumed dead, Tessa returns to Scotland, only to find her uncle struggling for his sanity and his life.

In the end, Tessa learns that the witches were correct, though they were cagey about it (as witches tend to be). Her trials prove that life is unpredictable, attraction is undeniable, and true love, when you find it, is never-ending.

William of Normandy and Matilda

Without knowing William the Conqueror personally, I've tried to portray him as accurately as possible. He was an illegitimate son of Robert I of Normandy (France) who believed he'd been promised the English throne. When England's council didn't agree, he decided to cross the Channel and take it.

At the same time, the Norwegian king planned a similar conquest, believing he had the strongest claim to the throne. Things happened as this story tells, with the English defeating the Norwegians first and then rushing back to fight William's men. They were unsuccessful, and in October of 1066, the Norman Conquest made England into William's territory.

William built lots of castles, tried to modernize farming methods, and began an accounting of everything in his kingdom, which he called a "Great Survey" and we call the Domesday Book. It's useful to today's historians because it gives a picture of life at the time.

William didn't meld England into his other lands. Instead he set up a separate administration, saw to it that it was working, and then returned home to the Continent and his wife, Matilda, daughter of Baldwin V, Count of Flanders.

I'm a sucker for historical love matches, and William and Matilda seem to be a good example. The story Lukas tells of William dragging Matilda around by her braids is probably myth. There was some question whether the couple could marry, since the pope said they were too close in blood. That didn't stop them. They went ahead with the wedding and then convinced the pope to lift the ban by promising to build two churches.

They worked as a team to administer their several territories and raise a large brood of children. Interestingly, the wording for Matilda's coronation included notice that the new queen was God's instrument on Earth, just as William was.

Matilda saw to William's holdings on the Continent while he turned his hand to making England into a strong, vibrant nation. He did encourage intermarriage between Normans and English. Though he was high-handed, even cruel at times, kings could do that back then. His defenses lasted for centuries; he spurred growth and creativity; and he was willing to work with the conquered "Ainglish" lords if they'd work with him. These things are to his credit.

I picture William and Matilda much as I portrayed them here: confident, direct, and oblivious to the fact that anyone might have a worthwhile opinion that was different from theirs.

Note: I did change Matilda's Coronation date. She waited a year before coming to England to see her husband's new territory and accepting her crown.

Peg's Historical Novels

Macbeth's Niece is available in e-format only these days.

The Simon & Elizabeth Mysteries are available from Five Star
Publishing in hardcover, large print, and e-format

Her Highness' First Murder

Young Simon Maldon and Princess Elizabeth Tudor recognize each
other's intelligence and wit. When they investigate the deaths of women
in London, they must be careful Henry VIII doesn't learn of his daughter's
dabbling in sleuthing. They don't realize the killer will eventually turn his
sights on the Princess.

Poison, Your Grace

When a poisoning occurs at the palace, Elizabeth is concerned, first
because she fears her brother the king might have been the target and
second because she's a suspect. Recalling her friendship with Simon
Maldon, she calls on him again for help.

The Lady Flirts with Death

Mary Tudor is Queen of England, and Elizabeth is imprisoned in the
Tower of London. Simon wants to help her, but he also finds another old
friend in trouble. While he tries to puzzle out what to do, his wife takes in
a mysterious woman whose fate will change everything for his
household.

Her Majesty's Mischief

Recognizing that no one in her court is impartial when it comes to Mary,
Queen of Scots, Elizabeth calls on her old friend Simon for help. While
he's in Scotland, avoiding bandits, his wife and son hunt down a killer
who's been operating for years.

There will be one more in this series, but it's still far on the horizon.
Tentative title: **Her Royal Highness Plots**

If you enjoy contemporary mysteries, please take a look at Peg's
Amazon page AND her Sleuth Sisters Mysteries, written as Maggie Pill.